YOUNG & OLD

Book Three of Missing Persons
A Detective Grace Novel

Adrian J. Smith

Supposed Crimes LLC • Matthews, North Carolina

Published in the United States.

ISBN: 978-1-952150-28-9

www.supposedcrimes.com

This book is typeset in Goudy Old Style.

Young & Old

AFTER HOURS

SMILING AT the girl sitting across from her, her brown hair, crystalline eyes and the way too big suit jacket that took over her petite form, Grace asked, "If you were a tree, what kind of tree would you be?"

"What the hell kind of question is that?" Kit snarked.

Grace narrowed her gaze. "It's a question an interviewer might ask, and your attitude might lose you the job."

Kit rolled her eyes and shook her head with her arms crossed. "I'm not answering a stupid question like that."

"Let me put it this way, I have been asked this rather stupid question during an interview at a grocery store, and my answer was the only reason I was hired. So answer the question, Kit, and cut the attitude."

"I would be a white birch."

"See? Was that so hard? And what the heck, kid, a white birch?" Grace put her notepad down and glanced over at her best friend, Crystal, who was in the middle of her own interview with another high school student. Grace had managed to bring in three other people to help with the interviews that day, but not every student had managed to be paired, so they were trading out when they could.

Kit shrugged. "I like them."

"Why?" Shock rang through Grace's tone.

"They're pretty on the outside, but they look just like any other tree if you chop one down. They're nothing special, but they look special. They're just like every other tree out there, soaking up the carbon and shooting out the oxygen."

Grace bit her lip, wondering if Kit realized just how she had moved from describing a tree to describing herself, which had been the point of the damn question from the beginning.

"Interesting answer," Grace responded. "I think I'd hire you."

"You're biased."

"So?" Grace wrinkled her nose at Kit and leaned into the very uncomfortable chair she was perched on. She'd run into the school straight from the station and an interview, hadn't had time to change into more comfortable clothes, so she was stuck in a suit just as much as Kit was herself. She shifted in her chair, recrossing her legs and straightened her back.

"You can't hire me."

Grace chuckled. "Well, when you get a real interview for a real job, I will coach you through that one, too."

"Good because as soon as summer hits, I'm getting a job."

"Summer, huh?"

"I can't stay in that house with them all summer." Kit's tone softened to a near whisper.

Moving in closer, Grace made eye contact then lowered her lashes. She felt for Kit. She knew what that house was like, how hard it was for her to stay there, but Kit did, she managed every day to stay there and show up at the school for her classwork. Weekends she often came to Grace's and Amya's house. Her parents didn't seem to care where she was most of the time, only when the social worker came calling.

"You know you are always welcome at our house as much as you need to be."

Kit nodded. "Thanks."

"Anytime, kid. Now, move along. I've got other people to interview today, and then I'll have to make my final decision on who to hire."

"You're having too much fun with this," Kit muttered, disdain lacing every word as she pushed from her chair and went to the large table in the center of the gymnasium to wait for the rest of the group to finish.

They were in the process of cleaning up when Crystal came

over and put a hand on Grace's shoulder. "You find any kids worthy of hiring?"

Grace snorted. "They're green, but they'll shape up. Thanks for coming."

"Any time."

Sighing, Grace shoved some paperwork into a box. Crystal had to take off work early to help out, and Grace tried to avoid asking her to join in when her program wasn't happening on the weekend, which was near never. Crystal was excellent for a resource, but Grace hated putting her in a position where she had to rework her schedule to be there.

Grace herself had enough issues juggling her schedule as a detective for Missing Persons, but she couldn't deny that she really liked helping the kids. She'd been reminded of how much of that when Kit had done her stint living at their house over the Christmas holiday. As much as that entire month had been a disaster, it had been good to reconnect with something she wanted and get her head out of detective work.

Peggy came into the room, and Grace turned, straightening her back. No matter how many times she told herself she wasn't a kid in high school anymore, whenever the principal showed up—even one she might consider a friend—she always felt a sense of impending doom. Doom for what, she had no idea, because she wasn't sixteen and skipping school before dropping out anymore. She was getting closer and closer to forty every year, though Amya would beat her to it.

"How did it go today?" Peggy asked.

Grace sighed. "We had twelve kids today, so we had to split them up and do mock interviews in shifts."

"Twelve is a good number."

"It is." Grace picked up one of the jackets she had brought with her and folded it, shoving it into a box. "I'm thinking maybe we do need to go through the summer."

"The school is closed up for that."

"I know. We'll have to find somewhere else to meet, but I think that's when these kids are really going to need the support, you know? Kit reminded me of that."

"How is she doing, by the way? She's always tight-lipped whenever I try to pry something from her."

Grace stopped and glanced at Crystal who gave her a glance simply telling her to tread carefully. They had been best friends for the better part of twenty years, so Grace knew she had to walk carefully if Crystal was warning her. "I think she's doing as well as can be expected."

"She's passing all of her classes except math."

Snorting, Grace shook her head. They had tried to do math homework together, and even though Kit wasn't her biological kid, it had resulted it an all out screaming match in which the two of them both gave up and ordered Indian food to drown their sorrows.

"Yeah, she needs a tutor."

"I may be able to help," Crystal said. "Remember, I went to school for this."

"You doing it for free?" Grace teased, knowing Crystal would. She'd done it before and would do it again. She was a teacher through and through, even if she only taught elementary-aged kids, she had a heart for all kids.

"I will. You set up a time, and I'll be there."

"I'll talk to Kit." Grace shoved another suit jacket and a tie in the box. They'd had one of the other officers Grace had worked with when she'd been on patrol come and show anyone who had wanted to learn how to tie a tie. It had been an experiential lesson for herself as she had no clue where to begin with that one.

"You do that," Peggy answered, "And she may just graduate on time."

"I'll keep her in school. You make sure she graduates."

"Deal." Peggy grinned. "I've got to run, but I'll see you next week."

"Yup." Grace finished packing up the stuff they'd brought, then she and Crystal cleaned the tabletops and chairs before stacking and putting everything away where they found it.

As they carried the boxes out to Grace's cruiser, she shoved them into the back of the SUV and shut the trunk before turning to Crystal and crossing her arms. "I'll trade you a visit to your classroom for dinner tonight."

Crystal scrunched her nose at Grace then stepped in close to her, too close for Grace's comfort. She walked her fingers up Grace's arm to her lips and moved in even closer. Grace's heart thudded hard, and she was just about to jerk back when Crystal burst out laughing.

"You're too easy."

"That was *not* funny."

"Sure it was!" Crystal was still laughing when she shook her head. "Amya gone?"

"She's at some Jesus Camp thing."

That sent Crystal into another fit of giggles, so much so that she had to wipe tears from her eyes. Grace was unamused and remained standing stoically with her arms crossed and glaring at her best friend. When Crystal had finally calmed, Grace turned on her toes and walked straight for the front of her cruiser.

"Wait! Wait! Wait!" Crystal ran over. "I wasn't...that's just...she's not at Jesus Camp, Grace."

"She's at some Jesus conference. She's gone all week."

"What about Peter?"

Grace grunted. "We can *not* talk about him."

Crystal gripped Grace's hand and squeezed, her look soft and pity-filled. "Then let's do dinner. I know how much you hate cooking."

"I like cooking. I just...don't want to cook tonight."

"Hmm. Sure. We'll stick with that story."

"You're the one who hates cooking," Grace muttered as she slipped behind the wheel. "The diner?"

"Sure. Like you would pick anywhere else to eat."

"Well, fine, then. You pick."

"Let's go to Langden's Club."

"Really?" Grace pulled a face. She'd been there exactly once before, with Crystal no less, and she still didn't ever want to step foot back into that place. The food had been subpar, the alcohol choices limited, and it was crazy expensive.

"Sure, because you asked, you're buying."

Grace shut her door and rolled down the window. "Fine."

Grace arrived ten minutes before Crystal, and she'd sat in the booth playing on her phone and texting Amya, who wasn't answering, but she figured she would text Amya random shit that she would get as soon as she got to her hotel room. The house, while full of Peter and all his stuff, was going to feel so empty that night, just like it had the night before.

It was the first time she had truly felt the house was empty when Amya left it. Kit had made that difference, she was pretty sure, but she didn't want to analyze it too much. Maybe Kit would come over for the weekend and that would give her some reprieve from the silence and the moping half-way adult who locked himself in his room most of the day and night.

Once Crystal slipped into the seat, their drinks arrived. A Shirley Temple for Crystal, and a nice ice cold water for Grace. She would have preferred a beer, but since she'd had to leave straight from work, she still had her cruiser, so it'd be inappropriate.

"So where is Amya exactly?"

"Chicago."

"That's not too far from here."

"Far enough," Grace grumbled.

"My dear Grace, is your life revolving around your girlfriend, for the first time like ever?"

Grace glared. Crystal was right, but she did not want to admit it. Amya being going for the week put a serious cramp in her routine, and it made it near impossible to sleep at night. She took another long sip of her water to distract herself and keep any snarky retorts at bay.

Avoiding the subject all together, Grace moved on. "She'll be home Sunday, I think."

"You think?"

"It might be Monday. Peter's supposed to pick her up. Yeah, so Monday."

"You're pining away after your woman and you don't even know when she is supposed to be home?"

"I've had other things on my mind." Grace lifted one shoulder and dropped it.

"Like what?"

The waitress came over to take their orders, and as soon as Grace saw the look in Crystal's eye, she knew their dinner was doomed. Now she knew why Crystal had wanted to eat there instead of the diner. Her night was about to take a not so fun turn. With their meals ordered, and Crystal flirting with the waitress, Grace kicked her under the table to get her to stop. Crystal shot her a glare. The waitress caught it and flounced away. Rolling her eyes, Grace took another long sip from her water.

"She's cute." Crystal beamed.

"Good Lord."

"Aren't you not supposed to say that?"

"Amya ain't here."

Crystal grinned before her look turned sly. "Hey, you have to be my wing woman. I haven't had a date in months."

"Probably a good thing." Grace took another sip of her drink and wished their food would get there faster. If Crystal was going to flirt with the waitress for five minutes every time she came over it was going to be a very long dinner, indeed. She slipped her phone out to see if Amya had written back, and when she glanced up, the look on Crystal's face was alarming. "What?"

"Are you seriously looking to see if she called?"

"Texted. And what's wrong with that?"

Rolling her eyes and pressing her forearms on the table, Crystal leaned in closer. "Look, I know you've been together nearly three years now, but you can cool your jets, you know."

"I'm sorry, what?" Grace snorted.

"Give it a rest. She can leave for a work thing for a week and not have you drooling and pining so badly you can't have a conversation with your best friend. You're not newly involved."

"Okay. Duly noted and point taken. Phone is going away."

"Good. Now, wing woman or no?"

"No." Grace took another sip.

Crystal pointed. "Fine, then tell me about Peter. Is he going back to school or what?"

"Who knows." Grace sighed. "He's in theory going to his AA meetings, but I'm not sure he actually is. I'm trying to give him space to figure his own shit out, but I don't know. I don't want to give him too much space."

"You shouldn't give him too much space. You said he was drinking at school, right?"

Nodding, Grace spun the glass between her fingers. "He got a DWI, did what he needed to do to fix it, since it was his first one, and he kept drinking, which was why he came home. He just hasn't left, and I don't think the change in environment was as helpful as he thought it was going to be."

"It's usually not." Crystal turned when the waitress came back and grinned at her.

Grace rolled her eyes before staring at her food as it was placed in front of her. She tried to ignore Crystal turning all her attention on the waitress, whose name was Helena, apparently. Shoving a forkful of steak between her lips, Grace ignored the flirting going on in front of her like it had happened a million times before, which it had.

"You should set me up with her."

"What?" Looking up, Grace realized it was just the two of them again.

"Set me up with her. Come on, bestie."

"Don't do that."

"Do what?"

"I'm not your wing woman. If you want to go out with her, then ask her out or give her your number and tell her to call you. I'm not doing this for you. Grow up."

"Like you grew up with Amya."

"Shut up. You're the one who wants to date. I did not want to date."

"And yet you're the one dating."

"Can't help that." Grace shoved another forkful between her lips, really hoping the conversation was near an end, because while she enjoyed the time with Crystal, the constant dating, the constant new woman was overwhelming some days, and Grace figured that today was going to be one of them.

Crystal narrowed her eyes. "Speaking of dating, did you and Amya ever figure out your problem?"

Frozen mid bite, Grace shook her head in confusion. "What problem?"

"I seem to remember Amya spending the night at my house in an utter upset because your partner was making the moves on you."

"Jesus." Grace set her fork down and pushed back in the booth, straightening her spine against the wood. "Paige was not making the moves on me. Nothing has ever happened."

"But it was going to, admit it." Crystal pointed her fork at her.

"No. Nothing was ever or is ever going to happen. Mind your own business."

"She made it mine when she showed up at my apartment." Crystal raised an eyebrow at Grace, daring her.

"She did not, and trust me, we had words about that."

"I'm surprised it wasn't you first."

"Me?"

"Who showed up at my place. I always figured you would show up first because of something you had done to piss Amya off."

"Why something I had done?"

"Come on, Grace. This is you we're talking about."

"Nice. Real nice. Totally want to help you get that girl's number now." Grace finished her water and set her cup down a little too heavy on the table. She did not want to have to stay there longer than necessary if this was how their conversation was going to go. It had been weeks since she'd been able to spend any quality time with Crystal, and she had not been expecting this kind of serious and obtrusive inquiry.

Crystal set her fork down. "No, we're having this conversation. You need to man up."

"I'm sorry, what?"

"Marry that girl, already."

"Oh my God. I'm done." Grace set her fork down and started to shift out of her seat. "I'm not having this conversation."

"Three years, Grace!"

"And three years is three years. We're not getting married. I had this whole conversation with her mother over Christmas. Amya is on the exact same page as me. It's not happening. I don't want to get married. She's fine with it. End of story."

Crystal's jaw dropped, and her eyes went wide. "But...but I was going to be your maid of honor."

"Fuck that. Can you really see me doing that? Honestly? A full out wedding?"

"No, you're right," Crystal muttered. "Get back in your seat, boss. I'll drop it."

"Good. As for the rest of it, nothing happened with Paige and me. It's done and over with."

"Is it really, though? I mean she is still your partner, right?"

Grace shrugged. "Sometimes. Depends on the case."

"Does she still push boundaries?"

Not answering, Grace took another bite of her food and stared at her plate. She knew the answer, and she knew Crystal knew the answer. She really did not want to talk about it. Amya had begged her to full out put a stop to it, to be blunt to Paige and tell her to stop, but Grace didn't have the courage. Instead, she did everything in her power to avoid any situation that could end up with Paige and her alone, which was not working to her advantage.

"Grace."

Shaking her head, Grace shoved another forkful of food between her lips. "We're done talking about this. Tell me about school. I miss the kids."

Conceding, Crystal sighed. "School is good. This is a good group of kids this year, unlike last year. They about took all my passion for teaching and stomped it under their feet."

"I remember."

"These are good kids. Smart kids."

"I need to stop by soon. Really, I promise. After spring break?"

"Sure. We can set up a date for it."

"Good."

They fell into a brief silence before Crystal broached the next subject she was clearly waiting for Grace to bring up but she hadn't. "Kit?"

"What about Kit?"

"She was there today."

"She's there every day we have the program."

"And?"

"And what?"

"Come on, Grace, give me something."

"What is there to give? She's still living at home, mostly. She's with us a lot when she can be. We still pay her phone because her parents are literally doing the bare minimum they have to. I'd rather her hang out at our house than get caught up with the kids she was hanging out with, and I fully expect she'll spend all of spring break with us once she gets the courage to ask."

"I expected nothing less from you." Crystal smiled and went back to her meal.

Grace gave in. She flagged Helena down as she walked by. Setting her napkin in her lap, Grace grinned at her and nodded toward Crystal. "My friend here thinks you're hot, and she would like to go on a date with you, although why she can't ask you herself is something I can't fathom. So...now it's in your court." She shot Crystal a look at the last bit.

"Gee, thanks, great smooth move there."

"I never claimed to be smooth."

Helena scrunched her nose at the two of them before turning to Crystal. "I would love to go on a date with you."

"Here's her number." Grace pulled out her notepad she always kept in her pocket and wrote Crystal's number on it, handing it over to Helena. "There, now you owe me."

"You're snarky today."

Grace's lips thinned. "I miss Amya."

"We're back to that?"

Helena interjected, "Who's Amya?"

"My girlfriend," Grace answered.

"The most patient fucking person on the planet," Crystal added. "Seriously."

"Interesting." Helena turned her head for a moment when another table called her over. She excused herself to go back to work and left the two of them alone.

Grace nodded toward Helena. "You know you're going to have to explain me in order for her to think you're really single, right?"

"Yeah, I always do."

"Just making sure."

Grace downed her second glass of water as she finished her meal. She was just paying the bill when Crystal started fiddling with her purse and looking around the room nervously.

"What's wrong?" Grace asked.

"Nothing."

"You gave her your number. You could always go get hers."

"That's not it."

"Then what is it?"

"I'm thinking about joining up with the band again."

Grace shoved her wallet into her pocket but didn't say anything in response. She honestly wasn't sure how she felt about it. Crystal had been sober for over two years, unlike Peter, she had been following the program and hadn't back slid. But the band had been what helped her hide her drinking for so long.

"Same guys?"

"Yeah. Their singer got pregnant and isn't planning on coming back."

Taking a deep breath, Grace mulled it over. "I think you should do it, but be careful about it. Singing was good for you, and frankly, you're good at it."

"Thanks."

"You don't need my permission."

"I feel like I do."

"You're a dork." Grace rolled her eyes but felt warm at the fact her opinion mattered so much to Crystal.

"But you love me."

"Of course I do. I have to go and check on Peter."

Crystal sighed. "Give him some time, but watch him close, Grace. He's young still. He wants to hang out with the crowd."

"I know. And he's so sensitive. I think he's just getting down on himself for falling off the wagon."

"I'm glad he found you."

Grace chuckled. "More like I found him, drunk in your school, remember?"

"Trust me. I remember."

Grace got out of the booth and headed for the door with Crystal only a few steps behind her. She said her final goodbye with a promise to talk to her in the morning about a date to meet up with her class. Then she headed home, to her empty and Amya-less house.

THE CASE

THE OFFICE was quiet when she strode in. Most of the desks were empty, but Grace was always early, and typically the first person there. For years she had been a morning person, and without Amya to keep her bed warm, she had been up on and off most of the night.

She loved when the office was like this. It gave her time to think before the crew headed in for the day and the noise started up. Grabbing a personal-sized bottle of orange juice from the mini fridge after she started the coffee pot, she sat at her desk in the middle of the large room and booted up her computer. It was the perfect way to start a day. Would have been better with Amya, but like she'd told Crystal, she would survive, even if she didn't like it.

Sitting at her desk, she downed half the bottle of orange juice before Paige came in for work that morning. Typically Paige, her partner, was always one of the last in, so it was odd she was there so early. Turning in her chair, Grace raised an eyebrow in Paige's direction, her brown hair mussed, dark rings under her green eyes, and a sorrowful look on her face.

"What the hell is wrong with you?" Grace asked, her voice pointed and firm in the quiet of the office.

Paige grunted.

"No, seriously. What happened?"

Paige's gaze slid from her desk to Grace, and she shrugged before she moved to Grace's desk and sat on the corner of it. With her arms crossed and her long legs still planted on the floor, Grace's gaze roved over her body up to her face.

"Break up?"

"How could you tell?"

"You've only been dating a month."

"Not all of us can be in loveless marriages, Grace."

"I am not...never mind. What happened?" Grace bit her lip but leaned in her chair to get a fuller view of Paige's face. The only time to get Paige to talk about this was when they were alone, and they only had ten more minutes before the rest of the crew arrived.

Paige moved a hand to rub her eyes and then her cheeks. "I have no idea. Something about being unattainable or not emotional. I don't remember. It was a long night."

"You look like you just got off a binge. I thought you were done dating."

"I thought I was, too. I definitely am now. I don't have time for this back and forth. I'll stick to drinks, sex, and home before dawn. Much better that way."

Snorting, Grace shook her head. "For you maybe."

Paige narrowed her eyes at Grace. "Like I said, we're not all in loveless marriages."

"First, I am not married."

"Oh, we are all aware."

"What crawled up your ass? Because this is way out of the ordinary for you."

"Sorry." Paige sighed and rubbed both her hands over her face this time. "Sorry. That was uncalled for, you're right. Ugh. I'm just going to do some paperwork." Paige pointed at her desk before she pushed off Grace's to stand. "Maybe in my morose state today I'll get it all done and get a sticker from Humbard for completion."

"I'm pretty sure if you finished all your paperwork on time or ahead of time, he'd buy you a six pack."

Paige's ears perked up at that. "You think?"

Grace snorted. "No, asshole. But I'm not sure you've ever been caught up on reports."

"Well, we can't all be perfect." She hit the button on her computer to turn it on with more force than necessary. Paige plopped into her chair after shoving her jacket onto the back of it, the white button up shirt she wore pulling across her chest. Grace's gaze lingered before she dragged it away.

Grace debated before speaking again. "Is this going your mood all day? Because if so, I'm not inviting you with me anywhere."

The look Paige shot her was the end of the conversation. Grace went back to finishing out her reports from the last week she had avoided then filtered through some of the old cases she had sitting in her desk, the cold cases she loved to work when there were no active case in her possession.

Within the next hour, the rest of the detectives in her unit filtered in for the day of work. Tuesday morning seemed rough for a lot of them, but she wasn't going to question why, not after her experience with Paige. She should have left that one alone when she had the chance.

When Humbard came in, he called Grace over before he even got into his personal office in the back corner of the unit. She pushed up from her chair, chugging the last of her orange juice before she stalked into his office to wait out whatever he had to say.

"Shut the door," he said as he put his briefcase and his jacket away.

Grace raised her eyebrows in curiosity before turning and shutting the door as he had requested. When she'd first started working in Missing Persons, she would have been nervous to sit in the room alone with her captain with the door shut. In her experience, that meant someone was getting in trouble.

Humbard sighed, adjusting his belt and pants up before he sat in his desk chair and stared right at her. "I've got an odd case for you."

"Oh?"

"It's been through about four other detectives hands, but they're not making any progress."

"Okay?" Grace gnawed on the inside of her cheek. Four detectives meant it was likely an older case, but she couldn't really imagine a missing persons case that wasn't a cold case by that point. And cold cases were for a completely different department.

Humbard brushed a hand through his thinning black hair and opened his desk drawer to pull out the file. "I want your full attention on this case."

Grace nodded, waiting impatiently for that file to be in her hands. She had no idea what he was talking about, but the file looked ridiculously thin for four detectives to have worked it.

Drawing in a deep breath, she let it out slowly then stared at him.

"Like I said, this is a weird missing persons case. Kind of a reverse case."

"What?" Grace furrowed her brow.

"Here." He shoved the file over to her, and as soon as the cool paper hit her fingers, Grace's stomach twisted.

She opened to the first page and read the file number and summary. There was no name of the missing, but there was a picture. Sliding it from the paperwork, she stared down at it. He must have been in his late teens. He was clearly in a hospital bed, tubes all over his body, protruding from his mouth and nose and his skin.

"I don't understand," Grace stated.

"That's it. No one does. This kid, Joseph is what everyone has been calling him, was found four years ago off Pacific Road just by the hay barn over by the strip mall."

"Okay, yeah, I know that place."

"Four years ago, some taxi driver found him. Who knows what the driver was doing over in that area, but he found the kid. No one knows *who* Joseph is."

"What?" Grace's eyes widened, then she stared down at the picture. "So where has he been for the last four years?"

"In the hospital on life support."

"You're kidding."

"The nurses and doctors have all fought to keep him on life support. No one knows who he is or where he came from, but they don't want him to hit five years in there alone. They want to find his family."

Shaking her head, Grace turned to stare up at Humbard. The same question she'd been asking the entire time slipped from her lips again. "What?"

He put his hands in the air with exasperation. "I don't know. But they pulled strings, got media going, and they are trying to figure out who this kid is."

"This is...not a missing persons case, is it? Was there ever a missing persons case for this?"

"Not one that we can connect to this kid."

"So you want me to ID this kid so he can what? Be taken off life support?"

"No, so his family can make the proper decisions about him."

"And you think a family who hasn't reported a teenager

missing for four years deserves to make those decisions about whether or not to continue life support?"

Humbard's mouth opened and closed like a fish out of water before he shook his head. "I don't know. But I was handed the case and told to do something about it. It's your turn to do something about it."

"I...I don't even know where to begin." She flipped through a few more of the pages, which had some medical information but not much. She only had the one picture, in which it was hard to even see the kid's face since it was bruised and cut and so covered in tubes and medical supplies that only one half-decent eye was even poking out. "There's no more photos."

"The case is yours, Halling. I expect you to figure out who the kid is."

"Are you serious?"

"Yes." Humbard glared at her. "Now get to work."

"I...are you sure? Isn't this a file for cold cases or something?"

"It's your case."

"What if I don't want it?"

"That's not how this works, Halling. Now get out of my office and start working on it."

Still in shock, Grace stumbled before heading to her desk. Sitting in her uncomfortable chair, she blinked at the case file before opening it up. No detective had written a report that was in the file Humbard had handed her. She opened her computer's file system and searched the case number. Only one additional report popped up. Printing it, she focused on the file in front of her.

This was insanity. Four years in a hospital, kid clearly an adult at that point, and no one knew who the hell he was. He'd been a minor when he was found, which meant he hadn't even graduated high school most likely. Running a hand through her hair, she shook her head at the file again. Whatever she had done to piss Humbard off to land this case must have been bad, but she had no idea what it was.

She snorted. There was nothing else she could do. She was as lost as if she'd been stuck as a detective her first day after the academy. Four fucking years, and this kid still had no name other than the one his doctors and nurses had given him—Joseph. Rolling her eyes, she sent a quick text to Amya telling her she just landed the weirdest case in Missing Persons history.

With her phone back in her pocket, Grace shoved the case file to the side and went to work on the reports she still had filtering around in her brain. She would finish those before she dove head first into the file Humbard had handed her. It had to be slow if Humbard was doling out four-year-old cases instead of fresh ones.

Grace's cruiser was warm as she went through the fast food drive-thru. Fast food was not her first choice, but she was avoiding. Massively avoiding. The hospital was only a few blocks away, and she had even brought herself a healthy lunch that day with her current favorite, dried mangos, shoved into the bag, but she had stared at the hospital and taken a detour.

She'd read through the case file three full times and had gleaned nothing other than the detectives who had the case prior had done nothing except let it sit on their desks. The first one had done up a report and an interview on the taxi driver who had found the kid, but that was it.

Her head reeled. She vaguely remembered the case filtering over the news, but she'd always assumed someone had found the kid's parents. Grunting, she grabbed her food from the second window and drove to a decently empty parking lot to stuff her face with greasy, unhealthy, and too-good food.

When she was finished, she had no more excuses. Grace swallowed all the weird emotions raging through her stomach and chest and pulled into the hospital parking lot. She walked slowly, which was not her norm, to the front desk. She'd been in the hospital before—many times actually, but she'd never really been to ICU when she wasn't the patient, which was exactly once, and she'd never been there to see a kid with no name.

Walking straight up to the information desk, she smiled at the elderly woman sitting behind the desk, no doubt a volunteer. "I'm Detective Halling with the Sheriff's Department. I'm here to see Joseph."

"What's his last name?" The woman pulled out a chart.

Grace shook her head. "He doesn't have one."

The woman narrowed her eyes at Grace like she had three heads and was smoking crack, which Grace could guarantee she was not.

"I swear to you." Grace smiled at her. "He's in ICU. If you just point me in that direction, I'll find my own way."

"Go down that hall to the elevator, up to the third floor, and then take a left."

"Thanks." Grace drew in one last bolstering breath then walked through the hospital.

Maybe she should have brought Paige with her because the case was just too weird. She was having such a hard time wrapping her head around it all and figuring out where to even start. She was just about to the elevator when Emma stepped around a corner. Confused, Grace's lips turned up.

"Emma."

"Grace!" Emma's equally surprised look was a nice change.

"What are you doing here?" Grace asked.

"I work here."

Raising an eyebrow, Grace was even more confused. "What happened to the Campbell Home?"

"They got shut down."

"What?" Shock rang through Grace. She had spent so many hours there with one particular resident before his brother had moved him out to Washington where he lived. She hadn't been back since, but she'd gotten Emma the job there in a roundabout way, at least a year before.

Emma shrugged. "After Harold there was an investigation. A lot of us jumped ship then, but they got shut down for mismanagement of funds."

"Crazy. I should have followed up more closely. I'm sorry I didn't."

"Don't worry. I got a job here in human resources, and I'm loving it."

"Good for you."

"Are you here on a case?" Emma's gaze skimmed down to Grace's badge which was hooked onto her waistband and then her gun on her left side.

Grace nodded. "Yeah, handed to me this morning. I was just heading to the room."

Emma's sweet face lit up in a smile. "Is this for Joseph?"

"Yes...?"

"We've all been praying for him, you know. We want so badly for you to figure out who he is."

"Well, I'm going to try my best."

"I've got faith in you."

A shiver ran down Grace's spine, settling into the base of it. Conversations like that always made her feel squicky. Tightening her jaw, Grace nodded. "I'll do my best. That's all I can guarantee."

Emma smiled. "I've got a meeting, but I suppose I'll be seeing you around a bit."

"You might be." Emma went one way, while Grace walked the other toward the elevator. That had been a pleasant surprise.

As soon as she got to ICU, she picked up the phone and waited to be buzzed in. She started with the nurses' station, her heart in her throat as she still avoided the room itself.

"I'm Detective Halling, and I'm here about Joseph's case."

The young woman smiled at her. "I'm Katie. I'll tell you what I can about him, but we don't know much other than his current medical status."

"Well, we can start there." Grace pulled out her notebook. "How is he doing?"

"As well as can be expected. We don't know if or when he'll wake up, so he's staying on the ventilator for now. We try to wake him up every so often, see if he'll start responding to stimuli, and he does sometimes, but not always."

Grace took some notes. "And no one has ever been to visit him?"

"There have been visitors, but no one who has claimed him as family."

"What kinds of visitors?" Grace shifted in her shoes, uncomfortable standing in the middle of the hospital. They always made her uncomfortable, but that day doubly so. She didn't want to see Joseph's still broken and lax face. He should have been found by now, found by family or friends or someone who knew something about him.

Katie sighed. "Mostly religious people."

"Like preachers?"

"Yeah, there have been two ministers and one priest who visit monthly. The chaplain at the hospital also visits weekly, praying over him. Other than that, just a few people who have worked with him who found an attachment."

"Do you keep any kind of record of his visitors?"

"Not formal, but I can get you their contact information."

"That'd be perfect. Thank you."

Katie rustled around in the desk and pulled out a piece of paper, writing the six names on it Grace had requested. As soon as she was done, she handed the paper over. Grace recognized one of the names, someone Amya talked about frequently. A pastor friend of hers who she often did studies with and helped with some programs.

"Thanks," Grace muttered, folding the paper and shoving it into her jacket pocket. "Is there anything else you can tell me about him?"

"Not much. He's the quietest patient on the floor and the easiest to work with."

Grace stared at Katie dead in the face. She couldn't quite tell if it was a joke or if she was really bad at being funny. Katie smirked and nodded her head toward a room.

"We keep him close by because we can."

Turning, Grace saw the room she had been avoiding all day. The sliding glass door was halfway open, but the curtain was closed. She pushed her pen and paper into her pockets and squared her shoulders. She could do this. Taking a deep breath, she stepped toward the room, her heart thundering.

Why she was avoiding him, she had no idea. The case was a strange one, like Humbard had said, but hospitals brought back some not so great memories too, including her own quick stint in ICU as a patient. Stepping around the curtain, she immediately saw him.

His light brown hair was cut and kept but had a slight wave to it as it sat at the top of his head. His cheeks were shaved. No doubt thanks to the nurses who took care of him. His eyes were closed, and Grace realized she had no idea what color his eyes were at all. The picture in the file hadn't even told her that nor had any information in the file itself. Joseph's skin was pale, but it had a darker tone to it that she'd suspect would make him a person of color, though she couldn't be sure.

Laying down it was hard to judge how tall he truly was, but she could ask that if need be. She'd guess he was on the shorter side and definitely under six feet. His body looked completely lifeless. The pressure of the machine breathing for him making his chest rise and fall in such an unnatural rhythm. Grace clenched her fist as she took a step in closer to the bed and to her newest case.

"Well, Joseph," Grace started. "I guess I will get to know you really well."

He didn't move, not that she expected him to. With her jaw tight, Grace moved in closer. The machines surrounded his head and didn't tell her much because she was in no way smart enough to figure them out. The room was eerily quiet, but there was a television on in the corner with an old western on it. Grace figured the nurses kept it on for him for stimulation.

"I really wish you could talk. That would solve the case rather quickly." Grace shifted her stance and glanced out the window. "Good to get a room with a view."

She had no idea why she was talking to a kid who couldn't even think about talking back. Shaking her head, Grace stayed there for another ten minutes before she took a deep breath and turned toward the door. She caught sight of a nurse's aide staring through the open doorway at her. She gave the small man a look then pushed passed to get out as soon as she could. Discomfort was the only thing she felt as she stumbled toward the front entrance to the hospital.

Grace knew she'd have to go back and visit Joseph again, but maybe next time she would insist Amya would go with her. Amya would no doubt know what to do in a way Grace didn't. Shaking the feeling from her arms and hands, she got into her cruiser and let out a breath. All right. She had a case. She had met the victim? No, the suspect? No...the missing? She had met the missing. That made no sense. Groaning, Grace put her head on the steering wheel and let out a large sigh.

It really was like she had been tossed back to her first day on the job when she truly had no fucking clue what she was doing or where she was even supposed to step. Fingering her phone, she called Amya even though she knew she wouldn't answer. As soon as it went to voicemail, she closed her eyes.

"This case is fucking weird, Amya. I'm telling you."

Then she hung up. She went to the precinct and took the long way to get there. She needed to clear her mind and wrap herself around the case Humbard had thrown at her before she ended up like the last four detectives on the case—the ones who did nothing.

FIRST DENIAL

BY THE end of her shift, she was no further into her case than she had been at the beginning except she had met the person she was finding. Which still threw her for a loop. Grace cleaned up her desk, putting everything in its orderly place and sliding it into the proper files in her drawers.

"We going, Halling?"

Grace knocked her chin up at Paige. "Yeah. Meet you there in thirty?"

"See you then."

Letting out a breath, Grace finished everything up and grabbed her keys. Peter was still moping at home so she hadn't really wanted to go there and hang out in a house without booze with no Amya to keep her company. She'd begged Paige once she'd proven a little better attitude with more caffeine to meet up with her at a bar and grill for a light dinner and drinks just so she could have a break from the monotony of being alone.

She also knew Paige would likely want to talk about her break up of her barely-a-month relationship. Grace headed home and switched out her cruiser for the car Amya had bought at the beginning of the year. If she was drinking, and planning on at least two, she could not be driving her cruiser around at all.

Letting the dogs out for a potty break, she changed out of her pantsuit and into a far more comfortable pair of jeans and a tight shirt. Knocking on Peter's door, she opened it when he didn't answer. He was a lump on his bed, which was not too much of a surprise. Sometimes she wondered if he ever moved.

"Hey, kid, I'm going out with Paige for dinner, so you're on your own."

"Okay," he muttered.

Sighing, Grace leaned against the doorframe with her shoulder and stared at his unmoving form under the covers on the twin bed. He had taken it hard when Kit had gone back home, but if she truly thought about it, he was already spiraling down the road of depression before then.

"Peter?"

"Yeah?"

Biting her lip, Grace waited until he popped his caramel-haired head out from under the blankets. She cocked her head to the side at him and let out a breath, knowing the serious conversation would have to wait until Amya was home for sure. "You tell me if you need something, okay, kid?"

"Yeah."

"I'm serious, Peter. We're here for you."

"I know."

"Just making sure you know. I'll be back in a couple hours, but I'm a phone call or a text away if you need me."

"I promise I'll text if I need something."

She could almost see the rolling of his eyes, but the dim of the room made it impossible for her to tell. She wasn't completely comfortable leaving him on his own, but she wasn't going to penalize her life for what-ifs either. She trusted he would be fine for the few hours she would be gone. He had been all day that was for sure.

Letting the dogs back in, she locked the front door as she left and got into the small sedan. It took her ten minutes to get to the bar and grill. By the time she parked, Paige was already inside waiting for her. Paige had invited her to her apartment, but Grace had declined, opting for a public location. That had been her norm lately because of everything that had happened between them.

It had helped. Kind of. She pushed open the glass door and smiled at Paige. "Booth or bar?"

"Bar. It's too busy in here to wait for a booth."

"Lead the way, then." Grace brushed her hand out in front of them. They'd been at the bar together several times throughout the year Grace had worked with Paige. She'd cut back on the number of times in the last several months, not only because her home life had gotten considerably busy since Peter moved in and they had taken on classes to become licensed foster parents to foster Kit, but because Paige had made some awkward and forward moves toward Grace, which she had been extremely uncomfortable with.

Paige slid onto the stool and patted the one next to her for Grace to join. Before she knew it, Paige had a beer and Grace had a whiskey on the rocks between her fingers. "So what'd you do to piss your girl off?"

Paige groaned. "I didn't piss her off."

"Obviously, you did."

Rolling her eyes, Paige took a long drag from her beer. "Apparently I'm too detached."

Narrowing her gaze, Grace studied Paige. "That's not everything."

Paige's lips thinned. "She thinks I like someone else."

Grace's shoulders stiffened. She would have asked, but she didn't want to know the answer because she was pretty sure she already knew. Taking a firm sip of her drink, she set it down and didn't look at Paige. "That sucks."

"Yeah." Paige rubbed her hands on her thighs. Silence fell over them. "Why are you not home with Amya?"

"She's gone, remember?"

"Oh yeah."

"She'll be back this weekend, I think."

"You think?" Paige's green eyes focused in on her. "See? You can't be that into her if you're going to make comments like that."

Groaning, Grace inwardly chided herself for letting her tongue slip. It was one thing to do it with Crystal, but another entirely to do it with Paige. "I'm not picking her up so the exact time doesn't matter. She's home Monday. Peter's picking her up."

"Peter? He still living with you? He get a job yet?"

Grace had to learn to keep her mouth shut. "Yeah, he is. He's going through something."

"Going through what?"

Shrugging, Grace spun her glass between her fingers, really wanting to down the entire thing to get a second drink before it was too late to have another one. Giving in, she knocked it back. "He's depressed, and I honestly wonder if he's drinking again."

"So get him help."

Grace's gaze moved to the corner of her eye so she could give Paige a sideways glare. "Don't think I haven't already tried that. Kid is stubborn."

Snorting, Paige sipped her drink. "Sounds like you."

Grace's heart warmed. It was the first nice thing Paige had ever said about the entire situation. Normally she just made comments about how Peter wasn't really her kid, and Grace would fire back with it didn't matter. But this time it felt different. She felt respected as the adult in Peter's life for the first time.

"Maybe he is a bit like me," she muttered. Grace's gaze caught a pretty blonde out of the corner of her eye. Pursing her lips, she tilted her chin up to stare in the mirror behind the bar to make sure she wasn't seeing things.

Sure enough, Crystal sat at one of the tables with the pretty waitress from the other night, except Crystal didn't exactly look like she was enjoying herself. *Oh, karma is a bitch sometimes.* Grace watched carefully to see if Crystal had even noticed she was in the same building.

When it was clear Crystal's discomfort and annoyance was reaching a pinnacle, Grace leaned into Paige and tapped her arm. "See that blonde over there? The one with the big blue eyes and the skanky little black dress? She's at the table with the brunette."

"Yeah, I see her." Paige's hand moved to cover Grace's on the counter of the bar, and Grace pulled her hand away immediately.

"Want to do me a favor that will win me some massive best friend points?"

"I'll do anything for you."

They stared at each other in the mirror, Paige's green eyes deep and serious, and Grace lost on how to respond. Clearing her throat, she barreled through to her request. "She's on a date, and she's having some issues. Her name is Crystal. She's been my best friend since middle school. Want to go pretend like you're her angry wife and drag her over here?"

"Absolutely!" Paige's sick grin made Grace chuckle. "Blonde one, right?"

"Yeah."

"She's hot."

"Don't even think about it, Delwin. I will beat your ass into tomorrow."

Paige raised her eyebrows up and down. "I could get on board with that."

"Shut up and go save the girl." Grace's cheeks tinged pink.

Paige slid off the stool and straightened her jacket she hadn't changed out of. Her suit fitted her form perfectly, her long lanky legs and broad shoulders. She always looked the part, unlike Grace who never quite felt like she fit into the detective uniform of a pantsuit.

"Crystal, right?"

"Yup."

"I got this."

Paige's walk had a swagger to it as she moved straight up to the table. Grace turned around with her new drink in her hands and watched everything unfold before her eyes. She couldn't quite hear what Paige was saying, but it wasn't much, before she bent down and planted her lips on Crystal's, digging her hand into Crystal's hair and tilting her back in her seat until she was half-covering her.

Grace choked and blinked wildly. That had not been what she meant at all when she'd sent Paige over there. Her heart beat wildly in her chest, wondering if Crystal was going to deck her for sending Paige over instead of just going to save her herself.

When Paige's mouth left Crystal's, Crystal's cheeks were flushed, her eyes wide, and the waitress—whose name Grace couldn't even bother to remember—was gone. Crystal looked up, and when Paige leaned in for another quick kiss before standing straight and holding her hand out for Crystal to take and stand up, Crystal finally saw Grace sitting at the bar.

Rolling her eyes, she gave a small bow to Grace then thanked Paige, who kept Crystal's elbow in her hand as she turned and beckoned Grace over with the crook of her finger. Cursing under her breath, Grace grabbed her drink and Paige's beer and went to the booth they were now apparently claiming as theirs.

She slid in next to Crystal, making sure to put space between Paige and Crystal, not to mention herself. She did not want a repeat of earlier, and she honestly should have thought that one through before sending Paige over. Crystal put her head on Grace's shoulder.

"Thanks."

"You're lucky I was here."

"I think your partner here did all the work."

"Hmm. Some work." Grace sent a glare in Paige's direction. "Crystal, this is Paige."

"I could only assume as much." Crystal put her hand across the table to shake Paige's.

Grace wasn't remiss to ignore the blush still lingering on Crystal's cheeks. "Date bad?"

"Awful. What was I thinking?"

"Pretty sure you weren't." Grace took another sip of her whiskey. "You eat yet?"

"No."

"Good. We haven't either." Grace flagged down the waiter so they could order. She did not want to be stuck there between the two of them longer than necessary. Something was going on with the looks they were sending each other, and it made her uncomfortable to say the least.

By the time Grace was heading home, she knew she had made a mistake sending Paige instead of just doing the damn job herself. The two of them had flirted for hours, insisted on dessert, and then when the bill had come, Paige refused to let anyone else pay it.

Grace could not have escaped faster to save her life. She hopped in her car and called Amya, hoping she would answer the phone this time. When it went to voicemail, she let out a sigh and closed her eyes.

"Well, I just accidentally hooked Crystal and Paige up. See what happens when you leave me on my own? Save me."

Hanging up, she put the car in drive and headed to her lonely house. Her week had gotten off on the wrong foot, and it seemed it was going to continue down that road for at least the next few days. She could only hope something would turn it around soon.

As soon as she got into the office in the morning, Grace started the paperwork to try and get a judge to sign off on getting her all of Joseph's medical records, which surprisingly hadn't been done yet. She couldn't quite tell what the other detectives had done—if anything—but if she had her guess, it was nothing. Nothing at all.

Groaning, she redid the ponytail for her hair and closed her eyes. When everyone else was in the office except Paige, she knew she should have thought better about sending Paige to save Crystal. She hadn't heard a single word from Crystal yet, which also meant only one thing.

She tried to push the thought from her mind because the image her head conjured was not a good one. At least hopefully it would get Paige off her back for a while, until it all blew up in their faces, which it no doubt would in at least a week but no more than two. Crystal and Paige were completely wrong for each other in every sense. Where Paige was rough and tough, Crystal was soft and tender. Paige would eat Crystal up and spit her out in two seconds flat.

When Paige did finally walk into the office, late as was her norm when she had someone to spend the night with, Grace cringed. She did not want to hear any details. At all. Ever. Shutting her mind off was harder than she expected it to be, but she finished filling out the paperwork to get the judge to sign off on getting Joseph's medical records in full.

When Paige finally swaggered over to Grace, and that was the only way she would ever describe that happy "I had sex walk" Paige did, Grace groaned and tried to escape to do work.

"What you working on?"

"My case," Grace answered aloofly. "What are you working on?"

"This new case Humbard landed me this morning."

"Good for you." Grace flipped around some papers on her desk, drawing out what she was doing to try and make it look like she was in the middle of something.

"Want to ride with me?"

Sighing, Grace tried to be smooth as she turned to glance up at Paige who stood over her desk with a hand on the back of the chair and near Grace's shoulder. "I've really got to get a jump on this case."

"It's a four-year-old case, Halling. It's not going anywhere."

"It's four years old, Paige. Don't you think I should try to make some headway on it, finally, unlike every other detective who has had it?"

"Sometimes you're too serious. Learn to take a joke."

Grace's chest tightened. Paige wasn't usually an asshole after she got laid, but because it was Crystal, it stung. If only Amya where there, she would escape down to the chaplain's offices and hide out.

"I can take a joke," Grace muttered and turned to her desk. "I just don't think sleeping with my best friend is very funny."

"Whoa! Slow down. What?"

Grace glared up at Paige. "You heard me."

"You think I slept with Crystal?" Paige's hand landed on Grace's shoulder.

Instead of Grace shrugging Paige's fingers off her like she wanted, she ignored them. "I know you did, and you can deny it all you want, but I know for a fact that is what happened."

"And how do you know that?"

Huffing, Grace leaned in her chair and crossed her arms, glaring at Paige with everything she had. "Because you came in late today, you are being smug, Crystal hasn't texted me all morning or said jack shit about last night, and you are a cocky son of a bitch."

"I know for a fact you don't know we slept together."

"Really?" Grace stood up from her chair, ready for the battle she knew was about to ensue. "And how do you know that, Delwin? Unless Crystal told you she wasn't going to tell me."

Paige's open mouth, blank stare, and flushed cheeks told Grace everything she needed to know and confirmed everything she had been thinking. Grace didn't even bother to grab the papers on her desk as she stepped around Paige and out into the hallway. Walking all the way down to the chaplain's offices, she cursed when she realized there was absolutely no point in her going there.

Grinding her teeth, she spun around and let out a breath. She needed a minute to calm down before she went to her desk to work. Slipping outside, Grace walked around the entire block before she went back inside. Paige sat at her own desk, and Grace ignored her.

With the files in front of her, Grace poured through them. Joseph was sixteen or seventeen when he was found most likely. They weren't sure. He could have been as young as fourteen or as old as twenty. It was hard to tell. She sighed. An age range of five years was a lot to work with when looking through old missing persons cases in the past ten years at least.

When he was found, he had been severely beaten and stabbed several times to the chest, neck, and head even. She had the photos to show everything in her case file she'd been handed. Pulling them out once again, Grace memorized every place Joseph had been injured. His cheek had been cut, the left side of his neck. Most of the stab wounds were on the left side of his body, indicating whoever had tried to kill him was right-handed.

Sighing, Grace put the photos down and focused on the initial investigative report. He'd been beaten and left naked in a ditch on the side of the road. There was no wallet, no ID, nothing to indicate who he was. His entire body had been completely stripped of everything.

No kid deserved that, nonetheless to sit in a coma for four years with no idea what his real name was. Grace gnawed on her lower lip. The only name she had was the taxi driver who had found him. She'd have to interview him soon enough, but first, she wanted to make sure she fully checked him out before walking into that interview.

She pulled his name up and ran it. She risked a glance over to Paige, who happened to be staring directly at her in that moment. Huffing, Grace turned to her computer and ignored Paige's glance. When she was about to skim through the taxi driver's record, she felt a hand on her shoulder.

"If you didn't want me to be with her, you should have said something before it happened."

Grinding her teeth, Grace looked up into Paige's eyes. Paige was right. She hadn't ever said they couldn't or that she didn't want them to. Still, she wasn't happy about it, mostly because she knew she would somehow end up in the middle of it all—she knew it.

"I know. Just...don't hurt her. She's my best friend."

Paige's fingers squeezed, massaging Grace's tense muscles. Grace drew in a deep breath and let it out slowly, still not quite sure how she felt about the entire situation. Figuring she should offer Paige an olive branch after getting so mad she ran away to cool off, Grace nodded her head at Paige.

"Tell me about your case."

"Really?"

"Yes, but no funny business. I'm not going anywhere with you today. I need to figure out something on this case."

"An interview for an interview?"

Grace gave Paige a sideways glance and smirked. "Maybe. We'll see. Who are you looking for?"

"Missing hooker."

"What?"

"Yeah." Paige's eyebrows rose and fell several times. "Go figure. She normally works the streets but hasn't been. Her working friends got worried so they called it in. Means I'm spending lots of time on Second Street."

The taunt on the tip of Grace's tongue was not going to be welcome, so she swallowed it down and went with a nicer one. "Not any place you haven't been before."

"You either, partner." Paige stared directly at her.

Grace's cheeks flushed hot. Every time Paige gave her that look, she couldn't stop her body's reaction, and she hated it. She didn't want to react that way. But with Paige's hand still on her shoulder, she could not stop herself.

"I still don't know where to begin with this case." There was the olive branch if she had ever seen one.

"Tell me about it."

Sighing, Grace turned to her computer and hoped the move would break Paige's grip, but it didn't. "The only person who was there before the cops was the taxi driver."

"So bring him in."

"I plan on it, but I want an objective or two first. It's been four years. I'm willing to bet his story has changed a bit, and I want to know how it changes. Got to figure out how to ask the right questions especially since I have no idea what he was asked four years ago."

"Good detective work right there, Halling. You've grown up on me."

Spinning in her chair, Grace grinned at her. "Why thank you, Delwin."

With one more squeeze to Grace's shoulder, Paige patted her back and walked away, the swagger still in her step. Once again, Grace had to bite back a retort. Concentrating on the reports in front of her, she learned her taxi driver was still a taxi driver in their city, which was a good thing. He'd be relatively easy to find. She could only hope he would be helpful, but she had a sinking suspicion he wouldn't be.

Pulling out a notebook and paper, Grace wrote down the first question that came to mind. *Tell me what happened that night.*

That would lead her down the rabbit hole she wanted to go on, the one that would hopefully lead her to some answers. She wrote out a few more questions, knowing she wouldn't get to ask them all but that some of them needed answered for sure.

She worked through her interview plan until it was time to break for lunch. Paige once again stopped by her desk and smiled. "Lunch?"

"Diner?"

"Really?"

"Yes."

"Fine. But I'm driving."

"Like you'd ever give me that option." Grace grabbed her gun, her badge, her wallet, and her keys. Together, she and Paige walked out of the station together. It may have been a rough start to the morning, but they were on track, now if she could only catch a break in her case, her day would be damn near perfect. Better if

Amya was there, but she would take what she could get.

SILVER ALERT

THE NEXT morning went far better than the previous morning, mostly because Paige didn't stagger in late to work, meaning she hadn't had anyone with her the night before and Grace could rest easy knowing Crystal was not with Paige. Her worry shifted from that debacle to Peter, who still hadn't really emerged from his room. It had gotten significantly worse since Amya had left for her trip, and if Grace didn't do something about it soon, she worried he would become petrified in his bed.

Paige worked on her own case, quietly at her desk. Humbard remained in his office. Other officers stayed in their lane, and for the first time in months, it was a very quiet day in the office. Grace wasn't quite sure what to make of it. Working the streets, she had always lived for the action of having something to do other than just sit in her cruiser and wait. As a detective, she had worried all she would do was sit and deal with paperwork and reports.

She'd been pleasantly surprised to find she often was running from place to place doing research, interviewing, and questioning people involved in her case. But that day, she had nothing to do other than sit on her ass on the phone. The unit was eerily quiet, granted spring break hadn't started yet, and she assumed there would be a few more cases as soon as that happened.

Letting out a sigh, she opened her bottom drawer and pulled out dried banana chips she had stored there to snack on whenever she got a chance.

Popping one in her mouth, Grace made a list of the neighboring counties. It wasn't every case she had to work with her counterparts in other counties, but she did have to do it on occasion, and she had gotten to be on a first name basis with some of them. Not all. Some were jerks but most were pleasant enough.

She would start with the ones she liked. Grace picked up her phone and dialed the number for her counterpart in Johnson County. It was a slightly smaller county than where she lived, and often she had teens that would run away there because it was a hub to escape from whatever they were running from.

"Detective Blake Miller."

Grace smiled at the detective's voice. She had enjoyed more than one drink with Blake on the occasion they'd been able to get together while one of them was in town for some case or another. It was a relationship she had wanted to foster. Blake was a young detective like herself, but Blake knew her stuff and there was no doubt Grace could and would learn from her. She was a good connection to have.

"Blake, it's Grace."

"Grace? What are you doing?"

Snickering, Grace leaned in her chair and relaxed. "I've got a case, and I was wondering if you could help me a bit on it."

"Sure, I've got a few minutes."

"This might take more than a few, but it doesn't have to be right now."

"Hit me. What are we talking about?"

Chuckling, Grace glanced around the room. Paige sent her a curious look, and Grace ignored it, focusing on the conversation at hand. She liked Blake, and it wasn't something she wanted to share with Paige either. It was a connection she had made and one she wanted to keep.

"Okay, so I've got this kid in ICU. He's been there four years. No one knows who the hell he is."

"You're kidding. You landed yourself Joseph's case?"

Furrowing her brow, Grace sat up and leaned over her desk and drew designs on a blank piece of paper she had lying nearby. "You know about his case?"

"I've looked at it every once in a while, curious to see if anyone had come forward to claim him yet, but that's all your county. Ain't got nothing to do with me."

Smirking, Grace popped a dried banana between her lips. "Oh, you know, I'm not too much of one for the rules. What do you know about the case?"

"*You* are a rule whore." Blake snickered. "I don't know much, just that he's still in the hospital and no one has come forward."

"Yeah, that's pretty much what I know. Boss just handed it to me a couple days ago. There is nothing to go on."

"Nothing at all?"

"Nothing." Grace's lips thinned. "Anyway, I was calling to see if you could pull some of the missing cases in your county for me to look at and see if I could match up with this kid."

"I could do that. How far back do you want me to go?"

"Ten years?"

"Halling! Are you serious?"

"I am." Grace sighed and rubbed the bridge of her nose. "This kid came from somewhere at some point. I'm thinking he may have been missing a whole lot longer than everyone else has been thinking."

"You sure about that?"

"I don't know, but I'm checking everything." Grace ran her thumb over the tips of her other fingers as she stared down at her hand. "I don't want to ignore this case like everyone else has."

Blake sighed her tone deeper than before with less joy to it. "I get that. I'll do what I can, but going back ten years is going to take some time."

"I know. But at least I also trust you'll do it."

"Lakin?"

Grace snorted. "Yeah."

"Try to go over his head."

"I'll try, but I don't have much pull with them yet. I haven't had to work with them too much and the one time...well, I'll just say it didn't go well."

"Lakin is an ass. He thinks because he's a detective that he has it made and can boss everyone around, even people in a different agency."

"Yeah, that was the sense I got from him, hence why we clashed."

"You wouldn't be the first, and I doubt you'll be the last."

Grace bit her lip, she knew their conversation was dragging on, but she wasn't going to lie, it was nice to talk to Blake, to someone who didn't know the ins and outs of her life except her work life, to someone she could easily talk shop with. "You got any interesting cases?"

"Just your run of the mill this week. Why?"

"No reason. Thought I'd ask."

"Polite?"

Grace flushed, heat racing to her cheeks as she was finally caught. "If you want to call it that. I should go. Got to call Lakin."

"Good luck with that. I'll email you what I find for now and give you an update on what I find later."

"Thanks."

It took almost all day for emails to start coming in from the other counties, but Grace was pleased with the information she was getting. She printed each and every file to read it over carefully. It would take her awhile to get through them all. She was just about to move on to the next file in her pile when Blake sent an email titled URGENT.

Her stomach full of anxiety, Grace opened it and skimmed the file itself. It was a missing persons case. The description matched her kid almost perfectly except the age would put him closer fifteen at the time of his disappearance. He went missing from Johnson County, but when Grace moved even farther down the file she noted it was solved but there was no more information on it.

She pursed her lips as she pulled up the Internet to run a search. Even if she hadn't gotten the full file from Blake, who might not have known there was more to it, she could see if the news media had reported on anything. Searching for the name and the word "found," Grace hit enter and let the computer do its work.

It took only a few seconds before it popped up. Sure enough, the kid was found dead. Funeral had been a week later. Sighing, Grace shot an email back to Blake with a snarky "He ain't Lazarus" and hit send. Amya would be impressed with that reference—Peter too if he was more with it.

Grace went to look through the other case files she had received. When her back ached, she moved around in her chair to try and ease the pain, but it didn't work. Blake sent her a response, and Grace chuckled at it. They could easily go on and on with emails all day if they were both stuck in the office.

When she opened the email, it was a missing persons file. One that again matched her victim or her missing. But this one too had been solved, by Blake herself. Confused, Grace shook her head and wrote back, asking if Blake had amnesia. She was in the middle of chuckling to herself when Humbard called her name.

"Halling."

"Yes, sir?"

"Case."

Grace shot out of her chair and headed for his office. He leaned against his chair as he handed her a thin print out. "Seventy-eight-year-old man is missing, first name, Eduardo."

"I've got it. You put out an alert?"

"As soon as you verify the information, I will."

Nodding, Grace turned on her toes and headed for her desk. She didn't bother to clean everything up as she grabbed her stuff and walked to her cruiser. She was just about to leave the building when Paige caught up with her.

"I'm coming."

"You're what?"

Paige rolled her eyes. "I gotta get out of here."

"So you're coming with me on my case?"

"Figured you could use a partner."

Grace let out a sigh and ignored Paige as she walked for her car. She got inside, Paige following dutifully. She wasn't even going to argue with her this time around. She was driving, Paige would have to suck it up and deal with it. Grace was out of the parking lot before Paige said a word.

"I like Crystal, you know."

"Jesus fucking Christ."

"Hey! You're not supposed to say that."

"Say what?"

"That."

"Why the hell not?" Grace ground her molars and stepped on the brake at a stoplight a little harder than necessary.

Paige snorted. "Because you're dating the chaplain."

"Just because she believes doesn't mean I do. And she cusses."

"She what?" Paige's eyes were wide.

"Sure. Rarely, but she cusses." Grace's shoulders tightened, her chest constricting. She hadn't anticipated the conversation taking this direction. Letting out a breath, Grace changed the topic back to the other one she didn't want to talk about. "I don't want to talk about you and Crystal."

"You should give me her number."

"Absolutely not." Grace took a turn and headed toward the house for the daughter making the report. "Why the hell would you want that?"

"I told you. I like Crystal."

"You like that she had sex with you the first night."

"No." Paige crossed her arms. Grace shot her a look. "I like her for more than that."

"Whatever."

"No, not whatever." Paige clenched her jaw. "Give me her number."

"I'm going to have to ask her first if she wants you to have her number."

Paige snorted in annoyance. "Fine."

As they arrived at the house, Grace let out a breath. Finally they had something to focus on other than the strange conversations the two of them had been having lately. She almost texted Crystal to warn her about Paige then decided not to. She wasn't sure she wanted to see the answer on that one while she was in the middle of her initial interview.

She didn't even wait for Paige to be with it before she was out of the car and walking toward the front door. The townhome was sandwiched between two others. It was small enough Grace could see why someone who was elderly wanted to live there, but she wasn't sure it would be something she'd ever want. She liked her space.

Knocking on the door with a closed fist, Grace stepped back and waited. Paige caught up, her hands on her hips as she turned and looked around the neighborhood. "I don't think I've ever been to this part of town."

"Lucky for you. This is my old turf."

"Really?"

"Yeah." Grace nodded to a house across the street. "Arrested a meth dealer there once. That is not a night I'd like to repeat. Ever."

"Why? What happened?"

Saved by the door opening, Grace turned to the woman and gave her a small smile. "I'm Detective Grace Halling. This is my partner Detective Delwin. We're here to talk about your father."

"Yes, come in. I'm Evangeline."

Grace didn't look at Paige as she walked into the small condo. It was decently furnished. Clearly an old person lived there. Grace could tell by the smell. They sat down on the couches, Paige next to her, and Evangeline across from them. Grace pulled out her notebook.

"Do you know when your father went missing?"

Evangeline bit her lip and shook her head, her eyes wide with fear. "I don't. I came to check on him this afternoon like I do every Wednesday, and he was gone. I come over Monday, Wednesday, and Friday for lunch, and then I'm here every weekend, too. I don't want to leave him alone if I can help it. He hasn't been the same since Mom died."

Nodding, Grace wrote those days down on her pad. "He was here Monday, though, yes?"

"He was. And I talked to him last night. My sister checks in when she can and said she talked to him this morning."

Grace thinned her lips because Evangeline did know about when Eduardo had gone missing even though she said she didn't. "Did she say if he said where he was?"

"He had to be here. It's a landline."

Grace's lips thinned. She had stupidly assumed cell phone, but she shouldn't have. Chiding herself, she wrote more information down. "Was you father upset about anything?"

Evangeline shook her head. "I don't think so. He's been so happy lately. I don't know."

"Does your father have any medical conditions we should be aware of?" Grace perched her pen over the paper, waiting for some kind of answer. Typically when the elderly went missing it was a sign of some impaired mental capacity. Not always, but she needed to know because it would affect how to approach him when he was found.

"He's been forgetting things a lot lately. We were going to bring him in to the doctor but haven't been to the appointment yet."

"All right. Do you have any idea where he might have gone?"

"I don't know. His car is gone."

"What kind of car does he drive?"

"He's not supposed to drive."

"Why is that?" Grace held in her sigh, but Evangeline was not very forthcoming with information, although Grace was pretty sure it wasn't intentional.

"His eyes are bad."

Grace scratched that into her notebook. "All right. So what kind of car does he drive?"

"A gray Volkswagen. It's newer. I don't remember the year, but it's a newer car."

"Is it registered to him?"

"Yeah. And it has my name on it."

"I can search for it, then." Grace made a note so she'd remember.

"Okay." Evangeline let out a heavy breath. "I'm so worried about him."

Paige interrupted before Grace could speak, her voice firm and serious as she answered. "We'll do our best to find him, ma'am. Grace here is the best detective we have, and she takes all of her cases very seriously."

Grace's cheek tinged with heat, but she didn't dare look at Paige. "I do. I'll work my hardest to find him. I promise."

"Thank you."

"Where are some places he likes to go and liked to go, particularly if there has been a specific decade or time in his life he's been remembering a lot of lately."

Evangeline wrapped her hands together in her lap, twisting her fingers. Her body had a slight shake to it like she was nervous. Her eyes were welled with tears, her nose red, but Grace couldn't quite make out exactly why she was having that specific reaction in that moment. They hadn't said anything to upset her on purpose.

Grace sent Paige a look to see if she had any idea why Evangeline was suddenly breaking down, but Paige shrugged at her—barely noticeable except Grace knew her so well. Turning back to Evangeline, Grace relaxed her stance.

"We'll do our very best to find him, but you have to help us, okay?"

"Okay."

"Good. Where does your dad like to go?"

"Um...he liked to go to the barber." Evangeline wiped her hands under her eyes and let out a breath. "He used to go there every week for the last forty years. Same place every time. Same haircut every time."

"Okay, and where is that?"

"It's in a guy's garage that he converted years ago. Umm...I think it's off Twenty-Second Street? His name is Jasper."

"Oh." Grace smiled. "I know Jasper."

"You do?"

"Yeah." Grace wrote his name down even though she didn't need the reminder. It would be easy to check there but harder to get away. "Where else does your dad like to go?"

"He likes to drive by the fishing ponds. He used to fish there when I was younger, but since he can't really do it any more, he'll go and park there some times and watch the younger boys do it."

Grace wrote that down. She was starting to get an idea of who her father was, a man stuck in the fifties but who loved his family dearly. "Anywhere else?"

"No." Evangeline sniffled again. "Not that I can think of."

"I want you to keep thinking, okay? You can call and tell me when you think of some place he might be."

"Okay." Evangeline's head bobbed as tears streaked down her cheeks. "Okay. I'm so scared he's not going to come home."

"We'll do our best to bring him home." Grace shifted on the uncomfortable couch. The room was suffocating, but it wasn't because of Evangeline. Paige's presence was making it harder for her to focus.

By the end of their conversation both Paige and Grace had reassured Evangeline they would to their best to find her father so many times Grace wasn't sure she could count that high. She'd slipped Evangeline her card, telling her to call if anything came up. They sat in the cruiser and called in the pertinent information to Humbard, and he started the Silver Alert before they even left the condo.

Grace pulled up to the first stop sign and chided herself. She knew she couldn't hold her tongue any more than Paige could. "Why do you want to see Crystal again?"

"I told you, I like her."

"You two are not each other's type. And she's my best friend."

"So is she off-limits?"

Grace wrinkled her nose. "I don't like to do those kinds of things. Crystal dates who she wants to date, but I don't think you're interested in her because of her."

Paige turned, her head against the seat. Grace risked a glance in her direction. For some reason, it seemed as if there was far more than a date with Crystal riding on their conversation. Their friendship too perhaps.

"You're right," Paige muttered.

"Right about what?"

"She's cute, she's hot, she's damn sexy, too, but she is not my type."

"She wants a relationship," Grace commented. "You don't

want that."

Paige chuckled. "Yeah, I do, but not with Crystal."

The tension in the cruiser intensified, the air palpable. Grace gnawed on the inside of her cheek, trying to find something to say. They both knew who Paige wanted a relationship with, and they both knew it wasn't happening—well, Grace knew. Paige for some reason kept holding out hope.

With a deep breath, Grace pulled into the station and parked her cruiser. Paige got out, but she stayed inside.

"What're you doing?" Paige asked.

"I'm going to go check out some of those places Evangeline told us about and talk to Jasper."

"Your choice."

"I'll be back in a few hours."

"Okay."

Grace waited until Paige was inside, not because she thought she had to but because she wanted to make sure Paige stayed at the station and didn't come with her. Grabbing her phone, she sent Amya a text with three simple words she'd never thought she'd say. *I miss you.*

Almost immediately the response came in. *I miss you, too. Only a few more days, love.*

Smiling to herself, Grace slid her phone into the cup holder and backed out of the station parking lot. She had work to do, two cases to solve, and a wayward son who needed a wakeup call. Bolstered by Amya's text, Grace set about her job and planned the conversation she wanted to have with Peter in her head in the meantime.

INTERFERENCE

SHE HAD talked to Peter for hours the night before, pulling him out of his shell. She had hoped it would work a little, but that morning when he'd come out for breakfast—which had been a miracle—he'd pulled right back into himself. Grace had made a hearty breakfast with sausage, bacon, eggs, and English muffins to try and get some meat back on his bones because of all the weight he had lost except he still looked puffy as if he had been up all night.

Grace had insisted he find a job the night before. She didn't care what kind of job, but he needed something to do other than hiding out in his room and three months of that had been plenty to wear on Grace's nerves. She and Amya had already talked through that. She'd just pushed to have the conversation a little earlier with him than planned.

He was, in theory, spending most of the day applying for jobs, although Grace would be happy if he applied for just one. When she'd left the house, she locked the doors behind her and slid into her cruiser, ready for the start of a brand new day.

As she pulled into the parking lot of the station, her cell phone rang. Putting the car in park, she grabbed her cell and grinned at the name flashing across the screen. "I didn't think I'd hear from you anytime soon."

"I had a few minutes before my next lecture, and I wanted to talk to you." Grace could hear the smile in Amya's voice.

Leaning into her seat, Grace couldn't wipe the smile off her face. "It's good to hear your voice, you know."

"Likewise, Grace. Tell me what you've been doing?"

Staring out at the doors to the station, she shifted in her seat. "I got a second case."

"Tell me about the first one."

"I don't even know where to begin." Grace chuckled. "But this second one is much easier. Missing elderly man. I checked some places out yesterday, will check more after I get inside and see if there was any calls about his vehicle."

"Sounds like you've got it handled."

"For now." Grace bit her lip. "How's Jesus camp?"

"Grace," Amya chastised.

"What? I never remember where you're at."

"It's a homiletics conference."

"I have no idea what you just said."

"Preaching, Grace. It's a preaching conference."

"Oh. Why didn't you just say that?"

"I just did."

Grace caught sight of people arriving for work, but she didn't want to hang up. Her heart raced as she fiddled around with the things she had brought with her. "Monday isn't that far away."

"It's not. How's Peter?"

Grace sighed, and she felt herself collapsing in. She had wanted to talk to Amya so bad about Peter in the last few days and even weeks, but they rarely had chance to sit down and figure it all out. "He's Peter."

"What's going on?"

"I told him he needed to get a job last night. Nicer than that, but still."

"He's the same?"

"Yeah. Maybe worse since you left. I don't even see him. Just a lump."

"We'll tackle that when I get back."

Grace nodded. "Good."

"I've got to go. My next lecture is starting, and I don't want to miss it. Cynthia Hale and William J. Barber."

"I have no idea who that is, but you go do your fan girl thing, and I'm going to go find an old guy."

Amya laughed. "I love you. See you soon."

"Love you, too."

Amya hung up first. Grace didn't wait any longer as she grabbed her coffee and orange juice and got out of her cruiser. She was inside within the minute. Grace drew in a deep breath as she walked into the office, stopping short. She normally was the first one there. With her coffee in one hand, orange juice in the other, Grace froze at the doorway to her unit. It was filled with people.

Grace's lips tightened, her shoulders tensed and her knees locked. She swallowed as she looked for one familiar face, one person from her unit, but she found no one. Then, in the back corner, she saw him—the one familiar face in the whole crew. Alonzo Esparza. His dark skin, his darker eyes, and his salt and pepper hair that he combed and glued down perfectly with so much gel Grace was sure she could take a hammer to it and not make a dent.

He stared directly at her. Grace's heart thumped, and she wanted to run out of the room and to her cruiser, restart her day and take more time on the phone with Amya. Whatever shit was about to hit the fan, it was going to spray everywhere. She knew it. They knew it.

If Alonzo Esparza, commander of Internal Affairs was in her unit, something was wrong. His crew were at every desk, including Humbard's, and she was pretty sure they hadn't expected her in that early. Biting her lip, Grace let out a breath, not sure where to go, where to stand, or what to do.

Alonzo headed toward her, and she glared at him. She'd met him twice before, had emailed him once, and talked to him on the phone once, but other than that, she wanted to stay as far away from Internal Affairs as possible. Those people were pariahs, and she did not want to end up like one of them.

"Detective Halling." His voice slid over and sent a shiver down her spine.

"Commander."

"A word."

"Not like I have much of a choice."

He gave her a smirk and nodded his head toward Humbard's office, which he had apparently taken over. With one nod to the investigator who was in there, the office was vacated.

"We're performing an investigation."

"No shit," Grace answered, sneering as she turned to look around the room. "I'm going to assume you can't tell me anything."

"A good assumption."

Grace spun in a circle and looked out at the rest of the office, where her desk was, Paige's desk, everyone she worked with. They would all be coming in shortly, so at least she wouldn't be the only one standing there like an idiot.

"Do I get to work today?"

"Yes."

Turning back to Alonzo, Grace nodded sharply. Without another word, Grace went to leave the office, but Alonzo's voice kept her still.

"Halling."

With a raised eyebrow, she stared at him. "What?"

"The offer still stands."

"I've told you what I think of that offer."

He sat on the corner of Humbard's desk, one leg propped up higher than the other, his hands on his lap as he stared her over. "Yes, you have. But the offer still stands."

"Why would it? I would have thought you'd get the idea that I don't want to transfer to your unit by now." She knew her tone was biting, but she couldn't help it. Walking into an ambush like this would make anyone defensive. But what his statement did tell her was that no matter who he was investigating, it wasn't her. No way would he offer her a job and a transfer if she was the primary reason for him being there.

"You're one hard cookie, Halling."

"I take pride in that, sir."

He chuckled and shook his head. "I like how you work. You are meticulous."

"How do you know how I work?"

Shrugging, Alonzo smirked. "You think today is the first day of our investigation?"

That had been a stupid question. Chiding herself, Grace turned to face the door and wondered when someone else would be coming in to save her from this conversation. Paige was in next. Grace heard her sharp curse at the door. She bit her lip and shifted her gaze to Alonzo.

"You're a smart detective, Grace. One who is thorough and puts her whole heart into every investigation. Not to mention, you like the rules, and you like ethics and morals. I need that in my division. You would make a wonderful asset to Internal Affairs."

She sneered again. "Not happening."

Grace stepped out of the office and met up with Paige by the door. Rolling her eyes, she stepped in close to whisper to Paige. "We're going to be shit at getting anything done for the next while."

"How long have they been here?" Paige whispered.

"Who knows. I was later than I planned, and they were all here by the time I showed up."

"This isn't good." Paige crossed her arms, nodding to Jackson and Kline as they came in. "Who are they looking at?"

"No idea," Grace muttered. "I have shit to do today."

"We all do, kid."

"Humbard's gonna blow a gasket."

"He's going to be late today."

"What?" Grace turned on Paige. "Why?"

"Dental appointment."

Grace snorted. "Prime day for that."

Paige licked her lips. She couldn't even manage to get to her desk, neither could Grace for that matter. Paige asked, "Say, you didn't call them in for something, did you?"

"Fuck no. I'm offended you even asked me that." Grace clenched her jaw. "But seriously, I've got shit to do."

"Better get your stuff before they do."

Groaning, Grace stepped through the throng of people to her desk. She grabbed her paper files, which she always made a copy of, very thankful she did not need to sit at her computer to print things, and stepped away from her desk. Paige gave her a funny look, but Grace ignored her as she booked it out of the room and down the hall.

She went all the way to the other side of the station, where she knew she could find some quiet, and where she hoped Alonzo wouldn't find her. No one followed her. She slid into the office, thankful the door was open. When she shut it behind her, Khloe stared up at her curious and confused.

"Grace?"

"I need some place to work, and hide out, but mostly work. Can I use Amya's office?"

"I'd have to check with her."

Grimacing, Grace looked at the second office she knew was hidden in the chaplain's suites. "Can I use the second office? She doesn't have anything in there that's confidential."

"Yeah, I suppose you could do that."

"Great, thanks! I'll bring you back a coffee when I go out later."

Khloe chuckled. "You don't have to, but I appreciate it."

"Amya appreciates you and everything you do for her, trust me." Grace didn't want to linger too much longer, so she opened the office door and slid inside, shutting it. It was a small room with a couch on one side and two chairs on the other. A small table sat in the corner with a mini fridge underneath it, which Grace knew had orange juice, water, and pop in it.

Letting out a breath, Grace sat on the couch and put her files on the coffee table in front of her. Without a computer, she was going to have to work extra hard on making connections and doing some of her research. Before she got started, she reached for her phone and called Amya, hoping to catch her on a break or something. When there was no answer, Grace groaned.

"I walked in and there was IAB, all over. I'm currently sitting in your offices, hiding and working. I have no idea what's going on. Call me. Please."

Putting her phone to the side, Grace focused on her elderly missing. He was her priority. Joseph had been missing for four years. He could wait a few more days without too much going on to disrupt that case.

Grace made her list of places she needed to go to try and find Eduardo. She did as much possible research as she could from Amya's small secondary office, but eventually her capabilities to work without a computer and pulling files hit her hard and she had run into more than one dead end.

Packing up her stuff, she formulated her plan. She could run in to her unit, grab her laptop, which she had forgotten earlier, and do the rest from her cruiser. She was used to doing work from there, she'd done it for years as a beat cop. It couldn't be that hard to do it again. The problem was going to be getting in and getting out without being stopped by someone, whether from Alonzo's crew or her crew.

As she walked down the long hallway, Grace prepared herself. She did not want to get sucked into the drama. She wanted to get in and get out as quickly as possible. With a last breath, she slipped into the room, which was still in utter chaos. Paige sat at her desk, Humbard stood outside his office with his arms crossed and a scowl on his face.

Grace bit her lip, booked it for her desk, and grabbed her laptop she had shoved in the bottom drawer, then headed for the door. Paige turned at her, and Grace stopped short. "I'm going to do some interviews."

Paige glared but nodded. Alonzo started toward Grace, but Paige stood up and stepped between the two of them, spouting off a complaint about how she couldn't do her job with his people all over. Grace took the opportunity for what it was and left the building.

As soon as she was in her cruiser, she backed out of the parking lot and headed to an empty parking lot where she knew she could sit and focus. It took her a little bit to get re-situated, but as soon as her computer was up and running, she focused on where she was going first. Finally able to check the computer, she saw there had been several calls in on the vehicle, but all of them had proven to be different cars. Nothing to indicate where Eduardo might be.

She had already called Evangeline to check in on her and see if she'd heard anything from her father. That had proven fruitless. With a plan in hand, Grace put her car into drive and drove straight to Jasper's. She wanted to check in with him again, just in case. He was a popular guy, and he'd been too busy to be super helpful the day before.

She pulled up outside his small white house. A knee height white picket fence surrounded half the yard, and the garage door was propped open with an old metal coffee can filled with cement. Grace rapped her knuckles on the screen door and headed inside.

It was dim inside but bright enough Jasper could do his work. Two chairs sat side by side with mirrors facing them. Grace let out a breath. She'd been in here before, with Daniel Mason Brady, her mentor for years before he passed away in a tragic car accident. He had never gotten his hair cut anywhere else, but Grace had only been with him two or three times.

"Jasper?" Grace called.

The small elderly man came around the corner of the garage. His apron he wore over his waist was tied tight across his hips, small instruments he no doubt used all the time tucked into the pockets on the apron. His back was far more twisted and curved than when she'd seen him years ago, but he was somewhere in his nineties from her estimation. She figured she would find out when he died and read his obituary.

"Hey there, Miss."

Grace gritted her teeth. She wanted to correct him but instead held her tongue. "Jasper, I wanted to talk to you about Eduardo."

"Oh, yes! He's a good man."

"Yeah. Have you seen him at all?"

Jasper shook his head, his gray hair he kept slightly long shaking with the movement. His curved spine worried her, but she was pretty sure if she made a comment about him almost breaking, he'd put her in her place faster than she could say uncle.

"Has he been normal lately? Like when he was here last, did the conversation repeat at all?"

"All our conversations repeat." Jasper chuckled, his voice deep as he moved to grab his broom and sweep up some hair on the floor. "I'm a barber, not a therapist, but everyone repeats themselves sooner or later."

She couldn't fault him there. "What has he talked about lately?"

"Oh this and that."

Grace clucked her tongue. "Jasper, I'm not asking to be nosy. I'm asking because I need to find him, and it's likely he went some place he was talking about recently."

That stopped him. His small frame and thin hands gripping the broom tightened. "His wife."

"He talked about his wife."

"Yup. And his daughters, but when they were little, not now. He was telling some story about when he took them to a zoo."

"That's very helpful. Thank you." Grace shoved her hands in her pockets and rocked back on her heels. It was good to focus on something she could do, something she could accomplish. "Was there anything else he's been talking about a lot lately?"

Jasper's lips thinned. "Hmmm. Nope. Just the girls and Julia."

"Julia? Who's Julia?"

Jasper didn't dare look at her. "His wife."

"His wife's name was Maria. Who is Julia?"

The color drained from Jasper's cheeks. "Oh, right, I mean Maria. All these names. I get them confused."

"No. Jasper, who is Julia?"

Jasper shrugged and turned his back to Grace to continue sweeping the floor. She was going to wait him out. Nothing in her research had indicated a Julia of any kind. Grace moved her foot so her toe pressed into the ground and twisted her knee as she stared at him. She'd wait one more minute before she asked him another question.

When he finished the floor, he glanced at her and had a look of surprise on his face like he was shocked she was still there. Sighing, he leaned the broom against the wall. "Julia was his girl."

"Like his girlfriend?"

"You could call her that."

"For how long?"

"What?"

"How long was he having an affair?"

Jasper snorted. "Decades."

Narrowing her gaze, Grace shook her head at him. "What's her last name?"

"I don't know that. A man don't go telling secrets he don't want revealed."

"He obviously told you about Julia, so he trusted you."

"By accident. I caught him one night out dancing with her."

"Dancing where?"

Jasper's brow furrowed, and his lower lip popped out. "An old warehouse off downtown. It was called The Emporium before it was shut down."

"That was like thirty years ago."

Shrugging, Jasper stared right at her. "You asked."

"Thanks." She asked him few more questions, once again told him to call if he saw Eduardo, and then she got in her car. Letting out a breath, Grace mulled it over in her head exactly where The Emporium was. She'd driven by it, remembered the sign that was so faded she could barely read it, but the exact location wasn't all that easy to remember as was the general area.

It took her twenty minutes to get downtown, and then another five to get to the outskirts of downtown, the part where the buildings were run down, right on the edge of where the train tracks were. Rubbing her lips together in a nervous gesture, Grace leaned forward in her seat as she looked around, eyes wide open, for the silver car he drove.

Sure enough, when she took the next left, she saw the sign for The Emporium just like she remembered it. Grace drove right for it. Once she pulled up by the front door of the large warehouse-like building, she saw his car. The license plate was a dead match.

Grace parked, and as she got out of the cruiser, she called for backup, but she didn't wait. The front door was broken in, the thin wood snapped by the door handle. She knew Eduardo had been unlikely to do that based on his health and how elderly he was. She pushed the door open and grabbed her gun, holding it out in front of her just in case.

"Eduardo?" she called. "Eduardo, I'm with the Sheriff's Department, are you in here?"

A rustling echoed at her, and not for the first time, did she wish she had a mag light to show her the dark corners of the room. With just the light from the broken in door and the random broken spots in the roof, she made him out. His gray sweatpants were dirty, his white t-shirt ripped on one side, but overall, Eduardo looked to be in decent shape.

Grace stepped up closer to him, lowering her volume and softening her tone. "Eduardo! I'm so glad to have found you. I'm Detective Grace. Evangeline is very worried about you."

"Evangeline?" he asked, turning to her.

"Yeah, your daughter." Grace holstered her weapon, although it wasn't without a sense of fear pricking the back of her neck. "I talked to her yesterday. She's worried about you."

He nodded. "I—I was waiting for Julia. She promised she'd meet me here."

Grace squatted next to him and put a hand on his knee. "You miss her."

Once again, his chin bobbed up and down, tears brimming in his eyes. "It's been a few weeks since I was able to take her out. She loves dancing, so I always take her dancing."

"I bet she probably is just running late. You want to come outside with me and see if we can find her?"

"Oh! Would you do that for me?"

"I would." Grace gave him a sweet smile. "Come on."

She stood up and held her hand out for him. Eduardo took it, holding on tightly as they made their way out of the warehouse and toward her cruiser. A uniformed officer arrived just as they stepped into the sunlight. Eduardo gripped Grace's hand hard, and she let him. She didn't want to lose the connection she had already built with him.

"I'm going to call Evangeline, okay?"

Eduardo nodded at her but still refused to let go of her hand. Grace pulled her phone from her pocket and hoped she didn't drop it as she unlocked it and dialed Evangeline's number. It was a good day, but it was going to be a long one of paperwork. She had found her missing silver alert in just over twenty-four hours. That was something to celebrate, even if the investigation back at the unit was going to interfere with the work she could accomplish on Joseph's case. As soon as Evangeline answered, Grace turned all of her focus onto the case at hand.

PANIC ROOM

FRIDAY HAD not come soon enough. Grace had spent hours bent over her computer finishing out her reports with Alonzo Esparza and his crew hanging around and watching every little thing she did. She had taken to escaping her desk as often as she could, but with a case closed, she couldn't just leave. She had paperwork to complete.

Paige was hitting a max on her patience level, too, that was clear to everyone in the vicinity. Grace had shot her a few dirty looks, silently telling her to calm down, but it hadn't worked. Paige's body language told Grace that Paige was worked up to the point Grace knew a rant was coming. It was a good thing Amya was still out of town.

She ditched the office an hour early like she did every Friday and headed down to Granville High School where her program ran. They were having a simple follow up from the interviews and talking about the different parts of a job, like paying taxes from a paycheck, the importance of showing up on time and not giving lip. That was going to be a fun conversation.

As soon as she arrived, Grace checked in at the front office and grabbed her stupid visitors badge they insisted she wear—though, she swore her police badge should be enough, she played by their rules, really not wanting to piss off the front secretary. Again. With the badge around her neck on the ugliest lanyard she was sure they could find, Grace stalked through the busy halls toward the classroom she'd been assigned.

Kit was already in the small room, but no one else was there as Grace entered. Puzzled, Grace cocked her head at Kit and rubbed her lips together. "Shouldn't you be in class or something?"

Kit shrugged. "They let us out early today."

"That's hella early to be let out. You better not be lying because you know I have no issue going down to the office and asking if you were present for your last class of the day and all your classes for that matter."

Rolling her eyes, Kit let out a huge sigh only a teenager with too much attitude and hormones was capable of. "Fine, I skipped my last class."

"Kit. We talked about this."

"What are you going to do about it?"

Grace didn't want to have this battle again. They didn't have a choice for Kit to go home. They would have much preferred she stay at their house where she was actually supported, respected, and safe, but the state had sent her home. Reunification always the goal even if it wasn't always the best.

Sliding into the seat next to Kit, Grace stared out the door of the small room, hoping no one would stop by in the next few minutes so she and Kit could have a real serious conversation. "What's with the attitude? Cut it, seriously. I don't want to hear it."

Kit growled, legit growled. Grace shot her a dirty look.

"Nope. I can walk out of this room right now, Kit. You want me to listen, I'll stay, but I'm not doing it if you're going to act like this."

Kit's nose scrunched before she stared down at the desk in front of her.

"Just because you have been given a shitty hand doesn't mean you can give up the hand you've been dealt. In the game of life, folding is not an option."

"What's that even mean?"

Grace closed her eyes briefly before opening them again to stare at Kit's crystalline eyes, that deep blue with specs of black that reminded her so much of Amya. They both had the same stubbornness to boot. "It means you've been dealt a crappy hand. You don't have a perfect life. Your parents are not great parents.

They don't treat you right, but that doesn't give you permission to act like an ass, to not go to class, to not learn, to not finish high school. If you don't do those things, it's on you. Not them."

Kit shrugged. "I don't care."

"Trust me, you will in about five years when you can't find a job because you don't have a diploma. That shit makes a difference."

"So you've said."

"And I mean it! I've been there. It's no joke. Get your diploma, then you can figure life out on your own, but until you're eighteen, you're stuck at your parent's house."

"Can't I just live with you?"

Grace's heart broke. She wanted to tell Kit yes, wanted to open not only her doors to her house but her arms, but she couldn't. Her hands were tied, and since Kit hadn't been kicked out of her house again and was living on the streets, Grace wasn't going to push it. She had to support the decisions made for a kid with the intentions of her best interest in mind even if Grace didn't think they actually worked for her best interest.

"Not right now, kid. You know that." Her voice was soft when she spoke, and she knew the disappointment and frustration rang through her tone as loudly as it did Kit's. Well, maybe not as loudly, but enough Kit would hear it.

"Spring break?"

"Yeah. Let's do Spring break." Grace watched as Annabelle slipped into the room—Kit's best friend and sometimes girlfriend—Grace couldn't figure that one out, but it did remind her. "But no sleepovers."

"What?"

"You heard me," Grace muttered. "You know the rules. If you want to crash out our house, you have to follow them."

Kit pouted, but she nodded. "Fine."

"Good." Grace patted Kit's shoulder and hunched over the table. They spent the rest of the afternoon going through the interviews, talking about more tips for when interviewing, and Grace teasing them when the moment was right.

As she released them for the evening, Grace turned her head up to find Peggy standing in the doorway with a smile on her lips. As soon as the last of the kids was out of the room, Grace cocked her head at Peggy with a raised brow, silently asking her what was up. Two visits in two weeks was out of the ordinary.

"Kit skipped."

"I know." Grace sighed. "She confessed it all under the hot interrogation methods by this fine cop."

Peggy chuckled. "She's been skipping all week."

"I'm not surprised." Grace straightened her shoulders. "She doesn't see the point. She's not interested in college, and any job she wants she doesn't need a diploma for, and if her parents don't care, why should she?"

"She's slipping back into old habits."

"I know. I talked to her about it, but I'm not sure what else I can do. She's not in my custody anymore." Grace couldn't figure out why they were going in circles.

"She respects you."

The warmth that seeped into Grace's chest surprised her. Staring straight into Peggy's eyes, Grace shook her head. "Have you heard the way she talks to me? She does not respect me."

"She does otherwise she wouldn't talk to you that way. Remember, there are two types of people guaranteed to be assholes in this life: toddlers and teenagers."

"I haven't been around many toddlers."

"Trust me, they're not that much different than teenagers except teens are quicker with words."

"I guess that makes sense. Amya's got a bunch of nieces and nephews, so some of them are toddlers, but I don't really see them ever." Grace packed up her bag, her stomach tensing at the thought.

"You don't go to family holidays?"

Grace shrugged. "I'm not really family."

"Haven't you two been together awhile?"

"Three years."

"That's a long time."

"For some." Grace wanted to escape. The conversation had taken an odd turn, one she was very uncomfortable with. Sure Peggy knew about her and Amya—she'd never tried to keep that secret, but she didn't want to dissect her relationship with Peggy either. "Hey, while I have you here, do you remember a case about a kid who was found on the side of the road, beaten, and in a coma?"

"No."

Grace nodded. "It was about four years ago. He was a minor. They figured he'd be about seventeen when they found him, but no one knew his name. They called him Joseph."

"I mean, I vaguely remember it."

"So you didn't have any kids go missing from school randomly during that time?"

Peggy shook her head. "I think I would remember if one of my kids went missing like that."

Pursing her lips, Grace nodded. "Right, but he might not have been reported missing. He may have just stopped showing up to school."

"I don't remember any. Sorry." Peggy crossed her arms, eyeing Grace carefully.

"It's fine. I figured it was a long shot to begin with, but I do have to get some work done on that case, so unless you needed something."

"Just to talk about Kit."

"Like I said, I think I've done what I can for now. She asked to stay for spring break, so I'll make sure she gets her homework done while she's with us, but I can't guarantee anything when she's home."

"I know. I just...I worry for her. It's funny. I never would have worried for Annabelle, yet she's the one who ended up in trouble."

"Hmm...she was the one in trouble. I have a feeling Kit is going to find herself in a whole lot more trouble than Annabelle was in. And, to be fair, Annabelle wasn't really in trouble."

"No." Peggy stepped out of the classroom, walking with Grace down the hall. "She wasn't. I meant trouble in the sense you were involved."

"I was, but that's the blessing of Missing Persons. We're not typically there because of trouble, only because someone has gotten lost in some way."

Peggy stopped and grinned at Grace. "I wish you'd be our Resource Officer, really. You have a way with understanding the world I think these kids could really benefit from."

Laughing, Grace pulled off the visitor's badge and handed it over. "I'll stick to my day job, thanks."

Without looking back, she left the high school and hopped into her cruiser. The sun was setting and a chill had taken over the air. Grace wished she'd remembered to bring her jacket with her, but in all the fuss with Alonzo's investigation, she had forgotten to grab it when she'd ditched the office. Hoping the heat caught up fast, she pulled out of the parking lot and headed for home.

When Grace pulled into her driveway, she narrowed her eyes

at the cruiser already parked out front. Gritting her teeth, she realized it was Paige's and knew she was done for. As soon as she stepped out of her car, Paige shot out of hers and came straight over to talk.

"Where the hell have you been?"

Grace shrugged. "The school, where I am every Friday. What are you doing here?"

"I need to talk."

Paige was tense. The energy simmering just under the surface of her body palpable. Grace glanced at her front door, knowing Peter was likely inside. She had wanted to try and coax him out for dinner and yell at him to change his sheets, but if Paige was coming over, she knew her night was going to be focused on her rather than on the wayward kid in her house who needed some motivation for life.

"About what?"

"This whole IAB investigation. It's freaking me out."

Sighing, Grace nodded her head toward her front door. "Let's go, then. No booze, though."

"Fine. I just need to vent."

Raising her eyebrows rapidly, Grace turned toward her house and unlocked the front door. Before she was even two steps inside, she knew the dogs hadn't been out at all that day. Roslin and Izzy jumped on her before racing to the back door and jumping again. Grace walked straight for the door and let them out to burn some energy and take care of themselves.

When she turned around, Paige stood right next to her, too close for comfort. Grace wished for Peter to come out of his room and into the room with her and Paige, a buffer of sorts, but she knew her wish wouldn't come true.

"I haven't been in the office much. Any idea what the investigation is for or who they're looking into?" Grace asked as she walked to her fridge to fill a glass with ice water for herself and one for Paige.

"No fucking clue, but I'm pretty sure they're after me."

"What? Why? What'd you do that would bring them in?"

"I don't know." Paige let out a large breath and plopped down onto Grace's couch before standing up again. "I don't know."

Pacing back and forth, Paige put her hands on her hips, then across her chest, then back down to her hips. Her energy ran everything. Grace stepped closer, handing her the glass of water as she slowly sipped from her own. She knew the investigation didn't involve her, but she had no idea if it involved Paige. She hadn't asked Alonzo, not that she thought he would actually answer if she did. In all the time they had worked together, she hadn't seen Paige do anything that would warrant an investigation, but she wasn't with Paige all the time either and they certainly didn't work every case together.

"You have to just let them do their thing, and we'll find out eventually what's going on." Paige glared. Grace swallowed hard, not sure what she'd said that was wrong. Paige clearly didn't like something she had said with the look she was receiving. "What?"

"They're after me."

"Paige, calm the fuck down. And sit down. Seriously." Grace rolled her eyes and plopped down into the chair next to her couch so Paige would have no option of sitting next to her, which she knew would happen if she did go for the couch. She had worked hard in the last three months to maintain as much distance from Paige, physically, as possible after some very awkward moments and a very jealous Amya. Having Paige in their house wasn't going to bode well for Amya's jealousy when she found out.

Grunting, Paige collapsed into the couch, grabbed one of the side pillows and shoved it on her lap like it would protect her from everything. "I know what they're after."

"What?"

"I don't want to drag you into my drama, kid."

"Paige, you showed up at my house in an all-out panic. You better tell me what the hell is going on otherwise I'm kicking you out. I've got other things to do with my time." Taking a sip of her water, Grace watched Paige carefully over the rim of the glass. Paige went from offended, to upset, to resigned in the matter of a split second. Grace admired how quickly Paige could work through all of that.

"Fine. I fucked up."

"On what?" Grace moved her head side to side, hearing the dogs at the back door and music down the hall from Peter's room.

Paige sighed. "You remember that case, ages ago, the one I took over when I transferred in?"

"Yeah. I remember that case." How could Grace forget? Her favorite resident at the Campbell Home gone missing for weeks before they found him. She'd done her best to help with the case but had met resistance in her own unit until Paige arrived. It had been what solidified their friendship, which perhaps hadn't been the wisest choice Grace had made. Still Harold held a special place in her heart, and she thought of him every Christmas and every Saint Patrick's Day on his birthday.

Letting out a heavy breath again, Paige fell into the couch, the small pillow pressed to her chest as she held it tight, not looking at Grace or really anywhere specific. "Well, I didn't follow all the protocols I should have."

"Really?" Grace wracked her brain. At one point, she had memorized that case. "Does it matter, though? That case was a year ago. Would IAB be investigating a case so old?"

"The brother threatened to sue."

"You think he's suing us?"

"Not us. Me." Paige's eyes were shut tight.

"What? If he was going to sue anyone, it'd be me. I was the one who dealt with him mostly."

Paige shrugged. "I may have had a few choice words for him, too."

"Did you really?" Grace raised an eyebrow, curious what Paige had said to him because the lecture she had wanted to give had carried with it an extensive amount of cursing and screaming.

"I did." Groaning, Paige sunk impossibly farther into the couch. "God, this could ruin me."

"You're close enough to retiring, aren't you?"

Paige snorted. "Sure...in three years I can retire with fifty percent of my pension. That's totally enough to live off. Get a grip, Halling. I don't make that much to retire after twenty years."

"Well, if you have to—"

"Nope. If they're taking me down, they're taking me down."

"That's fucking stupid."

"What?" Paige looked bewildered.

"That's stupid. Really. Don't let them take you down if you don't deserve it. You're better than that. In fact, I'm not sure I've ever seen you step aside and just take what was doled out or given up so easily."

Paige's green eyes connected with Grace's, and there was meaning in them far deeper than an IAB investigation. Grace swallowed and tried to push past it.

"You don't give up, Paige. I have never known you to do that. Ever. So why now?"

"I hate IAB."

"Who doesn't?" Grace chuckled and took a sip of her water. That was the precise reason why she turned Alonzo down every time he asked her to transfer. She did not, under any circumstances, want to be the scourge of the earth. She liked that the uniformed officers still liked her well enough to give her tips and help her out easily enough when she was in the middle of an investigation. She liked that she had friends in different units who called on her with questions, and even different agencies.

"Truth." Paige grunted. "I wish you had booze."

"Don't we all," Grace muttered into her glass as Peter's door opened and shut. She twisted in her chair to watch him walk down the hallway in boxers and nothing else. His hair had grown out so long that it brushed his shoulders, and it was massively askew. She wouldn't be surprised if he hadn't showered all week, and if he got much closer, they would no doubt be able to smell him.

He reached the entry into the living room, his footfalls stumbling when his gaze caught sight of Paige before he turned and made for the kitchen without a word. Grace pursed her lips. She had never thought she'd have a twenty-one-year-old kid living with her who acted more like an upset teenager. Shaking her head, she turned to Paige and shrugged.

"You should just chill about it. There's nothing you can do, anyway." Grace set her glass onto the end table and made sure to keep her eye on Peter. She was curious how long he'd stay in their presence before retreating to his room again.

Paige groaned. "I can't just leave it alone."

"What are you going to do?"

"I don't know, but they're supposed to interview me first thing Monday morning."

"Huh. I haven't been asked for an interview yet."

"Oh, you'll be next on their list, I'm sure."

Grace shrugged. She really had nothing to worry about. Alonzo had said as much in their all-to brief meeting before everyone else arrived. He'd been sly in how he'd told her, but she'd read right through the lines. Though, with how worried Paige was, there was probably something else she wasn't sharing that was bugging her and making her think her job was on the line.

One little lawsuit from a guy who was an ass to begin with wasn't enough for her to really be worried about her job, especially when that case was a year out. Yes, the ass had threatened it, but if he was truly going through with it all, they would have likely heard from him before then. Paige's story didn't add up, and Grace wondered for the first time if Paige was lying to her.

She'd have to keep her wits about her just in case. She needed to be able to trust her partner, and if Paige was lying, then she certainly couldn't trust her. Grace shot a look over at Peter as he shoved a plate in the microwave, no doubt making a Hot Pocket again. He lived off those things, and she was pretty sure he was going to turn into one if she let him.

"I'm sure I will be. Still, I want to finish this case before they get hold of me, or at least make some good headway on it. IAB interviews seriously slow me down."

"What do you mean?"

Grace froze. Maybe Paige didn't know about her previous encounters with IAB. Rubbing the back of her neck, Grace tried to backtrack. "On my last couple years in uniform I had some interviews with them because of a case I kept running into. Quite a few interviews later and I now have a thorough understanding of how they function and how they try to peck away at an officer's self-esteem, confidence, and trust in the job and the rules."

"Wow."

"Yeah." Grace pursed her lips and shot Paige a look before glancing at Peter. "You going to wash your sheets any time soon? The stench is reaching my room."

"Whatever," he muttered as he walked by them and turned the corner down the hall.

"Not whatever! Wash them!"

"Yes, Mom."

The whine in his tone actually gave her a surge of pleasure, along with the endearment he rarely ever called her. He'd meant it as a tease, but still, it felt damn good to have that title with him and that he felt comfortable enough to tease her in that way.

"Are we eating dinner?"

"What?" Grace turned to Paige sharply.

"Well, the kid got food, and it reminded me I missed lunch. I'm starving."

"Fine. Order pizza, but you're buying."

"Pizza?"

Grace shrugged. "Order whatever, then. You're still buying."

"You're an ass."

Smirking, Grace chuckled. "Only half the time."

Paige pulled out her cell phone to order some food. Grace

checked hers and realized she had missed a call from Amya in the midst of their conversation. Cursing, she set the phone on the arm of the chair in case Amya called again. She did not want to miss talking to her.

As soon as their dinner was ordered, they settled into an easy conversation about work and Crystal—as much as Grace tried to avoid that topic. She hadn't even dared ask Crystal yet if she wanted Paige to have her number. She was way too scared of the answer she might get and then the subsequent best friend dating her coworker drama and fall-out that would no doubt ensue.

Grace could certainly do without that. Before their food arrived, she heard Peter's door open one more time. Twisting around in her chair, she watched him walk—this time with pants on—to the hall closet where their washer and dryer were. He shoved his sheets into the washer before skittering back to his room. Grinning, Grace turned to Paige who had a look of astonishment on her face.

"That never worked when I was a kid," Paige commented.

"Does it work now?" Grace asked, grabbing for her water again.

"Ha! No. Not even now."

"Figures. He's a good kid at heart. He's just a little lost."

"Then I'd say he's landed in a damn good place to be a little lost."

The compliment took her off-guard. Paige had been full of them lately, since she'd had her last break up. Grace wanted to narrow her gaze at Paige but resisted. She didn't want it to come off as flirtatious, but she was definitely curious what was floating around Paige's brain as to why those comments and compliments had been running rampant in their conversations as of late.

"I suppose he has," Grace muttered, ending the conversation when the doorbell rang with their food order. Saved by the bell had never had a more perfect ring to it.

SECOND DENIAL

THE FLIGHT had been short, although Amya had to fly farther away from home to fly home, which never ceased to amaze her. It had felt like a long day and the end to an even longer week. While she always enjoyed religious events that were full of learning and camaraderie with other clergy and they rejuvenated her soul, she was left exhausted at the same time. It was an odd sensation.

Amya stood at baggage claim, checking her phone every once in a while. Grace was still at work and hadn't been able to sneak away to pick her up, which had left Peter or a cab. Since Peter was technically living off them for free, they'd told him it was part of his rent to pick up Amya. She wasn't quite sure what to do with him, but ever since he'd officially told the school he would be taking a hiatus for at least a semester, he had spiraled down faster than she had expected.

Amya grabbed her luggage and pulled out the handle to roll it behind her. She stepped outside to wait for Peter to show up and get her. She had enjoyed living there the past three and a half years, and it had been an excellent choice of a move for her to make after finishing up seminary. Ten years on the streets as a cop had been enough to wound her heart. She wasn't sure how Grace or some of the other officers she talked with did it some days. Ten years had been plenty for her until she'd finished her master's and applied to be a chaplain at several police departments.

She bounced in her tennis shoes, wishing she had brought a warmer jacket. While winter was nearly over, March always brought with it a chill she struggled to get out of her bones. It wasn't until well into summer that she felt completely comfortable leaving the house with a sweater or a jacket in hand. Grace teased her relentlessly for it.

Turning her head side to side, she looked for her tiny car she'd bought at the end of the last year when they'd thought Kit was going to be staying quite a bit longer with them. She'd realized quickly with Peter and Kit in the house, or even one of them, they were going to need another car since they had sold Grace's old Mazda for parts when she'd been issued a cruiser for work.

She shivered slightly and checked her phone again. No messages from Grace, none from Peter, and whoever was supposed to pick her up—which was Peter, but who knew—was already twenty minutes late. She could call a cab, but that would dip into finances they hadn't planned on. Not that they couldn't move things around, but if there was one thing she had learned in the year of living with Grace, it was Grace was obsessive about her finances and kept a very tight leash on everything.

Their finances were still mostly separate minus some of the house bills while Amya finished paying off all her schooling, but she hated relying on Grace when she didn't have to. Groaning when there was still no sign of a vehicle, she grabbed her phone and called Peter. It rang and rang and rang until it went straight to voicemail.

Scrunching her nose, Amya tried again with the same result. Next she called Grace just to double-check that Peter truly was the one picking her up because at that point he was hitting close to an hour late and it was way too cold for her to be standing outside in nothing other than slacks and a suit jacket.

When Grace didn't answer, she pulled up a search on her phone for an Uber. She was just about to hit pay when she saw her car coming toward her. Erratically. Amya watched. Everything happened in slow motion. The car swerved side to side, inching its way along the roadway to where she stood. Brakes were tapped. Multiple times.

Peter finally pulled the car to a stop in front of her. Amya's heart was in her throat. He didn't get out. Amya took a deep breath, fear racing down her spine and her stomach twisting with anxiety.

She had never anticipated needing to have this conversation with anyone again, nonetheless Peter. But she had been a cop. She'd done it before, she could do it again.

She opened the back door, shoved her suitcase inside, and then instead of getting into the passenger seat, Amya walked around the front of the vehicle to the driver's door and wrenched it open, the sickly sweet smell of alcohol flooding her nostrils. When she spoke, she made her voice low, deep, angry. She set her face in a look of disappointment. "Get out."

Peter reached for the seatbelt and pushed the button, depressing the release. Amya reached in and grabbed his arm to get him out faster. He was moving so slow, unlike anything Grace had ever told her when he'd been drunk before.

Amya took him to the curb and stood him before her. It was probably comical, a barely over five foot brunette middle-aged woman with her hands on her hips and a glare in her eyes, yelling at this twenty-something six-foot kid in the middle of the sidewalk, but it needed to happen.

"What do you think you're doing?"

Peter shook his head, not saying anything.

"Don't! Don't even think about avoiding this one. You're done for."

"What?"

Even his eyes told her he was beyond drunk. They were blood shot. The smell of alcohol churned her stomach the moment she had opened the back door. Standing in front of him this way was easier on her stomach, but she knew she'd have to get back in that car again.

"Don't what me. You're drunk."

Peter shrugged.

"No. You are an alcoholic. How long have you been drinking?"

"Just today."

She narrowed her gaze at him. "You better not be lying to me. Where'd you get it?"

"The store?"

Snorting, Amya crossed her arms and tapped her shoe against the ground as she debated what to even say to him. He wasn't her kid, and even if he was, he was an adult. She couldn't force him to go to rehab or talk to a drug counselor, or take him to an AA meeting. She could call the cops on him for drunk driving, but she wasn't sure that would get the results he needed either, since he'd already had a DWI which had landed him with them.

"Get in the car."

"Huh?"

"Get in the car." When he started toward the driver's side, Amya scolded him. "Don't even think about it. You're not driving anywhere."

She slid behind the wheel, rolled down all four windows and closed her eyes. She needed to talk to Grace about all of this. But it wouldn't be soon enough, she knew that. Grace still had a full day of work ahead of her, which meant she wouldn't be home for hours. For now, the weight of the responsibility was entirely on her shoulders.

Shoving the car into drive, Amya headed for home. She remained stoically silent the entire time. As they pulled into the driveway, she turned and raised an eyebrow at Peter. "Go take a cold shower, get some water, and start sobering up."

"Okay."

When he moved without another complaint, she knew he was far gone. She watched him walk into the house, which he had also apparently forgotten to lock. Good thing she was the one coming home to find that and not Grace. She leaned her head against the seat and closed her eyes. It was going to be a long day, indeed.

She didn't wait much longer before she grabbed her suitcase and headed inside. She stashed it just inside the door to their bedroom and walked straight for Peter's. He'd at least listened and was in the bathroom, which left the room to her. She didn't wait as she tore it apart, looking for where he hid all the alcohol.

She opened the closet, started on the upper shelves before she flipped the mattress up and looked under. All in all, she found nothing. No hidden bottles. Pursing her lips, she surveyed the room again before leaving it and walking to the guest room, repeating the process. She knew where Grace and her alcohol was, which was locked up in the bottom of the gun safe in their bedroom. They had talked for months about getting a second safe so guns and alcohol weren't stored together, but hadn't had the time to do it yet.

Sighing, she put the guest room back in order and started on the living room about the time Peter left the bathroom. She heard him curse and ask what she thought she was doing. Amya ignored him and continued her search. It took her a total of three hours to finish her first not completely thorough search of the rest of the house. She and Grace would have to do a much more detailed one later because she'd found absolutely nothing.

Collapsing onto the couch, Amya rubbed the bridge of her nose and her eyebrows and temples in an attempt to remove some of the tension that had built up there. Peter came out and grabbed a glass of water and some food, sitting at the kitchen table to eat.

She didn't want to talk to him. She didn't know what to say. She worried if she did start that conversation right then and there the only thing out of her mouth would be accusations and screams. They had done so much for him that she felt heart broken. Like it hadn't been enough, which Amya knew was her head telling her heart lies.

She could not control another person. She could not make them do what she wanted them to do. Peter proved that endlessly, but this was a whole new level of proof. Curling into her couch, she pet the cat who came to settle on her feet and stared at the dogs who were finally calm enough to settle on the living room rug.

Every answer she came up with didn't seem like a good one. All she wanted to do was yell and scream, which she knew was going to get nowhere, especially with him in that state. Amya closed her eyes. She'd just wanted to come home, take a nap, start her laundry, and pray Grace was able to sneak away from work a few minutes early so they could spend some quality time together before they both had to go to bed. Instead, she was left with this mess.

Unbeknownst to her, Peter moved around to stand in front of her and cleared his throat to get her attention. Amya opened her eyes to stare up into his dark eyes, eyes that reflected so much pain and self-hatred, stupidity, and drunkenness. She'd dealt with her fair share of addicts in her life, her younger brother to boot, but living with one was something she had never experienced before. Her heart went out for Lauren, her sister-in-law, in a whole new way.

"I'm sorry," Peter muttered. "I messed up."

"You did," she whispered. She wasn't going to sugar coat anything. He needed the reality check, and if he was going to initiate the conversation, she was going to give it to him. "You really did."

"So, I'm sorry."

Amya bit her lip before clenching her jaw. "Do you expect me to accept your apology?"

"I don't know."

"Do you know how many people you could have killed on your drive to the airport? The least you could have done was say you had something to do, and I would have found another ride, or hell, just told me you were shit-faced."

"I'm sorry, Amya."

Grunting, she shook her head. "No. I'm not doing apologies. If you're really sorry, this won't happen again."

Peter's facial expressions barely changed as he turned and left the room. Amya didn't have heart to follow him. He was lost, he was young and made mistakes, but more important than anything, he was an addict, and she had to remember that.

Grace had been at her desk most of the day, going through cold case files and trying to put a name to the face she had of the kid stuck in the coma, but she was coming up with blanks. She'd checked her watch and phone a half-dozen times, waiting for Amya to text about being home and wanting her home, but there was nothing beyond the text that she'd landed and a missed call with no message.

Grace stretched her back and had just popped a dried mango between her lips when Humbard shouted her name across the room. She turned to him, then he looked beyond her and called for another detective. Curious, Grace got up and followed the call to his office.

As soon as she and Kline were inside, he shut the door. "I want you two to work together on this case."

"Sir?" Grace asked, being the more senior officer.

"Just do it. I don't want IAB down here looking for more issues."

"Sure." Grace's lips thinned. She liked Kline, at least what she knew of her. "What's the case?"

"Missing teen." He handed a piece of paper over with an address scrawled across it. "That's all I have, sorry. Uniform officers are there now."

"Then we'll get going."

"You do that."

Grace sighed as she walked out of the office. She knew the neighborhood they were going to. She went for her desk, grabbed her stuff, and nodded her head at Kline. "I'm driving."

"Fine."

Grace turned to Paige who stared at her with wide eyes. Grace asked, "What are you doing that you couldn't come today?"

"Interview."

"Oh right! I forgot that was today."

"How could you forget? They interview you yet?"

"Nope, but I expect it'll happen soon enough."

Paige's lips pursed. "Yeah."

Kline walked right up to the two of them. "Ready?"

"Yeah." Grace headed for the door, following Kline. She was a tall lanky woman with salt and pepper hair, except her pepper was clearly fading red. Her eyes were a baby blue, and while she looked to be mostly leg, Grace was sure she had a good amount of strength to her.

When they got to her cruiser, Grace sighed and put the car in reverse. "Working in pairs ought to make cases interesting."

"It should." Kline was clearly a woman of little words. Still, Grace could work with some words.

"You have any kids?"

"I have two, a daughter who lives in California and a son who is still here. Both are grown."

"Not bad. We have a twenty-one-year-old kid living with us for the time being."

Kline didn't respond. Grace let out a breath. All right, maybe it was going to be harder than she'd originally thought. She pulled up to a stop sign and came to a complete stop before taking a left. "You liking Missing Persons so far? You transferred from...warrants, right?"

"I did. Missing Persons is different."

Grace chuckled. "It is, but it's worth it. Least I think so."

"This week has been interesting."

"Right?" Grace smiled. She'd finally found the topic that would open the ice queen up. "I've been a part of IAB investigations before, but never like this. This is something else."

"Yeah. Any idea what they're looking for?"

Grace's stomach clenched. They weren't supposed to talk about it. She had trusted Paige enough to talk, but she wasn't sure she trusted someone she barely knew. "I have no idea. I haven't even been interviewed yet."

"Me either. I'm set for tomorrow."

"I hope it goes well."

"You too."

Grace pulled up to the house with three cop cars still parked outside with lights and sirens off. They went straight to the front door, Kline a step or two behind her. Humbard hadn't actually told them which one was in charge, but it seemed Kline was deferring to her. Once inside, Grace started in on her questions.

She found the mother, a petite Latina, who had on a traditional garbed shirt. "Ma'am, I'm Detective Halling, and this is Detective Kline. We're here from Missing Persons. Would you tell us a little about your son?"

"Yes. He...I don't know. Lucas is usually so grounded." Her accent was very slight.

"Do you think he ran away?"

"I do. I really think that, but he's at risk."

"At risk for?"

"Seizures. If he doesn't take his medicine, which he hates taking and he didn't take it with him, he can have seizures."

"Then we better find him fast." Grace glanced at Kline over her notepad and their gazes connected. They both knew what they were looking for. "Why do you think he ran away?"

"I have no idea. I work every day of the week. I'm rarely home. He can fend for himself." Tears slipped down her cheeks, which she wiped away quite angrily. "He's so much like his father sometimes."

"How's that, ma'am?" Grace swallowed, ready to absorb all pertinent information.

"He gets caught up in the simplest things. I'm worried he left to go one place and what he'll find is something else entirely."

"Where do you think he went?"

"I don't know. Maybe to someone's house who he plays video games with? He doesn't really have a lot of friends, so he plays video games all the time and earns money off it even. I don't quite know how that works."

Grace wasn't completely sure either, but she'd have to do some research into online video games. "What games has he been playing?"

"Here." She went over to the television and pulled out a couple cases, handing them over. "You can take them. After this, when you find him, he's not playing any more for a long time."

Nodding, Grace shoved the cases under her arm as she continued to write. "Does Lucas have any friends he may have gone to?"

"I've called all of them."

"Well, what are their names, and we'll check them out, too."

She rattled off a list of about five or six other teenage boys. Grace let out a sigh. It was going to be a long night if she had to stop by all of these places just to see if the missing kid was there, with Kline in tow because they weren't allowed to split up any longer. She had just wanted to get home and see Amya. So much for that.

"Is there anything else you can tell us about Lucas? About why he might have run away? Was he having problems at school or with another student? Were there problems at home?" Grace's gaze skimmed up to lock eyes with her, making sure she caught every small reaction.

"No, no. He's pretty settled. This is so out of the blue. I have no idea why he might have run away."

"All right." Grace straightened her shoulders. She was not getting as much information from Lucas' mom as she thought she might. She'd have to take a new tact. "What's been going on in his life lately? You said he was earning money from gaming?"

"Yeah, on some streaming service. He's makes almost a thousand a month doing that."

"No shit!" Grace looked bewildered. "From playing video games?"

"Yeah."

"Crazy." Sending Kline a look, Kline shrugged. "Has he had any customer complaints? Or online bullying that might cause him to run away?"

"No, not that he's shared with me."

Grace sighed. "Okay, does he have a computer I can take to my tech people who can maybe find some things on it?"

"Yes." She led the way into Lucas' room. Grace scrunched her nose as soon as she walked in, deciding that at least Peter's room wasn't quite that bad, though, she'd done her best to keep it that way with making him do regular cleanings of it. The stench was near overwhelming: body odor, stale and moldy food, and something she didn't want to think about but she was pretty sure was teenage boy related.

"Here it is. Sorry for the mess, I can never get him to clean."

"It's fine." Though it wasn't. She hated it, but she had to do her job. Grace stood in front of the computer, a desktop rather than a laptop. She was going to have to pull everything apart to bring it in. Letting out a breath, she fiddled with the mouse to see if it was still on before turning it off and pulling wires.

Kline finally spoke up. "Ma'am, did your son have a girlfriend or someone he may have been interested in and was dating?

Someone he may have talked to daily outside of his friends?"

"No." She said the word firmly. "He's not allowed to date."

Grace rolled her eyes. Like any seventeen-year-old boy was going to listen to that rule. She made sure to keep her face out of the line of sight of Lucas' mom and let Kline take the next few questions, which proved to be almost as fruitless as Grace's. She really wanted to ask how much time Lucas and his mom actually spent together, but she had a feeling it wasn't all that much, and she was hoping his disappearance was mostly a problem of miscommunication.

Standing up, Grace looked from Lucas' mom to Kline. When Kline said nothing else, Grace sighed and took over the conversation again. "Do you think he may have left for something to do with his gaming?"

"I...I don't know. He's never done something like this before."

And they were back to square one. "What school does he go to?"

"He doesn't."

"What?"

"He dropped out just before Christmas, said he was bound to make enough money to support himself without high school, so he dropped out to play more games and raise his income."

"Got an entrepreneur on our hands, don't we, Kline?"

"Sounds like it."

"Which school did he go to?"

"Central."

"I'll check with them, just in case he didn't show back up wanting to get his diploma again." Grace nodded at Kline sharply. They would have to go there first if they didn't want to miss most of the students and teachers. "What else does he do? Any places he likes to go?"

"He goes to the movies a lot. He also does movie reviews online."

"Jesus, this kid is a genius if he can earn an income from playing video games and watching movies. Wish I had thought of it." Grace chuckled. "All right, does he have a phone?"

"Yes."

"Will you allow us to track it?"

"Absolutely! I don't know why I didn't think of that."

"Do you have a locate-me app on it?"

She shook her head. "No, I always told him I was going to

install one, but he's not exactly a kid that just leaves, you know. So I didn't do it."

Grace sighed. It would have been helpful and the easiest way to find him, assuming he still had his phone on him. "Okay. We're going to take his computer and do some research on what he's been up to online. Meanwhile, if you hear anything or think of anything, you call us, okay?"

Handing over her card with her work cell phone on it, Grace made eye contact with the small woman. "We'll do our best to find him."

"Thanks."

They wrapped up the rest of the conversation, took the computer and the games Grace had been handed and piled into her cruiser. "To the school?"

"Yeah," Kline answered. "I guess we should go there first."

Grace put the cruiser in drive and headed toward Central High School. It was going to be a long night unless Lucas randomly showed back up at the house. She'd have to find a minute to text Amya and let her know how late she'd be.

Too Old for this Shit

GRACE HAD been out all night. Her muscles ached in places she didn't remember she had. Her back hurt the worst from sitting in her cruiser with Kline most of the night as they tracked down wayward teenagers to interview and then stalked Lucas online to see if he was going to get on from anywhere. She was beat and her brain and eyes hurt.

They had found nothing. For a kid that was constantly online, he had gone completely silent in the last twenty-four hours. Kline had managed to find his streaming. He'd talked about a new game releasing soon, so after a few quick searches, they figured out it was releasing in two days. They both figured he'd surface—if he truly ran away—right around then with the new game in hand.

Groaning out her aching body, Grace pulled into her driveway and stared at the quiet house in front of her. It was about three in the morning. She had two hours before she normally woke up to go into the office, though she might sleep in an extra hour just because she could and needed it. Still, she wanted to find Lucas so she could go back to figuring out Joseph's real name.

She pressed the heel of her hand into the top of her thigh muscle and pushed down, sliding her hand until it reached her knee. She wasn't made for sitting for long periods of time. But it had been nice to be in the office without Alonzo's crew hanging over them.

With one last breath, Grace got out of her car and headed for the front door. She unlocked it, nonplussed when not even the dogs stirred at her entry into the house. The first thing she did was head straight for the fridge and her orange juice, pouring herself the largest glass possible. She shut the fridge after putting the juice back and jumped about six feet in the air with a hand over her heart as she stared right into Amya's sweet face.

"Jesus, Amya."

"Don't say that."

"What the fuck do you want me to say when you scare the shit out of me?"

Amya smirked. "I've been waiting for you."

"Obviously." Grace turned from scared to warm and stepped forward, wrapping her arms around Amya's shoulders and tugging her in for a long hug. It felt so good to have Amya back in her arms. It'd only been a week, but they rarely were apart for very long, often sneaking meals together when they could at work.

When Grace moved to pull away, Amya stopped her by tightening her grasp on Grace's back. Grace let the moment linger as much as Amya wanted it and buried her nose in Amya's neck and her loose hair around her shoulders. Just breathing in her scent calmed and eased her stress of the day.

Pressing a kiss to Amya's hot skin, Grace sighed and relaxed completely. It was then she heard Amya draw in a shuddering breath, her shoulders incredibly tense. Grace pulled back and narrowed her gaze. She turned the light on above the stove and stared at her girlfriend's face. Something was wrong. This wasn't just an "I missed you" embrace. This was an "I don't know what to do, help me" embrace.

"What's wrong?" Grace's face set, her shoulders squared, and she was ready to fight anything they needed to fight.

"You didn't answer your phone."

Grace cocked her head to the side. She had not been expecting that response. Rolling her shoulders, she clenched her fists as she tried to work through what the real issue was. "I was at work. You only called once. What happened?"

Amya sighed and flung her hands out in front of her. "I've been up all night."

Raising an eyebrow at her, Grace could have very much

pointed out she had also been up all night and since she didn't have the next day off like Amya, she really wanted to get some sleep, but she didn't. She kept her mouth shut, her lips tight. "Okay. I'm sorry I wasn't home earlier, but I was working on a case that got handed to me right at the end of the day."

"With Paige?" Amya sneered.

"No." Grace narrowed her eyes and resisted the urge to cross her arms in a defensive manner. "With Kline. But what difference would it make? It's a case. It needed to be worked. What's going on, really? Because I don't think you're mad at me about being at work."

"You're right." Amya grabbed Grace's juice and drank a quarter of the cup before she turned on her heel and headed straight for the couch, falling into it much like Paige had done days before. "Peter picked me up at the airport."

"He was supposed to. We talked about that. I wasn't able to get away from work if I wanted to be at the school this Friday. Humbard's really cracking down on that, and with IAB in the office every day, I really couldn't anyway." Grace slid onto the couch next to Amya, her back straight and stiff as she waited for the shoe to drop, which it hadn't yet.

Amya nodded and drank even more juice. Grace was about to say something when Amya handed it over and rubbed her hands over her cheeks and eyes. She looked a mess, an adorable one, but a mess nonetheless. Whatever was going through her head must have really been bothering her. Grace was going to wait it out. If it kept Amya up all night, it must be something big.

"He was an hour late."

"You're kidding? I'm so sorry. You could have taken a ride-share or something instead of waiting for him."

"Can't decide which would have been better," Amya muttered.

"What do you mean?"

"Oh, yeah, so Peter showed up to pick me up an hour late, but he was also so drunk it probably took him an hour to drive to the airport to begin with."

Grace's jaw dropped. She had no idea what to say or how to respond. Her heart clenched hard, her stomach twisted, her palms got cold and clammy. Setting the drink onto the coffee table, Grace tried to bide her time and find some answer. She had suspected he might be drinking again, but having it shoved in her face was an entirely different issue. Guilt tore at her insides. She should have known, should have looked for it better. She should have put a stop to it.

"I don't even know what to say," Grace finally answered.

"I searched the entire house, and outside of the alcohol in our safe, which I know he hasn't touched, I didn't find any."

"None?" Grace turned, her eyes wide.

Amya shook her head. "None at all."

"So...what now?" Grace asked. "I've been wondering for weeks now, to be honest. He can't just mope around here day after day. He's depressed. He needs to do something."

Amya sighed and leaned into Grace's side. "It's not that easy."

"I know. But...I hate seeing him like this." Grace wrapped her arms around Amya's shoulders and tugged her in tightly, dropping a kiss into her hair.

"Me too." Amya closed her eyes.

They fell into a gentle silence, both of their minds whirring with thoughts of Peter and what they could possibly do to help him this time. Grace had been through all it before, but Amya hadn't been too involved at the time, and even then, Peter had been willing to get sober. This time she wasn't so sure he was ready for that.

"We could tell him he has to go to AA meetings as a condition of staying here," Grace suggested.

"We could. But those meetings are kind of pointless if he's not wanting to be there."

"Agreed. But what can we do?"

"Other than not condone it and not give him opportunities for it? I don't know. He's lucky he didn't get caught driving, but I kind of wish he had. I almost called it in myself when I saw him. I was livid."

"I imagine." Grace stroked her hand over Amya's soft hair. Yawning, she tried to keep her eyes open, but it was getting harder by the second.

"We have to do something."

"But what?" Grace stifled a yawn again and dropped her hand to Amya's waist, nuzzling her nose into the side of Amya's head.

Amya shrugged. "I don't know."

"We'll figure it out when we've both slept. Come on. I'm beat, and I need sleep before I have to go back in."

"Yeah." But Amya didn't move.

Giving in, Grace shifted on the couch and settled into the cushions more, dragging Amya with her. She pushed her shoes off with her toes and wrapped her legs around Amya's. She ran her arms up and down Amya's back and arms as she shifted until she was comfortable. Amya followed suit and then very nearly sat straight up but leaned over Grace's prone form.

Grace had wide eyes as she raised a brow at Amya, wondering what the hell they had forgotten that would get Amya in such a tizzy with no warning. Instead of saying anything, Amya bent down and pressed their lips together then pulled back grinning.

"I realized I hadn't kissed you in well over a week, and I had to remedy that."

Snorting, Grace grinned. "Then come remedy it again."

With her hand tangled in the back of Amya's hair, she pulled her down for a much longer, much deeper kiss. She had missed this, and apparently Amya had as well. Lifting one of her legs, she rocked Amya impossibly closer and curved her hand around Amya's hips and up to her waist, pulling her thin cotton shirt with her.

Their tongues tangled as Amya moved on top of her. Grace reveled in Amya's hot skin, finally feeling like she could take on the world. With Amya by her side, she knew they'd be able to help Peter figure out his own life, help him come to terms with his addiction—again. Together they could tackle anything.

When Amya pulled back and grinned, putting their foreheads together, Grace grinned. She drew in a deep breath. "I love you."

"Love you, too. Now. Sleep."

"Yeah. We're sleeping here, right?"

"Oh yes. The bedroom is way too far away."

"Set an alarm on your phone. I've got to be up in a couple hours."

"Already done."

"Love you." Grace was already yawning again. When Amya settled her weight into Grace, she closed her eyes and let sleep take over. So long as she had Amya in her arms, she knew the world would be right.

Two hours of sleep was not enough. Grace rubbed her eyes and drank her third cup of coffee that day, grateful Amya had made the first two since she was much more adept at it. She shuffled her feet along the floor in her office, waiting for Kline to show up so they could get started on the case again.

As soon as she sat down, Kline joined her and slid her phone onto Grace's desk with a picture on it. "That's what he's after."

"What is it?" Grace picked it up and narrowed her eyes at it, trying to read the title.

"It's the new game coming on the market. Limited quantity drop, available only at one store in town. Drops at midnight tonight."

Grace turned her cheek to look up at Kline. "How'd you figure that out?"

Kline shrugged. "My son is in his mid-twenties and loves gaming. I called him this morning and asked."

"You've been holding out on me!" Grace made the image on the phone bigger.

Chuckling, Kline bent over the desk like she was sharing a secret. "It was a bit fun to watch you try and ask gaming questions."

Rolling her eyes, Grace handed the phone back. "What store?"

"Box store over in the old strip mall across town. They're a specialty gaming place."

"Figures. I'd never go near there. I do not do technology most of the time."

"You've got a fancy smart phone."

"Yeah. That's my limit and my son would probably tell me I massively underutilize it."

"Son? You never mentioned a son."

Grace paused. She had said that, hadn't she. With a deep breath, Grace shook her head. "Biologically no, but he lives with us and is as much ours as we are his. I mentioned him yesterday, remember?"

"Oh, yeah, I do."

"Anyway, he games sometimes, but mostly on his computer."

"This is a PC game."

"Okay. I'll take your word for that. Do you know if they got the trace on his phone?"

Kline shook her head. "They did, but didn't get very far with it. Phone is off."

"Wonder if the battery died. I mean, if he's standing in a line, then surely he wouldn't be able to charge his phone." Grace bit her lip and glanced at the clock. It was still super early in the morning for any store to be open. "Want to do a drive by?"

"Sure, you driving?"

"Yes."

"Figures."

Grace smirked and finished her coffee. She desperately wanted another cup, but if they were going out, she didn't want to be searching for a bathroom all day either. She grabbed her keys, her gun, and her badge and stood up. "Come on, let's get going. I want to find this kid so I can go home and sleep."

"Rough night last night?"

Shooting Kline a glare, Grace grimaced. "You're a night owl, aren't you?"

"I am."

"I am not. Give me five in the morning any day of the week to begin my day. Staying up past ten is rough." They made it out to the cruiser and slid inside. Grace drove toward the gaming store she had only seen once or twice in her life.

When they got to the parking lot, Grace was shocked to see the line of people nearly wrapping around the building. "You're shitting me."

"What?" Kline asked.

"Who would have thought a damn game would be this popular?"

Kline didn't answer. Grace drove down the line of people standing and waiting, most of whom didn't even bother to look up at her. The line went from six feet from the door to the gaming store, down the entire row of other outlet stores and around the corner. Sighing, she turned her cruiser around in the back of the buildings and drove by again.

"See him?"

"No."

"I'll do one more drive by, and then we can get out and walk it."

"Sounds like a plan."

Creeping her cruiser along, Grace craned her neck to see over Kline's head and out the window. No one jumped out at her as being Lucas. She wished she knew if he was there or not. It would make searching a whole lot easier.

"Did they get a last known location off that phone?"

"Yeah, but it wasn't near here. I'm betting he is here though, just hiding."

"Why would he hide? He doesn't know we're looking for him." Grace twisted the wheel in her hands and parked her cruiser in front of the gaming store. They were going to have to get out and walk the line.

Kline was out the door first, and Grace followed. They walked to the front door of the gaming store and stepped inside. Grace went straight to the front desk and asked for a manager after flashing her badge. Kline wandered around the near empty store. There was only one other customer in there.

When the manager came out, Grace showed her badge. "We're looking for a missing kid, and we think he might have visited here recently or will visit here shortly."

"A lot of people come in and out of here, and a lot more will by the end of day tomorrow."

"I assumed as much." Grace flashed him a smile. "This kid is about five foot eight, he's darker-skinned, dark black hair. He's seventeen-years-old."

"Do you have a picture?"

Grace pulled one up on her phone and showed it to the manager. After staring at the picture for a few seconds, he stepped back and shook his head. "I haven't seen that kid around here, but you might want to check the line outside."

"Plan on it. If you see him come in, call me, please." Grace handed her card over. "He's not in trouble, just missing."

"You got it."

Grace caught Kline's attention and nodded toward the door. The two of them left and started walking the long line outside. They made it seven people down when Grace stopped and smirked. There he was. Lucas. Hunched with a hood over his head, his hands in his pockets, and his face to the ground, no doubt trying to not be seen, and he'd done a damn good job of it until then.

"Lucas?" Grace asked.

His face jerked up at her. Grace's voice had caught Kline's attention who came over to join her.

"Lucas." Grace said. "We have been looking for you. I'm Detective Halling, this is Detective Kline with the Sheriff's Department. Your mom is worried."

He rolled his dark eyes and shifted his stance. "She probably didn't even notice I was missing for the entire day."

"Well, I spent hours with her yesterday, and trust me, she's worried. What are you doing here, anyway?"

"Game drops at midnight. I needed to get it so I can make money, and she wouldn't let me come because it's overnight, but I couldn't wait. I needed one of the first copies."

Grace sighed. "Well, I'm sorry to say that you won't be getting one of those first copies."

His lips thinned.

"Come on, get your stuff and let's go." Grace turned her body to face the front of the line and caught sight of a man moving awkwardly down the sidewalk.

The hair on Grace's arms stood straight up. Kline was talking to Lucas, but Grace's entire body was focused on this man. He walked with confidence, one foot in front of the other but like he had a hundred pounds he was carrying around each ankle. When he reached behind him, her shoulders tensed. Her jaw clenched. The ringing in her ears started.

When his hand came back around, Grace reached for her weapon at her left hip and pulled it out of its holster. The man had a hand gun neatly fitted into his palm. He drew it up and pointed, aiming directly at the first person in the line.

Grace barreled forward, her heart racing in her chest and moving up to her throat. When she yelled, her voice was loud and firm. "Put the gun down!"

Kline followed her rapidly, arms out in the same position. Grace kept her eyes on the man in front of her, aiming her weapon dead center of his chest. He turned to look at her, surprise etching on his face.

"Put the weapon down. Hands in the air! Sheriff's Department. You must comply!"

He had a sickening smirk on his lips, the lines deep set in his cheeks moving upward as he shook his head. His finger twitched on the trigger.

Grace didn't hesitate. She fired. The bullet flew from her weapon and hit him straight in the shoulder of his right arm, the one holding the gun. He jerked back.

"Put the weapon down!" she shouted again, Kline echoing her and flanking her as she moved out into the parking lot to get a different angle.

The man raised the weapon again, this time aiming it at her. Grace let out a breath, keeping her eye on him and making sure she was ready to fire once more. Her heart trampled over itself as she tried to find a better way to get out of the situation than shooting and killing him, but he wasn't leaving her much choice. She didn't even know who he was or what he was there for.

"Hands in the air!" Kline shouted.

Grace swallowed as he swerved the gun to Kline. His step was unsteady, no doubt from the first bullet wound finally making some effect in his addled brain and body.

"Put the gun down!" Grace screamed again, hoping he would listen this time.

He shook his head once more and re-focused on Grace. Then he charged. One tennis shoe digging into the gray cement after the other. He fired the gun, the bullet whistling as it blew past Grace's head to land somewhere behind her—hopefully not in anyone else who was in line.

Grace let out a short breath and braced herself to fire again. The bang echoed in her ears as the second bullet flew from her weapon and hit him in the upper arm. He didn't even try to dodge. She pulled the trigger again, the third bullet hitting his chest.

That one took him down. He fell face first onto the sidewalk, his cheek skimming and scraping against the smooth cement and his chin bounced. Screams echoed all around her as the ringing in her ears stopped, but Grace was focused on him and no one else. Kline still had her weapon raised as Grace ran forward and kicked the handgun out toward Kline. Grace put her knee into the center of the man's back and grabbed one of his wrists. She shoved her gun into its holster and pulled his other hand behind his back.

Holding him carefully, she pulled out the one pair of cuffs she still carried with her and slapped them onto his wrists tightly, double-locking them. Whoever he was, he wasn't going to get a second chance.

When Kline came over with his gun between her fingers, her chest rose and fell sharply. "You okay, Halling?"

"Yeah. Yeah, I'm fine. He missed me."

"Thank the Lord!"

Grace let out a breath, her limbs still numb from the adrenaline. "Call it in, will you? We're going to need a lot of help for this one."

"Yeah."

Kline raced to Grace's cruiser as she stayed leaning on the man on the ground. She eased up a bit.

"Call a bus!" Grace shouted over the crowd to Kline. She wasn't sure Kline heard her, but she could only hope she'd think of that.

Once the scattered crowd calmed down, Grace looked up and saw Lucas hiding behind one of the pillars out front of the store. She shook her head at him and relaxed. At least he was okay. At least everyone else was okay, except...*shit*. Narrowing her gaze, she saw someone lying on the ground a hundred feet down from where they were.

"Kline!" Grace shouted. "We've got wounded!"

Kline jerked her head up, spoke rapidly into the radio as she raced down the sidewalk to check on the victim. Grace moved off the man in front of her, and she started to pat him down, looking for more weapons or a wallet with an ID or anything to tell her who he was.

"What's your name?" she asked.

He didn't answer with anything other than a groan of pain. She pulled out a pocket knife, a second gun from the back of his pants, two clips in his deep pockets, and a bag of meth. Jesus, he had been ready to kill a whole bunch of people.

"What is your name?" she repeated.

"Daniel."

She scrunched her nose, thinking about her mentor briefly before bending down over him again. "Do not move an inch."

Sirens echoed in the strip mall, and immediately a uniformed officer came over to help her. Grace left Daniel in the uniforms hands as she jumped up and ran as fast as she could to Kline and the victim on the ground. Kline held her hand over his neck as blood oozed from between her fingers. The man choked, blood coming from his mouth.

"Where's the bus?" Grace shouted at one of the officers.

"Two minutes out!" was the only response she heard.

The victim wasn't going to make it. No way would he have enough blood left by the time someone got there to help. She pressed her hand against Kline's, increasing the pressure as much as she could. She wasn't going to give up so long as there was a chance.

"Hey," she bent down to the man, getting up in his face. "You're going to be fine. We've got you, and an ambulance is coming. We've got you."

She wasn't sure he understood anything of what she was saying. His lips quivered, more blood spurting from his mouth. His body was prone against the ground. The bullet must have hit him just perfect.

"Fuck," Grace muttered.

Kline shot her a dirty look, but Grace ignored her. She looked around wildly for the ambulance and heard it before she saw it. It rounded the corner at breakneck speed, coming into the parking lot and right up to them. Two paramedics jumped out, one slipping a hand under Kline's to take over. Grace and she stepped back, and

Grace wiped her hand out of habit on her pants before she cringed. The bright red stain on her tan pantsuit was obnoxious.

Holding her hands away from her body, she realized for the first time she didn't have a vest on. It wasn't part of her uniform. Jesus, she had walked straight into a gun fight without a vest. Amya was going to kill her. She would kill herself if positions were reversed. That was fucking stupid, but there was no one else around. Kline was in the same position she was.

Her heart still thrummed steadily, and she knew she was going to be stuck there for hours, so was everyone else. Lucas would probably get home before she did, and she was going to be on desk duty until Alonzo's crew could interview her and she could be cleared by the resident therapist, Kissik. Grace had been through the routine before, more than once. She hadn't ever thought she'd end up going through it again working in Missing Persons, but it was always a possibility.

"You okay?" Grace asked Kline as they walked toward Daniel, who was being tended to by a second ambulance crew who had shown up.

"Yeah. You?"

"Yeah. I'm fine."

"Where did he come from?" Kline sounded bewildered.

"Who fucking knows." Grace stopped, knowing a supervisor would be on scene soon enough to take everyone's statements. She was going to have to call her rep and let them know she once again had fired her weapon while on duty. She would be stuck in the office with all the drama there for sure. "Fuck."

"What?"

"I just realized I can't get out of being in the office now, and I'm going to have to sit around and listen to Paige whine about this stupid IAB investigation."

Kline snickered. "She's over the top with it."

"Beyond over the top."

One last cruiser pulled into the parking lot, and Grace knew it was the supervisor. Humbard would be there shortly since she and Kline were involved. Bolstering herself, she waited for the game of twenty questions to begin. She was too old for this shit.

EXPLICIT INTERVIEW

DISADVANTAGE NUMBER one to having her girlfriend be the police chaplain for the same force she worked with was what Grace knew was about to happen. As soon as Amya arrived, Grace relaxed. Their gazes connected over the supervisor's head while Grace continued to give her statement.

Amya checked in with Kline, touching her arm briefly as she consoled her no doubt. Amya also checked in with a couple of the witnesses who seemed particularly upset. They made eye contact quite a few times while Amya walked around the scene of the crime.

When Grace was done, Amya came straight over and gripped Grace's elbows. Her eyes were wide with fear as she stared into Grace's face, those crystalline eyes watering like she was about to cry. "Are you okay?"

"I'm fine. At least for now. I have no idea where he came from."

"No one does."

Grace nodded. "I'm fine. Really. I didn't kill him."

"You didn't have a vest!" Amya whisper-screamed, her eyes going wide.

"I know." Grace let out a breath. "I don't wear one every day. It's not really expected I'll need one. I'm not going into those types of situations anymore."

"Except you are."

"Don't argue with me. I really can't right now." Grace bit her lip and looked around. "I'm fine. I promise you that."

"But you might not be."

"Amya, right now I am. Leave it at that. I don't have time analyze what happened at the moment." Grace bit back her angry tone when she glanced down into Amya's worried gaze. Doing something she never did before, she reached down, cupped both of Amya's cheeks and pressed their lips together, sighing into the kiss. Grace kept it short, but she gave Amya a peck when she moved away. "I'm fine."

"Okay, but to be honest, doing *that* makes me worry more."

"Shut up." Grace rolled her eyes, but she had a smile on her lips. Grabbing Amya's hand, she twined their fingers together and held still, all the while hoping Amya couldn't feel her shaking. She had wanted to get better at showing Amya affection not only in public but in front of other officers specifically. Today was as good a day as any.

Kline sent them a look, which Grace challenged but didn't say anything. She stayed where she was with Amya's hand in hers. It felt good. It felt complete in a way their relationship hadn't been before. Amya stepped in closer and whispered into Grace's ear, "Don't scare me like that again, please?"

"I'll try, but I can't guarantee anything. You know that."

"I know."

Grace let out a breath and snorted. "Want to maybe go home since you're not really supposed to be working today anyway and get me some clean clothes? I really don't want to be walking around with blood all over me. In a uniform is one thing. The dark blue makes it next to impossible to see. In this? Crazy visible."

"Yeah, I can do that as soon as we're done here."

"Thanks."

Grace was finally released from the scene two hours later when everything was cleaned up. They'd gotten word the victim had died en route to the hospital, bleeding out to death, which hadn't been too much a surprise. The perpetrator had made it, the wound to his chest high enough to not do much damage.

Apparently he was staying in the hospital a few nights before he would be transferred to the jail. Daniel had been planning his little gun shindig for weeks, specifically wanting to kill at least two people he knew would be there. He'd been unlucky Grace and Kline had been present. Almost everyone else had been lucky.

But she was still stuck on desk duty. Kline finished up their case while Grace had sat at her desk and waited for Alonzo's crew to come interview her. It was going to be the longest week ever. Between Peter and the IAB investigation still ongoing and now this new IAB investigation, she was done and over work. She needed a vacation.

Yet, she still had one case she could at least work on. One she had been wanting to work on but had been distracted by other cases incoming. Since she wasn't allowed any new cases, Grace hunched over her keyboard and did some deep digging. She hadn't been down to see Joseph again and was pretty sure it would be a bit longer before she made it that way because, well, restrictions.

She pulled the files again and stared them over. There had been very little work done on the case, and it astounded her each time she looked at the old files. One interview popped up that she had somehow missed before. Biting her lip, she opened the file and printed it along with the accompanying report.

She skimmed through the report. The person who had found Joseph had been a taxi driver, or ride-share, or something. He worked for a private company in town that someone could call for a ride anywhere in town and sometimes out of town.

Grace wrote down the name of the company on a sticky note. She would check them out as soon as she finished reading the interview notes. She wished she could watch the interview, but she wasn't sure the file was anywhere to be found. Most often interviews with witnesses weren't even recorded, though, so unless they thought he was suspect, it was unlikely there was any such video to find.

The man who had found the kid had presumably been driving along and stopped to take a piss in the woods for whatever reason—she couldn't fathom why he thought that was a good idea—and had seen Joseph unconscious down off the roadway where the forest began and the road ended. He'd called the ambulance immediately and that was that. No follow-up interview, no talk about what he was doing there.

"Fucking hell," Grace muttered. It was a poorly done interview to say the least, or it could have been the best, but the notes in the report were slim. She would have to interview him again, but now that she knew where Joseph had been found, roughly, she wanted to go visit the area and get more of an idea of what it looked like. She'd have to talk to the driver first to get a better idea of where it was, maybe even bring him with her.

She glanced over at Paige who sat hunched over her desk, the scowl that had been on her face for a week still very much present. She'd had her interview the day before, had told Grace it had gone decently, but she was still worried for her job and left it at that. They weren't allowed to talk about those things at all until the end of an investigation, and neither wanted to get into more trouble than they already may be in.

Focusing on her work, Grace listed out questions she wanted to ask the driver, then reworked them to get the best answer and outcome possible—the truth. She wanted to leave no room for him to lie or change his story. It had been four years, but Grace was sure the memory was still at the forefront of his mind.

Paige stepped over to her desk and bent down. "When's your interview?"

"Which one?" Grace muttered as she typed away at her computer.

"Can't they combine them?"

"Apparently no because it's two separate cases. I can, however, choose to do them back to back if I want."

"You going to?"

"Probably not. Those things are exhausting."

Paige shrugged. "So when is it?"

"In an hour."

"Oh. I wish I'd been with you today."

"No, you don't."

"I do." Paige insisted. "You know I always want to be with you on those kinds of cases."

"It wasn't the case that brought that on. Kid just happened to be in the wrong place at the wrong time, which is why we were there. He wasn't involved."

"Or was he?"

Grace tilted her chin up at Paige, looking at her bewildered. "This is not some conspiracy theory you get to try and find connections where there are none. Don't you have a real case to work on?"

"Yeah."

"So go work on it and stop bugging me."

"When do you meet with Kissik?"

"Jesus, Paige. Do you have to know everything? I haven't set up that appointment yet because I can't until IAB clears me. You know how the procedure works, no matter how slow it is."

Paige tensed. "I'm just trying to figure out when you can work with me again."

"Not today. Probably not even tomorrow or this week. Just chill."

Shrugging, Paige stood up and went to her desk. Letting out a huff, Grace bent over the report again and re-read every word on it. She wanted to memorize it if possible, and probably would before the case was over. Next she went over Joseph's initial injuries, though there was no explanation as to why he was still in a coma.

Searching through the news reports, she found quite a few on Joseph from four years prior and a couple more recent ones. She found a social media page that was built for fundraising to support his stay with a few pictures and updates, though they were rather unspecific. Probably because the information couldn't be shared.

She worked through who the owner of the page was, which took longer than she thought it should, and immediately planned to interview them as well. It was going to be a whole lot of questioning as soon as she was back on active duty. She wanted to be there sooner than she would be, but the next few days were going to be telling. She could at least do this work for now. Making sure to also add on another visit to Joseph with Amya in tow, Grace planned out her days as soon as she was released. It was going to be a lot of work, but it'd be a good distraction.

Alonzo was the one who showed up next to her desk. Grace sighed. She had hoped it would be someone else but had figured since Alonzo had taken some weird sort of special interest in her that he would be the one to interview her.

"You ready?" he asked.

"As ready as I can be."

"We can go to my office."

"Great," Grace answered sarcastically. She stood and followed him, the new clothes Amya had brought her clean and perfect for the rest of the day. Amya had even taken the other ones to the cleaners for her.

They made the slow walk through the halls and up to the second floor where IAB was located. Grace sat in Alonzo's office, crossing one leg over the other and pressing her forearms into the chair, nervous as fuck about what was about to happen. She didn't want to say anything to jeopardize her job.

"So, Grace, do you want to start with our initial investigation or the one from today?"

"We're doing both these interviews?"

Alonzo turned his dark eyes on her, his face not betraying any emotion. "Would you prefer to only do one and come back up here tomorrow?"

"No," she said quickly, ignoring everything she'd told Paige. "Today is fine."

"Good." He had a smile on his lips, but it made Grace's stomach twist with anxiety. "It actually makes this easier. Shall we start with today? I think it'll be easiest."

"Sure. Ask away." Grace waved her hand in front of her in a circle, indicating he should continue. The faster she could get out of his office, the better.

"Tell me what happened today at the strip mall."

Grace let out a breath, her mind flashing back to that moment she saw Daniel pull out the first gun. He never made it to the second. "Kline and I were talking to our missing kid we had literally just found. He was in line to get some video game. We were about to get him in the cruiser, when I turned and saw the perp coming toward us. He was walking different."

"Different how?"

Grace shrugged. "I don't know. He was on a mission. He knew why he was there and what he was doing. He didn't hesitate in his step. When he got to the sidewalk near the front of the game shop, he reached behind him and pulled out a gun. I pulled my weapon and aimed it at him. I ordered him to put the gun down. He didn't comply."

Her heart raced. She couldn't make it stop as much as she wanted it to. Her mouth went dry, and she stared at the shiny pen in the cup holder on his desk. She wondered briefly if he ever used it or if it was just for show.

Swallowing hard, Grace continued, "That's when he aimed the gun at someone in line. I stepped closer, and I fired."

"Did you tell him to put his gun down again?"

"I did. I don't remember if it was before or after I fired the first shot. Definitely again after because I said it multiple times, but I don't remember if it was before, too."

"All right, continue." Alonzo made a note on his paper.

Grace desperately wanted to know what he was writing down, but at the same time, she didn't. It was probably just what she'd said in short hand. It was what she would write down. "Um...so I fired my weapon and hit him in the shoulder. That didn't stop him, but it did turn his attention on us. He fired at me and missed, hitting the guy who was behind me I guess. Kline was out to my left, flanking me. I shot him twice more. Once in the arm and once in the chest just below his collar bone. That's when he stopped, and I cuffed him."

"Okay. Good. Then what?"

"Then Kline ran to check on the victim while I tried to get some information from Daniel, like his name, and I gave him a quick pat down. Kline called it in, and soon enough we had other officers there and then the supervisor showed up and then Humbard and now I'm here."

Alonzo pursed his lips and stared down at his paper. "Hmmm...when did Kline call it in to dispatch?"

"After I cuffed Daniel and had him under control."

"All right. And then she did what?" Alonzo's dark eyes locked on Grace.

"Went to check on the victim." Repeating herself during these interviews always got annoying.

"While you?"

Grace groaned. "While I patted down the suspect and tried to get some information from him."

"What did you say to him?"

"I asked him what his name was."

"And he told you?"

"Not the first time I asked, but yes."

Alonzo nodded. Grace bit her lip. She was tired of running through everything again and again. She'd already told the story at least a dozen times that day. "Okay."

"You keep saying that," Grace muttered. "Does my story match everyone else's?"

"It matches what information I have, yes." He eyed her carefully. "I didn't think you would lie or that there was much beyond the story than what had already been told."

"Great. So why are you interviewing me then?"

"Because, Detective Halling, I think you have impeccable interviewing skills, you're smart, you cut through a lot of the bullshit—like now—and try to find the truth which is always somewhere in the middle of what people say. I trust your judgement, so to say, and I figured if I want you on my team, then I have to earn your trust."

Narrowing her eyes at him, Grace clenched her jaw. The man just did not give up, and he was also correct in his assessment. If he wanted her to work for him, he'd have to gain her trust first. "I don't want to work in Internal. I have...never mind. I don't want to work in Internal."

"No, tell me." He put his pen down and laid his palms flat on his desk. "Off the record, I promise."

Grace chided herself. She should have watched her wording better. She hadn't wanted to ever tell anyone what she'd experienced as a police officer that wouldn't be considered ethical or moral. But she'd kind of walked right into this one on accident.

"Fine. I have always been the pariah on the force. I don't really want to continue that."

Alonzo gave her a confused look before he reached into his desk drawer and pulled out a file. He slapped it down onto the desktop and opened it. "I think you have an interesting view of your time in the force. What makes you think you were a pariah?"

"Start with the fact I'm a woman. That's not too uncommon now a days, but there are lot of officers who see this as a man's job and don't think women should be doing it."

"I've seen that viewpoint, but not everyone has it, not even the majority."

Grace sighed. "No, not everyone, but enough to make it so women don't often fit in as well as men."

Alonzo sighed then turned a piece of the file around so she could see it. It was a commendation written by Toulouse, her former supervisor, about the good work she had done. Then he handed her another one and another one. Paper after paper listed all she had done in the past eleven years that had been good and just. Grace flushed, her cheeks heating as she stared at the papers in front of her.

"Each one of these tells me a different story."

"I...I don't know what to say." Grace's voice was barely above a whisper.

"One more question, and it's one I probably shouldn't ask, but I want to be clear where I stand on the issue, all right?"

"Okay." Grace handed the papers back and stared up at him.

"Is the other issue because you are in a relationship with

Chaplain Stone?"

Grace's shoulders tightened, her stomach clenching. Her palms sweated to the point she had to brush them against her pants, and her toes curled in her shoes. "H-how...?"

"First, it's in your file, as is any relationship between two employees. We want to make sure there is no conflict of interest going on." Alonzo stared straight at her. "But I have reports from today, Detective."

"Oh." Grace flashed to when she'd drawn Amya in for a kiss, their lips touching in front of everyone. She had done so well to keep everything hidden and below the radar for three years, and then suddenly she had broken her own rule, and while it had felt good in the moment, she was pretty sure she was going to learn about the consequences.

"So is it because you're dating the chaplain?"

"No." Grace's cheeks still flushed hot.

Alonzo grunted. "Then what is it other thing that makes you feel like a pariah?"

"It's not because she is the Police Chaplain," Grace answered, saying what she wanted to say without using the words. She'd only ever truly come out twice in her life. Once to Daniel Mason Brady and his wife Carol on her eighteenth birthday, sure they were going to throw her out of the house, which had been why she had waited until then. The other was to Crystal, who had pretty much laughed, kissed her, and said she'd known all along. No one else had she explicitly said those words to, and they still felt foreign to her mouth.

Nodding, Alonzo closed the file and put it back in his desk. "Well, that is something we have been working to deal with here. There is no room for bigotry in this department or in the Sheriff's Office in general. It is not only one of my mandates as an officer of the law, but it is one of my personal passions to get rid of any kind of homophobia or sexism."

Grace's stomach untwisted, and she stared at him with wide eyes. She wasn't sure what to say. She hadn't anticipated the conversation taking this turn when she had come up to his office. No way had she figured it would go that direction. She whispered her only word, "Okay."

"Now that I've made that clear, let's talk about our other investigation."

"Sure." Grace cleared her throat.

"Have you noticed anything going on in your unit that has made you feel uneasy?"

"Like what?"

"Answer the question."

"Hard to answer without specifics." Grace crossed her arms. She would defend Paige's work to a fault if she had to. But if his line of questioning pertained to some of things Paige and done with her, then that was a different story.

Alonzo sighed. "Detective, I realize you have never been a part of an investigation quite like this one, but my questions are vague for a reason. Please answer."

"No."

"No to answering or no is your answer."

"No is my answer."

"Are you sure?"

Pursing her lips, Grace ran through every scenario that popped into her head at the moment. There had been multiple times she had been uncomfortable with some of the decisions Humbard had made, including times he refused to put out an Amber Alert solely because he didn't like he had to when he probably should.

"No," Grace answered. "There have been times."

"Tell me about them."

Grace hesitated. She did not want to be the reason anyone got into trouble. "There was a case in December when Humbard refused to put out an Amber Alert for a missing kid with downs, she was also the daughter of a corrections officer."

"Is that the only time something in the office has made you feel uneasy since you have been there?"

Grace shook her head. "When I first transferred in, there was a detective who had issues with me. He was transferred out, I think? I'm not entirely sure, but he wasn't there much longer."

"Did you file a formal report on him?"

"No."

"Why not?"

Grace bit her lip, staring directly into Alonzo's dark eyes. "Because I don't want to be your poster girl."

Alonzo nodded. "Did he have issues because you are a woman or issues because you are gay?"

"Both, honestly."

He wrote something down on his notebook, and not for the first time, did she wish she could see what he was writing. "What do you know about his leaving your unit?"

"Not much. I was told he left, or was transferred out, I can't remember. But that he wouldn't the there any longer. That's when Detective Delwin joined and transferred in."

"Okay. Any other times?"

"None that I can recall off the top of my head."

"All right. If you think of any more, please make sure to tell me."

"I will." Grace rubbed her lips together and sat up a little straighter in her chair. "Am I done?"

"For now, but I'll probably be seeing you soon. Here." He handed her a piece of paper that had his signature on it. "You'll need that in order to make your appointment with Kissik."

"I'm cleared?"

"You likely will be tomorrow. There were videos of what happened, and your story has not changed once, and it matches everyone else. You did what needed to be done, Detective. Take that to heart."

Grace nodded. "When do you think you'll be done with your other investigation?"

"These take time. We've been investigating already for a while, to put you at ease, now we're in the final stage of it and gathering all the interviews we need to make our case."

"Your case?"

Alonzo cocked his head at her. "Yes. But that's all I'll share. If you think of anything else, please let me know. It will help immensely no matter what it is."

"All right." Grace stood up and stepped out of his office, confused as to what had just happened. That was the easiest and most basic interview she had ever partaken in. Confused as much as she was relieved, Grace went to her office to set up a time with Kissik, praying he had time early the next morning.

GIVE ME A BREAK

FRIDAY COULD not have come any sooner, Grace had about enough of the week and really just wanted to get back to her job, which she was still restricted from doing because the final paperwork hadn't been filed yet. She sat at her desk, toying with a pencil and glaring at anyone who dared try and talk to her.

She was over it. Over being on desk duty. Over not being able to find Joseph's family because she wasn't allowed to do any work. She should have just taken the rest of the week off in paid time off. Heaving another sigh, probably the twenty millionth time that hour, she closed her eyes and hit her forehead against her desk.

"Don't do that."

"Do what?" Grace narrowed her gaze and looked up to find Paige leaning over her. Paige's hand touched her back before moving to the desk top.

"Mope. I'm so sick of seeing you mope."

Grace glared. "You try sitting at your desk for a whole week."

"Been there. Done that. So have you before too, by the way."

"Doesn't matter." Grace sighed yet again. "I'm stuck here. I can't even really work on my case."

"Sure you can."

"No, I can't."

"Yes, you can."

"Paige, quit it. I'm stuck here. I can't go do interviews or anything. I'm not even allowed to call to do interviews. All I can do is plan. Plan interviews, plan who I'm going to see, research people and add it to the piling amount of papers I already have."

Paige chuckled. "What if I told you that I sprung you?"

"You can't. It's against protocol. I haven't been cleared for duty yet."

"You're as cleared as you can be. What's a little paperwork?"

Grace narrowed her eyes with suspicion. "Paige, this is ridiculous. I'm not going out into the field today."

"Humbard gave you permission. He just told me when I went to beg him to make you stop sighing and groaning about being stuck here yet another day."

"Seriously?"

"Yes, Halling. Now get off your ass and get to work."

Still, Grace hesitated to get out of her seat. She wasn't sure if Paige was telling her the truth or not. Either way, if she were to leave and go into the field it was completely against protocol. Just about everyone knew that.

Standing, Grace went to Humbard's office and knocked on the door lightly. He looked up her and shook his head. "Didn't believe her?"

"I just...no, sir."

He chuckled. "You're free to go out today. I got your paperwork in about twenty minutes ago."

"Really?" The grin on Grace's face lit up in her eyes. She hadn't expected it.

"Really, really. Now scram. I'm as tired of you moping as Delwin."

Laughing, Grace went to her desk and grabbed her keys, but Paige put a hand over hers. "Nope. I'm driving."

"You're coming?"

"We still have to work in pairs, remember? At least until this whole IAB thing blows over."

"Right." Grace pocketed her keys. Any time she and Paige went out together on a case, Paige insisted on driving. It was rare she forced Paige to sit shot gun. When they got out to the cruiser, Grace let out a breath. A chill was in the air, so she turned the heat on, but Paige turned it off.

"It's not warm yet."

"Fine," Grace muttered. "Where are we going?"

"We've got a special stop to make before we go wherever you need to go."

"We're not working your case?"

"Today's all about yours, kid. I know you've been itching to get some interviews under your belt, so now's the time."

Warmth spread in Grace's chest. She had been waiting forever and a day to get back into the field, so it was good they were going to spend the rest of the day on her case. They only had about four more hours until it was the end of their shifts, but she could manage to get quite a bit of work done in that time. She'd talk to Amya over the weekend about setting up a time to go see Joseph.

"What's this special stop?"

"You'll see." Paige shifted a sly look to Grace, and Grace's stomach tightened again.

Something in that look didn't sit right. Paige was being deceptive for a reason, probably because Grace wasn't going to like where they were going. She sat in the passenger seat and glanced around, trying to see if she could figure it out before it was too obvious.

When Paige pulled up outside of Hamilton Elementary school, Grace was about to object. Paige parked and got out before she could say anything. Scrambling to catch up, Grace followed Paige closely behind.

"What are we doing here?"

"You'll see," Paige answered with a smirk.

"No, really, because if we're going to see Crystal, I typically give her a massive heads up before I just show up, and I plan shit for the kids."

They walked through the front doors to the building and right toward the administration office. They checked in, signed their names on the visitor logs, and then Paige turned to Grace with hands on her hips.

"Lead the way, oh faithful one."

"Tell me what I'm leading the way to."

"No. Just tell me where her classroom is."

Grace shook her head vehemently. "Paige, this is a bad idea. She's going to flip out and not in a good way."

"Just shut up and let me do this. You won't give me her number, she told me she worked here, so yeah, this is my last resort to get her number."

Pursing her lips, Grace planted her fists on her hips. "Horrible idea."

She led the way up the stairs on the far end of the building then backtracked one classroom. They came up to the room. Both doors were open, which meant they weren't taking a test or something. Grace breathed out a sigh and knocked on the door as she stepped inside. As soon as she had Crystal's attention, Crystal's face went from curiosity to a smile to panic. Grace shrugged and stepped to the side.

The kids all recognized her and their conversations jumped to a new decibel as they saw her. Shouts of "Detective Grace!" could be heard over each other as they all vied for her attention. Crystal put her hands out to quiet everyone and walked up to Grace.

Whispering, Crystal eyed Paige over Grace's shoulder. "Why are you here?"

"Trust me, this was not my idea. I didn't know we were coming. She just drove us here, and I don't think you're going to like what's about to happen, but I tried to stop it."

"Crystal," Paige said. "Mind if we talk?"

"Here? I can't leave my class."

"Grace can watch them."

"No, she can't." Crystal raised a perturbed eyebrow.

Paige's cheeks paled. Grace clenched her jaw. This was the worst idea on the face of the planet. If Paige had asked, she would have told her that a million times over, but she hadn't asked. She'd railroaded Grace into the entire situation, and she was about to railroad Crystal.

"All right." Paige drew in a long breath. "I like you, and I want to know if you'll go on a proper date with me."

Crystal's jaw dropped. The kids cheered, much to Grace's surprise. She didn't want to look at Crystal's face for her reaction, but she did. Crystal went from shock to livid in two second flat, but she masked it well as she stepped closer to Paige.

"You should not have done this here."

"I know. I tried to get you in the hall."

Crystal paused. "I will go on *one* date with you."

Grace knew that tone, and it did not bode well for Paige. Crystal would go on one date, or she would make the date and break it. Paige had thrown out the only chance she had of dating Crystal by messing with her classroom and her kids. Crystal loved those kids like they were each her own, and she did not take kindly to unexpected disruptions especially ones like this and of this magnitude. She wouldn't be able to calm the kids down for the rest of the day. Not to mention the flack she could get for it from parents which would turn into flak from her administration. Paige had been stupid to think this was remotely a good idea.

"Thank you!" Paige grinned, her cheeks flushing.

Grace still couldn't believe what she had just witnessed, not to mention, she knew it was another stupid idea for either of them to think they'd be good together in a relationship. Neither wanted to settle down, but their personalities were way too different to even be remotely compatible. Grace kept her mouth shut. They were adults and could very well make their own mistakes. She just didn't want to hear the drama later.

Giving the newly semi-happy couple a minute, Grace turned to the class and clapped her hands once. Some of them copied her. She did it again, but twice. More kids joined in. She got all the way to five claps before every kid was following her command.

"All right, since today was a bit impromptu for a visit. How many of you want to ask Detective Delwin here how many bad guys she has tackled in her very long career at the Sheriff's Office?"

Hands shot in the air.

"Ask away then!"

Grace made them stay in the classroom for another forty-five minutes before she told the kids they had to leave to get some real police work done. She promised candy the next time she came back. Shooting Crystal and apologetic glance, Grace shoved Paige out the door. They checked out with the front office and got into Paige's cruiser.

"That was fucking stupid," Grace said as soon as Paige's door shut. "Do you realize how you could have just fucked up her job? You didn't even think about that, did you?"

"What do you mean?"

"Jesus, Paige. You ask Crystal out in front of her class. Now what happens if one of those students goes home to a family who isn't okay with LGBTQ and more? Huh? That parent goes to the principal who then has to deal with Crystal, and you know what might happen? She could lose her job if it gets bad enough. You can't just walk in and pull that shit."

"I'm sorry. I didn't realize—"

"Of course you didn't. But I'm not the one you should be apologizing to. Also, not cool, that is a shitty way to ask someone out. Talk about pressure to say yes. She didn't even have a chance of saying no."

Paige's responding grin made Grace realize that had been part of the goal from the beginning. Fuck that. She rolled her eyes and crossed her arms over her chest after she buckled herself in. She stared straight ahead and let out a breath.

"We're done here. Let's go talk to my driver."

"Sure thing, boss." Paige's chipper tone only added to Grace's mood.

They went to his house, and he wasn't there. Once they got back into the cruiser, Grace grabbed her phone and dialed the phone number she had inadvertently memorized after staring at the files most of the week. It rang twice before he picked up.

Grace's stomach dropped when she heard his slick, "Hello?"

"Hi, I'm trying to reach Diego Narvaez."

"You've found him."

"I'm Detective Halling with the Sheriff's Office. I'm looking into a case you were involved with years ago, and I'd like to follow up with you about your interview." She really wanted to throw her fellow officers under the bus, tell Diego they'd taken shit notes and so now she was having to redo all the work they had done except she didn't. It would be unprofessional, and at that point it time, there was no benefit to doing it. She would have wanted to interview him again even if the reports had been detailed and there was a video of it.

"Is this about Joseph?"

Curiosity piqued, Grace slid a glance to Paige who raised her eyebrows at her. "It is. Where can my partner and I meet you to talk?"

He sighed, and Grace couldn't tell if it was a sigh of frustration or something else entirely. "I'm at work."

"Are you still driving?"

"Yes, but I have my own company now, and I'm very busy."

"Diego, you need to make time for this today. Otherwise it'll only drag out even longer."

Silence echoed on the other end of the phone, and she was worried he had hung up on her, but when his smooth voice finally reached her ears, she was pleasantly surprised. "You can come now."

"Where is your office?"

"My house."

Grace furrowed her brow and turned to face the house they had just gone up to and knocked on the door of. Rubbing her lips together, she shook her head at Paige. "And where is your house?"

"I live near Old Lion's Park, off Jasmine Lane and Fir Street. 1211 Jasmine."

Grace did a quick mental map of the area but didn't garner any information. Paige would either know where it was or they would look it up on a phone. She jotted down the address in her notebook and shifted it over so Paige could see. "Okay. We'll be there in five minutes." Hanging up, Grace slid her phone into its holder at her waist before strapping herself in with a seatbelt. "Apparently, he doesn't live here."

"Then why is it his registered address?"

"Maybe he moved recently? Who knows. That's his address. Know where it's at?"

"It's like three blocks from here."

"No shit, really?"

"Yes." Paige's gaze roved over Grace's form. "I'm sorry about Crystal."

Grace froze. "Sorry about what?"

"You were right. I shouldn't have done it that way, but I was afraid if I didn't do it today that I never would."

Drawing in a short breath, Grace kept her eyes on Paige. She wanted to ask, wanted to probe, but she wasn't sure she was going to like the answer. "Why did you want to do it to begin with? It's been weeks since you two hooked up, and it's not exactly like you were hitting it off before that happened. In fact, you'd never met her before."

Paige pulled away from the curb of the house and drove slowly down the street. Grace didn't take her eyes off Paige's profile. They hadn't spent much time together lately because Grace purposely put distance between them. Paige had pushed the boundaries of their relationship one too many times, and Grace had worked hard to keep their conversations neutral.

"Honestly?" Paige's voice was quiet, demure, which was so unlike her. "If I can't have you, at least I can have her."

Grace's stomach sank. Her heart sped up then slowed down. She was struck speechless. She had no idea how to respond, but she could think of two ways off the top of her head she wanted to.

However, having a pissed off Paige in the car with her while driving did not seem like the grandest idea out there.

"That's a stupid reason to be with someone." Grace turned to look out the front windshield and pushed back into her seat. "If you want to be with her for her, then do that, but don't do it because you want to be someone else."

Paige didn't answer. Silence filtered through the car for the rest of the two blocks until they arrived at Diego's house. He had a clearly marked taxi cab out front of his house, and then he had some simpler vehicles parked in his driveway.

After Paige parked, Grace got out of the vehicle and shifted into detective mode. She couldn't think about Paige and Crystal while she was interviewing Diego. She had to run through the questions she had spent the better part of the week thinking to ask. Something Alonzo had said in her interview with him had struck her, and she had changed up some of her questions to try it out and see if it garnered any information she wouldn't normally get. It might do well for her to be vague for a reason.

Grace marched right up to the front door, formed a fist with her hand, and pounded on it four times. It took Diego another minute before he answered, and he looked disheveled to say the least. He wasn't the tallest man around, but he had deep caramel eyes and dark hair that was clearly an uncombed mop on the top of his head.

His clothes were ragged as well. His gray T-shirt looked to be five times too big, stretched out, especially right around the neckline, his pants were barely hanging on to his hips, and his plaid over-shirt looked oddly out of place, like he was trying to be a punk and a prep at the same time. Grace narrowed her gaze at him.

"Diego?"

"Yes," he answered.

"I'm Detective Halling. This is Detective Delwin. We want to talk to you about the kid you found four years ago."

Diego nodded. "I assumed as much, come in."

The house wasn't in much better shape than Diego. He led them into the small entryway, through a living room that had two chairs, a television, and an insane amount of beer bottles. Most of which, Grace assumed, were empty. They went into a small office, where Diego sat in the chair at the desk. The room was barely big enough for the three of them, but there was even less room with the amount of papers stacked literally everywhere: the floor, the chairs, the desk top, the singular bookshelf, the filing cabinet. Grace wondered briefly if the cabinet was filled as well.

"What do you want to know?" Diego asked.

Grace swallowed. "I just received this case and am starting to work through all the witnesses and reports we already have, but I wanted to get a sense of what happened for myself. First, can you tell us exactly where you found him?"

Diego nodded. He pulled out a map, which was a surprise to Grace, and pointed on it. She glanced at Paige before stepping forward and leaning over the desk to see where he pointed. Sure enough, it was right behind the newer strip mall in town, behind one of the big box stores. There was nothing but woods behind those buildings except for the pass through street and the Hay Barn. Grace made a mental note of it.

"All right, can you tell us a little bit about what happened that night?"

"I guess." He rubbed a hand over his eyes like they had just woken him up from a deep sleep. "I was driving that night, and I stopped by the side of the road out back between jobs to take a piss. In the middle of that, I saw something weird right by the edge of the forest, so I walked down to see what it was, and I found the kid."

"How was he laying?" Grace pulled out her notebook. These were all questions not present in the reports she had.

Diego groaned. "Uhh...on his back. His head was turned toward the forest. He was completely naked except for this ring he hand on his finger."

"Ring?" Grace's eyes widened. That had been nowhere in previous reports, and it seemed like information that should be.

Nodding, Diego pointed to his left pointer finger. "Yeah, it was big and bulky. Had a giant red gemstone in it."

"Like a school ring?" Paige interjected.

Diego shrugged. "I don't know. I didn't spend much time looking at it. I went back to my car, grabbed my cellphone, and called the cops."

Grace backtracked slightly. "All right, so you found him naked on the ground. What else do you remember?"

"He didn't look good. Like it looked like he had the shit beat of him. His face was all swollen and bloody. His chest looked just as bad. Blood everywhere."

Grace wrote everything down as if she was getting the information for the first time. She'd seen the initial damage report to Joseph's body, which had included a couple stab wounds to his chest, neck and head, with a short knife, like a pocket knife, which explained a lot of the blood Diego was describing.

"So you called the cops, then what?" Grace asked, trying to get him to continue.

"I dunno. I waited for them to show up. Talked to them, told them I didn't know nothing, and then they sent me home."

Grace stopped at that. "Did anyone come talk to you after that?"

Diego shook his head.

Inwardly cursing, Grace could have beat someone bad. All the detectives before her had fucked up the case. Joseph hadn't even stood a chance, and the fact no one had figured out nothing had been done on his case since was a travesty.

"Okay, so the ring, what did it look like?"

"I don't know, lady. I didn't look that close. Give me a break, it was four years ago."

"I know it was four years ago." Grace softened her tone and shot Paige a look of frustration. "But Joseph is still in ICU from the beating he took that day, and we still don't know who he is. I'm trying to figure that out so at least someone in his family can come see him."

Diego paled. His fingers rubbed together before he shifted in his seat and rubbed his palms over his thighs. "I don't know anything else. I did what I had to do. I saved the kid's life, for Christ's sake. Can't you just let a good man off the hook?"

Grace stiffened and let there be a pause of silence before she asked her next question. Grace changed the subject, hoping it would help ease Diego's anxiety a bit. She wasn't after him, she just wanted to know more about Joseph to try and figure out who he was. "Do you remember or have record of what calls you were going to that night?"

"I have the records here, somewhere." He indicated the room, and Grace knew she never stood a chance of finding those names.

"Okay. If you think of anything else, especially about that ring, give me a call, please. I'm going to be doing my best to find out who Joseph is and find his family. I'm sure they've been missing him for the past four years."

Once again, Diego paled, but he took the card Grace offered him and refused to look her in the eye. Paige and Grace got into the cruiser, saying nothing until they returned to the station. "Think it's a school ring?"

"Good bet with it being a kid that age. I don't know many boys who walk around wearing rings on their left pointer finger that isn't a school ring."

"I'll check it out." Grace rubbed her lips together as they walked inside. They said not another word as they went to their respective desks and sat down. As soon as Grace pulled up her computer system, she couldn't help but think about Paige's words. If Paige couldn't have her—whatever the hell that meant. Grace had never given any implication she was interested in Paige. Ever. And she wasn't about to start then, but she maintained, dating Crystal—or anyone for that matter—because of some reason other than interest in them was disaster waiting to happen.

THIRD DENIAL

GRACE PICKED Kit up at school that day on her way home from work. Kit shoved a duffel bag into the trunk of the cruiser before hopping in the front seat. Grace waved at Peggy as she drove off with Kit in tow. They'd canceled the afternoon program that day, knowing the kids wanted to get gone for spring break.

"Amya's cooking," Grace stated.

"Good, because you suck at it."

Rolling her eyes, Grace smirked. "Thanks, kid. Love the compliment."

Kit shrugged. "Can Annabelle come tonight?"

"I guess, but no staying the night."

"I know the rules," Kit mocked.

Grace wondered how much longer Kit was going to keep the attitude and verbal assaults up in her life. It was so clear she was desperate for attention and desperate for someone to love her for who she was. She craved it, which was why she kept coming back to Grace's and Amya's, but the attitude was beyond repelling.

"I'll text her to come over."

"Tell Amya, too," Grace added as she drove toward their house. They lived on the other side of town from Kit's school, which had been decently annoying when Kit lived there and they insisted on dropping her off and picking her up every day. It took far more time than it should have to keep up with it, but they didn't trust Kit to come home by the public bus system, not to mention after checking routes, it would have taken her over an hour to use it to get a mile from their house and having to walk the rest. The public bus system was a joke.

As soon as Grace pulled into the driveway, she let out a breath. She needed the break the weekend would afford her. The interview earlier that day had been good, but she still had to shift through the information, and the ring she wanted to research before she brought it up again.

Stepping inside, Izzy ran straight for Kit, licking all over and trying to jump up onto her. Kit pushed her off like she didn't like it, but they all knew better. Izzy was Kit's dog, obsessed with her and wouldn't leave her side any time Kit was in the house. Kit didn't hesitate as she walked to the guest room and dropped her bag in it.

Grace walked right up to Amya, who had clearly just gotten home from her own shift and stood at the stove starting dinner, and kissed her on the cheek. "Kit text you?"

"No."

"Figures. Annabelle is coming, too."

"Okay. There should be plenty."

Grace wrapped her arms around Amya's shoulders and hugged her against her front before kissing once more into her cheek. "I was cleared for duty today."

"Really? That was fast."

"It was. Who knows. Humbard let me go out today."

"Good." Amya turned and kissed Grace's lips.

Grace sighed. "What's for dinner?"

"Enchiladas. I needed something easy."

"They're easy, and they're good." Grace moved away to grab some water to drink. "You'll never guess what Paige dragged me to do today."

"What?"

"Well, Humbard has us working in pairs because of this whole IAB investigation, right? So Paige came with me for my interview this afternoon. But first she dragged me down to Crystal's classroom to ask her out."

"What?" Amya turned, her eyes wide. "How does she even know Crystal?"

"Oh God, I forgot to tell you the whole story! Paige and I went out for drinks while you were gone, and Crystal was there with a date. It was bad, she needed rescuing. Anyway, we rescued, and they hooked up that night. Paige has been begging me for Crystal's number ever since."

"And you haven't given it?"

"No, not without Crystal's permission."

"And you, of course, didn't ask Crystal if she wanted her number handed out." Amya's tone was full of attitude.

Grace froze, caught. She shook her head. "It never came up."

"You avoided." Amya pointed a finger at her. "What if Crystal wanted to go on another date with Paige?"

"It wasn't a date. Didn't you hear me? They hooked up."

"So? What if she wanted a proper date?"

"Jesus." Grace put her glass down a little too heavily on the counter. "This is ridiculous."

"No, it's not. Why didn't you ask Crystal?"

Grace fisted her hands and put them on her hips. "Because they would be horrible together."

"That's your opinion. A lot of people could say the same about us."

"No, they wouldn't."

"Not now but in the beginning, well, maybe even now. We have a lot of major differences, Grace, and those aren't easy things to navigate, but they can be navigated."

"Things like what? We're perfect for each other."

Amya's eyes widened, and she shook her head slowly. She bent down and slid the casserole dishes into the oven before straightening and pegging Grace with a look. Grace knew she had just stepped in some kind of shit.

"Grace, you are a staunch disbeliever in God, and not only that, but you repel any kind of conversation about God, Jesus, faith, or religion. You want absolutely nothing to do with it."

"So?" She knew where the conversation was going, and she also knew Amya had a point. She just didn't want to admit it.

Amya rolled her eyes. "I'm a chaplain. Religion, God, faith—that *is* my life."

"I thought I was your life."

Laughing, Amya stepped in closer, putting her arms around Grace's waist and pulling her in. "You're a dork, but I love you."

"My point still stands. They would be awful for each other."

"As does my point, sometimes love is weird, and you fall in

love with people you least expect. I'd think you could attest to that."

Grace's lips thinned. The words were on the tip of her tongue, but she wasn't sure it would do any good to tell Amya, who had been jealous for the entire year she and Paige had worked together and it had reared its ugly head in a massive way last Christmas. But there would be fallout, she knew, and Amya would be dragged into it.

"Except today Paige told me she asked Crystal out because if she couldn't have me, Crystal was the next best option."

"What?" Everything in Amya's body tensed, and Grace feared she should have kept it all to herself.

"Yup. So...this is going to fail, and it will not be good for anyone."

"No, it won't."

The knock on the door interrupted them. Amya leaned up on her toes and kissed Grace quickly on the lips before she headed for the door, but Kit was faster. She raced to it and opened it, revealing Annabelle. Amya waved out the window at Annabelle's parents who had dropped her off. The girls started talking a mile a minute before Amya interrupted them.

"Dinner will be ready in about fifteen minutes, so if you two would set the table."

Kit glared, but Annabelle smiled. They moved together as one. Grace got out of their way and walked around to stand next to Amya. "Peter?"

"Who knows if he'll be joining. I'll go check, but I doubt it."

"It'd be good for him."

"It would, but I'm not going to push him do it."

While Amya disappeared, Grace slipped into their bedroom and changed out of her pantsuit and into far more comfortable clothes of a loose T-shirt and well-worn jeans. It was her standard uniform when she was at home relaxing.

When they were all at the table, Peter excluded, and they had said the required prayer Amya had them do, Grace looked from one kid to the next. They were clearly still together in some form or fashion, Grace wasn't quite sure, and she didn't want to pry, but it was obvious there was an underlying sexual tension between them. Hence why Annabelle was not allowed to spend the night, which was a decision they maintained.

"I think I'm going to go see Lauren and Clyde after the baby is born," Amya added.

"When's that, again?"

"August."

"Do they want you there?"

Amya shrugged. "Clyde says he's going to rehab after the baby is born, so I figure I can go help Lauren for a bit since she'll be wrangling three kids at once."

"Might not be a bad idea."

"Is it a boy or a girl?" Annabelle asked.

Amya shook her head. "I don't think they know yet."

"I love babies."

Grace had to stop herself from snorting. She'd never been that kid. Not once. Babies were not her thing, in fact, kids weren't so much her thing either, and she'd never really wanted any. Amya did, but that was a different story, one they often conflicted on.

"What are you working on, Grace?"

"Huh?" Grace looked over into Annabelle's eyes. Kit shot Grace a look she didn't quite understand, so Grace looked back to Annabelle.

"What case do you have?"

"Oh. I have a weird kind of reverse missing persons case. I have the kid—the missing—but I have no idea who he is."

"He can't tell you?"

Grace shook her head. "He's in a coma."

She took a large bite of dinner to try and avoid any more questions. She wasn't going to give them too much more information, but she wasn't going to lie, the entire interview with Diego weighed on her mind heavily. She wanted the time to sit and pick it apart, and she really wanted to know what happened to the ring Joseph was supposedly wearing.

Nowhere had it been mentioned. Not in the previous interviews or paperwork. Not even in the hospital intake. Grace froze. She turned to Amya then narrowed her gaze. Amya sent her a curious look back.

"What?"

"I just realized something."

"About your case?"

"Uh huh."

Amya rolled her eyes. "Can you at least wait until we're done eating to deal with it?"

Grace chuckled. "I'll do you one better and wait until Monday to deal with it."

"Really?"

"Yes, I need the break after this week." She turned to Annabelle and Kit. "What are you two going to be doing this week, since you have the whole week off?"

"We still have homework," Kit muttered.

"And you'll be doing that, right?" Amya added.

"Yes." Kit glared.

"We thought we'd go to the movies. I just got my license last month, so I can drive."

Grace's stomach twisted. They had been working on getting Kit's license when she'd been pulled from their house and put back with her parents. Now her parents would have to sign all the paperwork, which Grace sincerely doubted they would, so Kit would likely have to wait until she was eighteen to be able to legally drive. Didn't mean Grace couldn't take her to an empty parking lot and teach her.

Grace shot Amya a look to see how comfortable she was with that, but they both knew they treaded the line of being parents when they had no real authority. If Kit truly wanted to ride with Annabelle, there wasn't much they could to do stop her, since they weren't her legal guardians. Neither of them said anything about Annabelle driving. But the hole in Grace's heart where it concerned Kit grew just a little bigger.

She'd gone to bed Sunday night hopeful the morning would bring her good news and good ideas about the ring on Joseph's finger. Grace had kept to her word and not done any work the entire weekend. She had managed to spend time with everyone, including Peter, and was rejuvenated for sure.

What she hadn't been expecting was to wake up to a phone call at three in the morning. The phone rang shrilly, and she grabbed it half-asleep while answering. "Hello?"

"This is Officer Massey down at the county jail."

Grace's heart sank, and suddenly, she was sitting upright in her bed. Amya still slept soundly next to her. "What's going on?"

"I was given your number to call by a detainee."

"Okay?" Grace rubbed her eyes. She didn't know anyone in jail currently, but that didn't mean some of her former arrests still didn't have her number to call in case they got collared again. It wasn't uncommon before she'd been a detective, and there were a few throughout the last year who had called. "Who is it?"

"A kid named Peter Schultz."

"Oh God." Grace's heart plummeted. Reaching over she shook Amya's arm, trying to wake her up while still focusing on the phone call. "What happened?"

"He was in a vehicular accident."

Grace was out of the bed in two seconds flat. She hit every light as she went through the house, including the one in their bedroom to rouse Amya's still sleeping body. She headed straight for the front window to stare out at her driveway. Sure enough, the car Amya had bought last December for Peter to use was gone.

"Is he okay?"

"He's fine. The passenger in the vehicle is also fine but has been taken to Saint Patrick's for observation."

Grace's mouth went dry. She felt like she was going to puke. Walking as fast as she could back the way she had come, she flung open the door to the guest bedroom and flipped the light on. The bed was still made, Kit's clothes put away in the dresser. She kept the room impeccable. But there was no Kit in sight.

"Fuck," Grace muttered. "What did he hit?"

"He struck another vehicle."

"So he's arrested for DWI?"

"And distribution."

"What?" Grace's eyes went wide. She leaned against the doorframe, her head against the edge of the wood, and she wanted to smack it really hard.

Amya popped out of the bedroom, completely confused. Grace waved her over and gripped her hand. Without another beat, Amya squeezed her fingers, looked in Kit's room then went to Peter's, turning the light on and coming back after not finding him.

"How long are you keeping him?"

"We will release him after a seventy-two hour hold."

"Good. We'll be there to get him. Thank you for the courtesy call."

"Any time, Detective."

Grace hung up. She glanced at Amya, and her voice trembled, "Peter crashed your car."

"What?" Amya's eyes were wide. "Is he okay?"

"He's in lock up. He was drunk driving. But he had Kit with him. She's at the hospital."

"We're going, right?"

"Yes." Grace pushed up from the doorframe and walked

straight to their bedroom. "Yes, we're going. Now."

She got dressed as quickly as she could, Amya following suit. When they slipped into Amya's beat up car, Grace let out a breath. She was about to break a rule to find out where Kit was, but she didn't care. It was for a good cause. Amya took her hand as she drove, which steadied her racing heart and helped tamper her anger.

"Peter will be released in three days."

"Leaving him there?"

"Yes. He needs it. It'll sober him up good, too."

"I agree with that decision."

"Good." Grace clenched her jaw. "He apparently gave Kit alcohol."

"What?" Amya turned, surprise lacing her tone.

"He's been arrested for a DWI and distribution of alcohol to a minor."

"Damn it, Peter. We should have done something sooner."

"Probably." Grace drove through the quiet streets and headed straight for the hospital. She had grabbed her badge before she'd left the house, and she was ready to use whatever means she had to find out where Kit was and what medical information she could find.

When they got to the hospital, Grace and Amya walked confidently into the emergency room, the only doors open that late at night. Amya took Grace's hand and stepped in front of her as they went to the desk. She slipped a badge Grace had never seen in front of the receptionist. "I need to know where Kit Umptree's room is. I'm Chaplain Amya Stone."

The receptionist glanced at it then turned to her computer and typed into it. "She's still in the ER, in curtain seven."

"Thanks. I know the way."

Amya dragged Grace with her. Grace glanced at the receptionist, who gave them a curious look. Grace turned on Amya. "What the hell badge is that?"

"My religious credentials. My standing, essentially, as an ordained minister and as a Chaplain. Gets me into places you can't go."

"What even? Why didn't I know about this before?"

Amya shot Grace a look, reminding Grace of their earlier conversation that night, and then turned toward the patient area. She found Kit's bed and opened the curtain, smiling as soon as she entered. Amya went to one side of Kit and Grace the other. Grace touched Kit's shoulder briefly before she realized she might be bruised under the hospital gown.

"Hey, kid," Grace said.

"Hey," Kit answered, tears swarming in her eyes. "I'm so sorry!"

Grace wanted to lean down and hug her, but she wasn't sure the move would be accepted, and she certainly wasn't sure Kit would be up for it after being in a car accident. "Don't worry about that. We can talk about it later. First, are you okay?"

"Yeah." Kit sniffled. "Yeah, I'm fine. They won't let me leave."

"You're a minor, so that's not unexpected."

Kit shook her head, tears brimming over her eyes and falling down her cheeks. "No, they won't let me leave with you. They made me tell them my parent's phone number or they were going to call DCFS. I can't do that again."

Grace gave in and brushed her fingers over Kit's brown hair and slid her gaze from Kit's broken face up to Amya's. They were both thinking and feeling the same thing. There was nothing they could do. The hospital was following protocol as they should.

Amya's voice rang true. "Kit, you're going to have to go home with your parents unless they allow you to come home with us. But let's talk about that when it comes to it. Are you sure you're okay?"

"Yeah. I'm fine. They took some x-rays of my chest."

"Why?"

Kit shrugged. "Don't know. They won't tell me much."

"I'll deal with it." Grace glanced at Amya. She left the curtained area and found a nurse at the nurses station. Flashing her badge, she nodded her head. "I need to know what's going on with Kit Umptree. She said x-rays were taken, but she doesn't know why. You need to inform your patients of what you are doing. She might be a minor, but she is old enough to understand."

The nurse paled. "They were checking for internal bleeding."

"Why? Was there evidence of it?" Grace gave her a pointed stare.

"Yes. There is bruising on her chest and back."

"Consistent with a seat belt?"

The nurses lips parted, and she didn't say anything, but she shook her head. *Damn it.* Grace closed her eyes. "Thanks. Her parents answer the phone?"

"No, we are still trying to reach them."

"Good luck with that. They'll likely show up when I drag them down here."

The nurse gave her a curious and blank look. Grace ignored her and went back to Kit and Amya. As soon as she entered, they quieted. What the nurse hadn't said was the x-rays were to look for more than just internal bleeding. They had suspicions, and now so did Grace. A month home had already taken a turn for the worst.

"What were you doing with Peter?"

"He said he'd get me some beer."

"And did he?"

"Yes."

Grace wished she could tell Amya what she suspected, but there was no way she was going to do that with Kit right there, and she certainly wasn't going to leave Kit alone. She wanted to ream Kit a new one asking her what she was thinking going to get drunk with Peter, and she wanted to ream Peter a new one. She wanted to let her anger fly, but as soon as she looked down at Kit's prone form, she stopped short of it.

"We'll stay here with you as long as we can, okay?" Grace said.

"Okay." Kit wiped her tears away.

"But when your parents come, what they want takes priority, and we will likely have to leave. But remember this, Kit, please remember this, you are always welcome at our house." Grace made sure to make eye contact with Kit, her meaning clear.

It took until nine in the morning before Kit's parents arrived, mom and dad in tow. Grace and Amya had wondered, along with hospital staff, if they were ever going to show. They'd finally answered the phone around seven and clearly hadn't rushed over to see their only living daughter who was in the hospital. As they walked into the curtained area, Grace's spine stiffened as she prepared for battle.

"Get out." Her mother's voice was firm.

Grace put her hands up. "We're here to make sure she's okay."

"She's clearly not, and this is all because she was with you. Disgusting is what you are. Get out."

Amya stepped between Grace and Kit's parents. "We will leave. We wanted to make sure Kit was okay before we left and that she had someone here to be with her."

Amya, the perfect mediator. Grace, however, wasn't through. She sneered. "It took you six hours to get here. What kind of parents does that make you?"

"*Her* parents!"

"Some parents. Did you even know she was with us until this

phone call?"

Kit's father paled, but her mother's face tightened with anger. "We know exactly where our daughter does and does not go. It was your son who got her drunk. Your son who drove while drunk. Your son who crashed the vehicle. Maybe you should think a little more about your family and leave ours the hell alone."

Grace's fist curled tightly, her nails digging into the palm of her skin. Amya gripped her hand, trying to soothe her, but Grace saw red. "My son has a whole lot more love for your daughter than you do. You could very easily take lesson from him on how to love someone. And frankly, we love her more than you seem to. Care more about her well-being. Kit is a blessing. She's an amazing young adult who is just trying to find her way in this crazy world, her way when she's getting absolutely no guidance from the likes of you. Grow up, get over your shit, and raise your daughter."

Without another word, Grace stormed through the curtained area and left the emergency room. Amya stayed behind, probably to soothe ruffled feathers, but Grace was too angry to calm down. She wanted to punch something, needed to get rid of the anger as it built in her chest and grew in ways she hadn't seen it in years.

Kit did everything right, or at least she tried to. All she wanted was to be loved, cared for, safe. She'd never find that in her own home. When Amya showed up and ran a hand over Grace's shoulder and down so their fingers could entwine, Grace let out a breath.

"They took the x-rays because of bruising that was already on her."

"She bruised that fast from the car accident?"

Grace shook her head, her own tears brimming in her eyes, and she realized it wasn't anger she was feeling. She was scared. She was scared shitless that if she sent Kit back to her parents' house the next time she saw her would be in the morgue, naked on a slab of cold metal.

"No, for bruises *already* on her, from before she came to stay with us."

Amya's eyes widened. "What did they find?"

"No clue, but I doubt she got them from falling down stairs."

"We have to call Doreen."

"Yeah. Yeah, we'll call DCFS. I'm sure the hospital has already done it if they verified any of their suspicions." Though even then, she wasn't sure how well Kit would do being in foster care again.

They no doubt wouldn't send her to Grace's and Amya's with the argument they'd just had with Kit's parents. Leaning in and kissing Amya, Grace put their foreheads together. "Come on, let's go home and get ready for work. We're both late."

"Worth it."

"Yeah. We can figure out Peter's problem tonight."

"Sounds like a plan."

THE COCK CROWS

WHEN GRACE had gotten to work that morning, which was far closer to noon, she'd had to sit in Humbard's office and explain why she was late. The conversation had gone decently enough, but she couldn't help but feel there was an underlying tension throughout it all. Perhaps he was also feeling the weight of IAB's investigation into the department.

Finally sitting at her desk, Grace pulled up her computer and closed her eyes to concentrate. She had to make a list and a plan for what she needed to do in the few short hours she was there that day. Otherwise she wouldn't get anything accomplished. Who thought teenagers and young adults would cause sleep deprivation? She hadn't. That was for babies. Sighing, she pulled up the Internet to start a search.

Paige came over, sitting on the corner of Grace's desk like she typically always loved to do. Looking up at her, Grace shook her head. Exhaustion seeped into every bone she had, making her eyes want to droop. She needed more coffee.

"You look like shit, Halling."

"I feel like it. Be helpful, please, and go get me some coffee."

Paige's lips thinned, her green eyes staring at Grace unnerving, but she did get up without another word and go over to the coffee maker. Grace hoped it was newer coffee, but when she saw Paige changing everything out, she figured it had been so old even Paige wouldn't drink it.

She typed quickly into the search bar, trying to find places that made school rings. She really wished she had known what else was on the ring other than a red gemstone. Typically, from what she remembered which was not much at all, class rings held a bunch of information. But if this kid had a class ring on his finger, wouldn't that mean he had graduated and wasn't as young as they thought he was?

She redoubled her focus, skimming through the ads. It would be helpful if she knew which company was used by schools locally because there were so many and none of them were located in their fair town. It would take her decades to get the proper paperwork to filter through them all, which was not a prospect she was looking forward to.

Paige came back over with the coffee in hand and slid it in front of Grace's nose. Grace grabbed it immediately and took a long sip from it. Paige made excellent coffee, which Grace preferred to let someone else make it all the time since any time she attempted to make it, it tasted like muddy water.

"Thanks," she muttered into the cup before she took another sip. It was hot, but it was good.

"Any time."

Once again, Paige sat at the corner of Grace's desk as was her norm and crossed her arms over her chest as she stared out at nothing. Grace didn't say anything and went back to her search results. Paige would get around to whatever she wanted to ask soon enough. She was hesitant for whatever reason because normally Paige was a bull in a china shop and barreled straight through whatever she was thinking, but on occasion she did something like this, and it was normally when she had a huge revelation about something.

Grace moved through the second page of search results and shook her head. Her brain was not functioning up to par. Lack of sleep was one thing she used to be good at dealing with, but as she got older and into more of a routine at home, it became harder and harder.

Paige shifted. Grace skimmed her gaze up over Paige's profile. She looked so deep in thought and lost. Grace ignored her. Paige would figure it out. She always did. On the third page of search results, Grace realized she wasn't retaining any information and there was a much better method to trying to figure this out. She closed out of the search and pulled out her cell phone.

"She didn't give me her number." Paige sounded morose, so beaten down that Grace had to look up at her to make sure it was the same Paige she knew.

"Who didn't?"

Paige turned, staring down at Grace with a sad look on her face. "Crystal."

"Oh. But she agreed to go on a date with you."

"Hindsight is always twenty-twenty, isn't it, Halling? I shouldn't have asked her the way I did. It was reckless and awful of me. You don't think she's had any fallout has she?"

"Not that I've heard, but it is spring break this week, so she's not at the school right now. Crystal tries to keep most of her life private from the kids, at least what she can."

"She invites you to her classroom all the time." Paige rubbed her lips together.

"Yeah, to teach the kids about shit not to ask her on a date." Grace cringed. She knew that had come off as far too harsh. She had zero interest in Crystal. They were first and foremost best friends. They'd kissed exactly one time when they had been fourteen and stupid, trying to prove Crystal didn't like girls in the basement of Crystal's house.

Grace rolled her eyes at the memory and took another long sip from her coffee. That had not been an entire disaster because she'd realized herself she also liked girls, just not Crystal, in that way. Crystal, however, had always been the one to date and be far more in the public eye with her sexuality. Grace just stood in the background as she liked it and didn't really date until after she'd dropped out of high school and started working.

"That was harsh," Paige finally responded.

Once more, Grace glanced up at her. This time, she leaned back in her chair, her coffee mug between her hands as she stared up at Paige. There was something different about her compared to normal. She debated. Crystal had agreed after all, if she didn't want to go on a date, she would have said no.

"I'll give you her number."

Paige narrowed her gaze. "You refused before."

"Yeah, but before Crystal didn't agree to go on a date. Call it flustered or whatever when you asked her out. She agreed. So I'll give you her number."

"Really?" The light that blossomed on Paige's face was brilliant.

If Grace didn't know better, she'd think Paige actually had an interest in Crystal beyond the fact she was Grace's best friend. However, Grace still had her doubts on that one and was pretty sure Paige had been honest on Friday when she'd said it was all because Grace was taken.

"Yes. Here." Grace reached forward after setting her coffee down and grabbed a standard yellow sticky note. She had memorized Crystal's phone number years ago when she'd put her down as an emergency contact on literally everything. Scrawling out the seven numbers, she handed it to Paige. "Call her any time. She's on break and doing nothing. I know because the texts have been blowing up my phone."

Grace picked up her phone to prove her point. The screen was littered with texts and missed calls from Crystal, only three of which she had actually answered. Crystal knew better and didn't expect her to respond until after work. Grace also knew Crystal would likely be over at their house every night that week. Sighing at the thought, she closed her eyes. For the first time in four months, their house was going to be empty for three nights. It was going to be weird as fuck.

"Thanks!" Paige whipped out her phone, inputting the number into it. "I'll text her."

Standing up, Paige walked to her desk. Grace snorted and then unlocked her phone and called Peggy like she had wanted to do halfway through that conversation. Rubbing her hand over the back of her head, Grace waited until Peggy answered.

"Hey, Grace."

"Hey." Grace let out a breath. "I'm actually calling on business."

"Oh?"

"Hmm. Yeah. I've got this case, remember?"

"Yeah. I remember."

Grace licked her lips, the coffee flavor lingering on the tip of her tongue. "Where do you send students to get their class rings?"

"Oh! Hold on, let me pull it up on my laptop."

Listening as Peggy clearly moved to a different room and rustled around, Grace realized too late it was also spring break for Peggy, which she didn't think about principals taking, but they probably did, especially when they had their own kids at home, at least as much of a spring break as they could. Grace was pretty sure they still worked during it.

"How's your break?" Grace asked, realizing she should probably make small talk but her sleep-deprived brain wasn't functioning so great.

"It's good so far. Actually didn't work this past weekend and only a half-day today. Wilson is spending most of his time with his friends because his parents are lame."

Grace snorted. "I get that."

"Kit's with you, right?"

Pursing her lips, tears bit at Grace's eyes unexpectedly. She blinked them away. "She was. She's home now."

"What happened?"

"Another time, another day. I'm sure you'll hear soon enough."

"That's vague."

"It is." Grace took a sip of her coffee, wishing she had gotten the entire pot to herself, but she could already see it dwindling.

"Here it is."

A few clicks echoed over the phone line, and Grace grabbed her pen, ready to write. She waited with bated breath for Peggy to finally speak.

"We send families to Finnegan's for their class rings, but that doesn't mean they can't get them elsewhere."

"Like where?" Grace wrote the first name down.

Peggy popped her lips. "Well, anywhere really. They can get them at jewelers or at some box stores even if they're looking for a cheaper place to get them. There's a whole variety. We send them to Finnegan's because they can get package deals with graduation stuff like invitations and announcements."

"All right." Grace's pen moved swiftly as she copied down all the information. It was at least some place to start. She could check with Finnegan's, and if they had no answers, she could check with someone else. She hoped Finnegan's would be the answer. "Thanks so much."

"Did the kid have a ring?"

"I can't really say about that," Grace answered.

"I get it." She could hear Peggy smiling through the line. "Hey, by the way, when school's out for the year, we should do some type of backyard party or whatever. You, Amya, Crystal. All the people involved with the after school program."

"Sounds good, just let me know when and where and we'll be there."

"Good. Good."

"I've got to run. More bad guys to chase down."

Peggy chuckled. "This is why I love you, Grace. You're always about the making the world a better place. I'll see you around."

When Peggy hung up, Grace was left with a strange warm and tingly feeling in the dead center of her chest. That had been an unexpected compliment, and Grace wasn't even sure how true it was. She wanted to do her job and do it well, and she wanted to figure out exactly who Joseph was. He deserved to have his family around as much as possible even if he was in a coma for the rest of his life. No one deserved to be that alone and isolated. Focusing on the case at hand, Grace got to work.

When Grace got home that night, she passed out in bed for two hours before Amya arrived. She woke up to Amya's steady hand along her back, rubbing soft circles into her skin. When she blinked and stared up into Amya's rounded face, crystalline eyes, and soft brown tresses, she knew she was done for. She'd always been in love with her.

"Come here." Grace pulled Amya down onto the bed and threw an arm and a leg over Amya's body, tucking Amya into her side. She nuzzled her nose into Amya's neck and let out a breath. "It's so damn quiet."

"It will be for a few more days."

"Yeah." Grace kissed her hot skin. "How was work?"

"Exhausting. I imagine your day was, too."

"Yeah. Talked to Peggy, though, she wants to have a backyard barbecue this summer."

"It's March."

"You know her. She plans ahead."

Amya chuckled. "I worry about Kit staying in that house all summer."

"Me too."

They fell into a comfortable silence, and Grace was about to fall asleep again when Amya stirred under her. "We need to do something."

"About what?"

Amya sighed. "I need to do something."

Grace kissed her skin again. "I can think of a few things."

"Not that."

Slightly disappointed but not surprised, Grace pulled Amya in tighter to her body. "Then what?"

"We need to go through his room and this house."

Grace groaned. She did not want to be doing that on only a few hours of sleep. She kept her eyes closed and wondered for a second if she pretended to sleep if Amya wouldn't make her do it, but she knew that tone in Amya's voice. It was going to happen that night whether Grace participated or not, and if she chose not to, well, it wouldn't be good for anyone. "Can't it wait until tomorrow and some actual sleep?"

"No."

"Amya, he's not coming back tonight."

"And if we find alcohol? Do you want him to come back at all?"

Grace pushed to sit up, her eyes wide as she used one elbow to prop herself up and over Amya's body. "What does that mean?"

"I mean he's only gotten worse here. We haven't done a good job of helping him. In fact, I think we've done quite the opposite."

"Since when am I the patient one?"

"What?"

Grace sighed. "We can't force him to do anything, Amya. He has to come to that idea and conclusion on his own. All we can do is be here to support him."

"We gave him the car and the house and essentially the ability to have the funds to buy the alcohol."

"That's not true, and you know it." Grace scrunched her nose. "We did not buy him alcohol. We did not make him drink. We have given him a safe place to rest his head and figure his shit out. That's exactly what we need to be doing."

"Grace, we're enabling him."

"Jesus." Grace rolled over onto her back and rubbed her hands up and down her face. She did not want to be having the conversation at all. She wanted Peter to come home, get his life back on track, get back into AA.

Amya leaned up onto her elbow, looking down on Grace, her eyes wide with fear. "Don't do that."

"Do what?"

"Close yourself off because you disagree with me. You have to see how providing all this stuff for him is enabling him."

"I'm not kicking him out to live on the street!"

"I'm not saying we should." Amya put her hand on Grace's belly and splayed her fingers out. "Really, I'm not saying that."

"Then what are you saying? Because that is what it sounds like."

"I'm saying that even in trying to help him we have enabled him to keep drinking."

Grace's face was set as she mulled over what Amya said. Amya wasn't wrong, but that didn't mean she was going to kick Peter out any time soon either. Amya bent down and pressed their mouths together.

"I will go get him when he's released. They'll call, right?"

"They should if he tells them it's here he wants to come, but I'm sure they'll call to let me know anyway."

"I could only hope." Amya's voice became soft, almost a whisper. "We have to go through his room."

"You already did that."

"I did a basic search of it. Unlike you, Grace, it's been a long time since I've done a proper search of someone's residence." Amya smirked. "You're much better at it than I am, but we have to go through his room and this entire house—outside and in."

"Tonight?"

"Yes."

"Why tonight?" Grace whined. "I'm exhausted. You're exhausted. Let's get some sleep and do it tomorrow."

Amya bent down and kissed her again, this time drawing out the embrace. The hand on Grace's belly moved to her side and held her in close. Grace's left hand came up and threaded into Amya's hair, holding her still. When Amya pulled away, she was smirking again.

"That's not fair."

"I'll give you more if you help."

Grace narrowed her eyes. "Still not fair."

"Come on." Amya rolled out of bed and grabbed Grace's hand, tugging her until Grace at least sat on the edge of the bed.

Groaning and whining even more, Grace planted both bare feet on the hardwood floor and let out a sigh. "Really, can't we do this tomorrow?"

"We need to start tonight. I'm betting it takes us more than one day."

"That's what I was afraid of, but I swear to you, Amya, I'm not doing this past nine tonight. I'm way too tired."

"Deal." Amya stood up and tugged Grace to stand with her. Together they walked out of their bedroom and into Peter's. The dogs following them, confused as to what was going on but always wanting to be in the know.

His room had a distinct odor to it if Grace thought about it. Now that he'd been gone for more than twenty-four hours, the scent it normally was faded, and she could pick up the stale smell of alcohol and something else other than boy.

"Fuck," Grace muttered.

"What?"

"Can't you smell that?"

"Smell what?"

Grace pursed her lips and sniffed again. She was right. "Pot."

"No." Amya's eyes widened, and she took in a deep breath. "All I smell is BO."

"I bet we'll find alcohol and pot in here."

"Where?"

"He's good, trust me. He's in a house with two cops."

"Chaplain."

"Fine, former cop and a cop. He knew he needed to be subtle. I bet he never smoked it in here and it's just on his clothes."

Grace didn't wait. She grabbed the sheets on his bed and pulled them off. They needed washed anyway. Everything in there needed to be washed. She ran her fingers along the corners of the fitted sheet and then threw it into the hall before going back to the bed. On second thought, she changed her mind and started the wash with the sheets in them before going back to the bed.

Amya helped her lift the mattress and drag it out of the room. They were going to empty it and then fill it back up exactly as it was before. When they got to the box spring, Grace propped it on the side and bit her lip as she stared at Amya.

"Did you look here?" Grace asked.

"Kind of. Why?"

Grace pulled away the edge of the fabric on the bottom of the box spring. It had been clearly cut. She pulled away just a few inches so it wouldn't be that easily noticeable. When she stuck her hand in, she pulled out a bag of pot that had been taped to the side of the bed.

"Shit," Amya muttered.

Grace smirked. She always loved it when Amya cursed. It was cute because it was so random and odd coming from her mouth, unlike from Grace. "Yeah."

Going to the kitchen and grabbing a knife, Grace peeled away more of the fabric to make sure they didn't miss anything, but there was only the one small bag taped there. It would only be enough for a handful of joints.

Surprised Peter was heading into different drugs and vices, she set the pot on the desk and moved the box spring out into the hall with the mattress. They started on his dresser next. Grace pulled in a laundry basket and they went through each and every piece of his clothing before tossing it in. Together, they shifted the dresser from side to side until it was in the center of the room.

Sure enough, underneath the bottom of it were two small bottles of whiskey that had been hidden under the back legs. Amya grabbed them and put them next to the baggie of pot. Grace could only hope that was all they found. She really didn't want to stumble into Peter's porn stash, although, that was most likely on his computer.

"I can't believe I missed this stuff," Amya whispered, more to herself than to Grace.

Grace wrapped her arms around Amya's shoulders and kissed her cheek. "You were angry, not with it properly, and you said yourself you didn't do a full search. Also, let's be clear, this all could have shown up after that anyway. It's not like you searched yesterday."

"That's true." Amya leaned back into Grace's body. "Come on, let's at least finish his room tonight."

"Okay." One last kiss to Amya's cheek, and they went to work.

WHEN IN DOUBT, ASK AGAIN

PETER HAD gotten out at noon, somehow bypassing the seventy-two hours and getting out in just over twenty-four. Amya had gone to get him, since Grace had been at work, but the entire time, she couldn't get him out her mind, wondering if what they were doing was the right thing. Amya had a point. He'd gotten drunk and high on their watch, and they had given him the space to do it. Guilt swept over her, but she had to ignore it and focus on the job.

Joseph deserved as much of her attention as possible. Four years was long enough to be without a name, without a birthday, and without family around. She pulled up his file, wanting to interview the cab driver again to see if he remembered anything else about the ring or knew where it might have gone since there was absolutely no record of it.

She'd already called down to the hospital three times to check and see if they had the ring, and she'd gone personally down to evidence. There was nothing anywhere. Grace put what she needed in order and shifted her shoulders back and forth. She would likely have to find someone who had time to go out with her otherwise she'd have to convince Diego to come in, which she doubted would happen.

Kline, her first choice, was busy, and after the last time they'd gone out on a case together ending in a shootout, she wasn't so sure she wanted to ask Kline again so soon. When she glanced over at Paige, Paige was staring directly what her.

Smirking, Grace got up out of her chair and walked to Paige's desk. She balanced her weight on both her feet then stood still. "Want to head out?"

"Where?"

"Interview."

"Who?"

"Diego."

Paige grinned. "Uh, yes! Yes, let's go."

Grace chuckled. "Not this second. I want a plan first."

"What's the plan?"

"I don't have a plan, yet."

"Grace, don't tease me."

Wrinkling her nose, Grace shook her head. "Not teasing. I wanted to know who was coming with me before I formulated a plan. You know, different personalities and rapports make a whole lot of difference."

"Oh, I'm aware. So why are we going back to this guy? We just interviewed him last week."

Grace nodded. "Exactly. It's been four years since he talked to anyone, so maybe now that he's been thinking about it for, oh, five days, he's remembered a whole lot more."

Paige narrowed her gaze at Grace. "You have something specific you want."

"Of course I do. Don't you whenever you go into an interview."

Shrugging, Paige pushed into her chair and crossed one ankle over her knee. "Sometimes I do, and sometimes I don't. Depends on the interview."

"Well, this is a second interview, and he dropped that information about the ring last time that no one knew about, so I want to know if *he* has it."

"Why do you think he has it?" Paige's forehead wrinkled.

"Because no one else does." It was the only scenario that made sense to Grace.

"Where do you think it is?" Paige cocked her head.

Grace narrowed her gaze and pursed her lips. "How the fuck do I know?"

Rolling her eyes, Paige turned toward her computer before glancing back at Grace. "You figure out what you want to ask while I look into some more money trails. Let me know when you're ready to head out and I'll be ready."

"Got it." Grace went to her desk and pulled out a piece of a paper and a pen. She always preferred to work this way compared to on a computer like Paige. She wasn't old school, per se, but it did help her to think more clearly if she wrote everything out by hand before figuring out the wording when she typed it up.

She made a list of questions, then split them out into three trails she could potentially see them following. She hoped it'd be one of those three because she didn't really want to have to think that much on her feet to bring their conversation back around to her questions. Each time she ended with the same question. *Where is the ring?*

She wanted to know where that ring was, wanted the specific details on it that she didn't already have. It would make her job much easier if she could find it. Sighing, Grace typed up her questions, memorized them and the order she wanted to ask them in, and then she stood up after hitting print and stretched her back.

Paige must have caught sight of her because she shifted, her feet flat on the floor as she leaned forward like she was ready to spring the joint. Snorting and chuckling, Grace nodded at Paige in acknowledgement that it was time to leave. Paige didn't hesitate as she stood and grabbed her light jacket off the back of her chair and swung it over her shoulders.

Grace did the same and went to grab her papers while Paige went to tell Humbard where they were going. They had worked together so much in the past year they were able to do it without talking sometimes. It was a good feeling until Grace remembered Amya's jealousy, Paige's inability to keep boundaries, and it all came crashing down around her. She should have waited for Kline to be able to join her instead of asking Paige.

Shoving that bit of guilt to the side, they went out to Paige's cruiser and got in. Like always, Paige would drive and Grace would work on memorizing her questions while Paige tried to talk her through them so they could be on the same page when the interview started up.

When they pulled up outside of Diego's small house, Grace was surprised to see a few more cars parked outside. She wasn't sure he could have fit them on his property, but somehow, he did. They were parked haphazardly on his front lawn. She had no idea how much money he actually earned from his business, but she assumed from the way things were looking, he wasn't doing too great at it.

It might have been a flourishing business at one point, but it didn't seem like it was then. The cars he had were older vehicles, they weren't kept super clean. As she walked through the field of them and peeked through some of the windows on her way to the house itself, she noted trash littering the inside of some of them, broken windows that had at one point been taped over with plastic to keep the inside nice and clean but hadn't been kept up or fixed because the tape had come off and the plastic flapped in the light breeze.

"You think he's still even in business?" Grace muttered to Paige as they got to the front door.

Paige shot her a discerning look. "You didn't dig into that to find out before dragging me all the way out here?"

Shrugging, Grace rapped her knuckles against the door. "Slipped my mind."

"You're better than that, Grace. What's going on?"

"Got shit going on is what." She knocked again when there was no answer. "Diego, open up. It's Detective Halling and Detective Delwin again. We had a follow up question to ask."

Paige shook her head. "You don't just forget shit."

Grace turned full on to Paige and glared at her. "Yes, I do, and I did. I'll look when we get back to see how his finances and business is going. I also didn't really have too much of a reason to look because he's only a witness."

"Grace! Haven't I taught you anything? No one is ever only a witness."

Rolling her eyes, Grace moved to pound her fist against the door again, but it cracked open in the slightest. Diego popped his head out and winced at the light from the open door coming in. He rubbed his head and his eyes, the scent of stale alcohol swimming off him in waves made Grace's stomach churn.

"Diego, glad you could wake up to join us," Grace commented. "We've got a few more questions for you."

"Yeah." His voice was gruff like he really had just woken up. She was pretty sure he hadn't wanted to talk to them again but also pretty sure he truly had been asleep or at least passed out in some drunken state.

"We coming in or are you coming out?" Paige interjected, her lack of patience getting the best of her.

Grace also knew Paige was trying to play the one who kept him on his toes so Grace could play the role of getting closer to him. It was a dance the two of them had done so many times Grace had lost count. They worked together like a well-oiled machine.

"Come in," he grumbled and rubbed his head again before opening the door wider.

He took them down the hall to the room filled with papers that looked as though the stacks they were in would fall over to join the rest of their friends on the floor. Even if he wasn't in financial distress, how he kept anything straight in there was beyond her.

"I wanted to run through what happened that night four years ago once again."

"How many times are you going to make me do this?"

Grace sent Paige a look of curiosity. "Until we figure out who Joseph is. Please. This is to help a young boy find his family."

"Fine, fine." He waved a hand at her. "But I'm drunk, so who knows what I'm going to remember."

One more look at Paige told her they had an understanding. Grace let out a breath and knelt down so she was closer to Diego's level as he sat in the tattered old chair. She moved into a squat, sitting on her toes while Paige stayed by the doorway and kept an eye out for whatever might be happening outside of Grace's view.

"What do you remember from that night?"

"I don't know. I was driving like normal. I went to take a smoke break and I stopped behind the buildings so no one would see me."

Grace shot Paige a raised eyebrow and focused on Diego. "What were you smoking? And before you answer that, I'm not going to arrest you for something you did four years ago."

He nodded. "Pot."

"Thanks for being honest." Grace gave him a soft smile to try and entice him out of his shell. "So you stopped out back of the buildings, and then what?"

"I heard something funny, some groaning, so I went down to see what was going on, and I found the kid there. I called the cops, they came, that was it."

"Okay, so walk me through it."

Diego rolled his eyes and let out a huff. "I just did, lady."

"Answer her question," Paige grumbled from the corner.

Grace glanced up at Diego then to Paige. "One more time, I

promise."

He sighed. "I parked my car out back of the buildings to have a smoke break. I was minding my own business when I saw the kid laying there down by the woods, so I walked down because I thought it looked funny and saw him there."

"What did he have on him?"

"He was naked." Diego's eyes got wide as he stared directly into Grace's gaze before he looked down at his shoes and then off to the floor somewhere to his left, then back to his right.

Grace bit her lip. "You said before he had a ring on him."

Diego nodded but didn't respond verbally.

"What did the ring look like?"

"It had a red stone on it."

"Do you have the ring?"

He froze. His entire body tensed from his toes to his head. His jaw worked back and forth as his gaze didn't raise to meet hers. "No."

Grace nodded. "Any idea where it's at?"

Once again, he refused to look at her as he shook his head and gnawed on his lower lip. Grace patted his knee. "Did you see if he still had it on when the ambulance came?"

"Don't remember," he muttered, his voice so quiet, Grace almost missed it, and she knew Paige hadn't heard him.

"All right. Thanks, Diego. If you remember something, you give me a call, okay?"

He nodded as she handed him her card again to make sure he had it. When she stood up, Grace cocked her head at Paige with a smirk on her lips.

"I'll see you around, Diego."

He didn't answer. The two of them walked out of the house and to the cruiser. As Grace moved to grab the door, Paige pushed it shut and leaned in closer to Grace. Grace's heart ratcheted up a notch as Paige came closer, her breath brushing Grace's cheek.

"What was that about?" Paige's voice was quiet but controlled and firm.

"He's lying." Grace pressed her lips together, moving her gaze up to Paige's green eyes. "He knows where the ring is."

"You didn't press him for it. I thought you wanted that answer."

"Maybe next time, when he's not so drunk." Grace's chest rose and fell unevenly as Paige moved impossibly closer to her. If Grace didn't know better, she'd think their conversation was a whole lot more intimate than it was. Whatever was happening made her uncomfortable. She swallowed hard as she grasped for an out. "Wanna talk it out over lunch?"

"Would love to." Paige grinned and pushed away from the cruiser, giving Grace space.

As soon as Paige walked around the front of the car, Grace let out a breath and rubbed her sweaty palm on her slacks. It had been a long time since Paige had pulled something like that. They'd almost gotten back into their normal rhythm before that moment, but Grace felt has if she'd been tossed right back into last December when Paige hadn't let up either.

Slipping into the cruiser, she tensed her shoulders and tried to relax the stress in her jaw. "Diner?"

"Where else?" Paige chuckled.

Grace didn't answer as Paige drove.

As they sat down at the table near the front of the diner, Grace felt more at ease. She was back on level footing with Paige, who kept her distance, thankfully, since they left Diego's. With Sally already taken their orders, Grace shifted in her seat and glanced toward the front door and the back door before she fully settled in for their meal.

"So, why didn't you press him for the ring? Really."

Grace pursed her lips. "He was so drunk and high, I don't think he could tell me anyway."

"Sometimes that's the best time to get information from people."

Shrugging, Grace lifted her orange juice to her lips. "Sometimes, but it's also not reliable, and I'd rather be chasing actual information rather than ghosts. This whole case is ghosts. I want something concrete."

"I get that." Paige sipped her coffee. "So the different stories? What do you make of that?"

"Is this twenty questions?" Grace set her drink down and drew in a deep breath. "Normally I'm the one asking you these things."

"Maybe I want to see if you've learned anything in the past year."

"Whatever." Grace rolled her eyes. "It could be nothing. If he was high that night four years ago, he probably just remembers it different. Or he was lying then to cover the pot use. It was four years ago."

"Or...?"

"Or there could be something to it. He was definitely lying about the ring. Lying about what he did with it, I have no idea, but he did not want to talk about it. I'm betting he didn't want to tell me originally and it slipped." A sharp movement caught Grace's attention. Turning toward the front door, she heard the boisterous laugh that sent shivers up her spine. She hadn't heard that laugh in months.

She stared at the front door to the diner before she saw them. They were at the low counter that lined the front with seven stools bolted into the floor. Peter, in all his glory, sat at the stool closest the cash register. His brown hair at least looked clean as it was fluffy atop his head, but his cheeks were red with intoxication, and the boy—yes, Grace deemed him that—Peter hung his arms over to plant kisses on his lips looked just as drunk.

Her watch told her it was barely past one in the afternoon. Grabbing for her phone, she went to text Amya but stopped herself. Amya had handled getting him from the jail, which this was most definitely a complete violation of his release. Grace could handle this situation easily enough. Paige's hand on hers shocked her back to reality.

"What's going on?" Paige asked, concern lacing every bit of her tone. "You look like you've seen a ghost."

"No, just a very troubled kid who has gone too far down the rabbit hole. If you'll excuse me, I'll be right back."

Pushing to stand, Grace squared off her shoulders, prepared her speech in her head, and stalked toward Peter and the boy. When she reached them, the joviality in Peter's demeanor skittered away. He turned to stare up at her and looked like a lost puppy.

"Peter," Grace stared.

"Hey there!" The boy dared to speak, his tone happy. "I'm Dick."

The name registered immediately. He was the boy Peter had been interested in and was dating in seminary, the boy he'd gone to the club with, the boy he'd been involved with when he'd gotten his first DWI out there that he had refused to tell them about. Grace didn't even bother to give him any of her attention.

"You, one, should not be here at all, and two, should not be drunk. You're violating the terms of your release."

"Release?" Dick asked, turning to Peter. "What release?"

Peter let out a heavy sigh but didn't move his gaze from Grace. "We were having a little fun."

"You can give me every excuse in the damn book all you want, Peter. Trust me when I say I have heard them before. 'Lying lips are an abomination.'" She put her hands on her hips and glared.

Peter's eyes narrowed. Dick reached out and gripped Grace's hand. She flipped her right hand over his and twisted his wrist to bend it at a painful angle with a glare. He cried out when she dropped his hand and shook his wrist out to get rid of the pain.

Peter put a hand on Dick's thigh. "She doesn't like to be touched."

"Who is she even?"

Grace snorted. "Nice to know we can be a place for you to run but not a home for you to share."

"That's not how it is, Grace."

"I will only speak to you when you are sober. You know how I feel about you being drunk, and I swear, Peter, the next time I see you drunk I will bring you in myself. You're out of chances from me." She got down into his face to make her point. "Don't come home until you're sober, and don't come home with this idiot. I don't like him."

"You don't know him."

"Don't need to know him. He went and got drunk with a drunk. That's all I need to know."

"Wait, what?" Dick asked.

Grace turned to look Dick dead in the eye, then. "Guess he keeps quite a few secrets from you. What happened, Peter?"

Peter's eyes went wide. With what, she couldn't quite tell. It had a touch of fear in them, but it also held defiance, one thing she rarely ever saw from Peter. He always wanted to please her and Amya; he always wanted their approval, their love, their praise.

"Tell me, what happened that you suddenly lie?"

Peter's lips pulled tight, his chin raised a notch. "What happened that you suddenly quote scripture?"

Smirking, Grace winked. "I know more than you think. But seriously, don't bother coming home if you're not planning on sobering up any time soon. You're not welcome if you're going to continue to kill yourself slowly."

Without another word, Grace stood up and walked back to the table where Paige continued to sit. Their food was set before them, and Grace slid into the booth. She grabbed her orange juice and took a long and slow sip, and she glanced over at Peter and Dick, who still sat in shock.

She watched them shake their heads when the owner asked for their orders. Peter tossed money onto the table, grabbed Dick by the hand, and stalked out of the diner. Grace let out a breath and downed the rest of her orange juice. When she glanced at Paige, she knew she was going to have to confess everything.

"What the fuck was that?"

Grace snorted. "Stupid decisions."

"No, seriously."

"That's Peter."

"Your kid."

"Yeah. And he's...he's in a downward spiral. He was arrested for drunk driving, got released, and shows up here drunk. He wanted to be caught. There is no other fucking reason he would come here of all places. He knows this is where cops hang out."

"So you're going to let him drive drunk to wherever?"

"No." Grace snorted and shook her head. She reached into her pocket and dropped a pair of keys onto the table. "I swiped his keys while I was at it."

"You sneaky bitch!" Paige snatched the keys up and stared at them. "Where the hell did you learn that?"

Grace froze. "That's a story for another day."

"No. Now."

Sighing, Grace took a bite of her semi-warm food. "I lived on the streets for a bit. You learn a lot when you have to survive."

"You stole shit?"

"Yeah, you would have too."

"Why haven't you ever told me before now?" Paige settled the keys back down and grabbed Grace's hand. "You can trust me, you know."

Grace glanced at Paige's fingers then moved her hand into her lap. "Sure. It just never came up, and it was so long ago, it's not like I really talk about it to anyone."

"Does Amya know?"

Tingles raced up Grace's spine. She wasn't sure if Amya knew, honestly. She'd told her about her childhood, but she couldn't remember if she specifically shared how she had survived for the year she'd spent on the streets before Daniel Mason Brady had caught her stealing. She would have to remedy that. Shrugging, Grace shoved another forkful of food between her lips.

"I need to interview Diego again in a very controlled environment, but I want a hell of a lot more information before I go into that interview."

"Way to avoid," Paige commented.

Grace shook her head and let out a sigh. "I need to concentrate on this case, Paige. Nothing else to it. I don't have enough space in my head for Peter and his problems at the moment. Joseph deserves my attention, and I'm going to give it him."

She had hoped saying it out loud would help, but it didn't. She could only think of Peter and Dick and their drunk asses trying to find a way home because she knew they wouldn't walk back in there to confront her. She finished half her plate in silence before she dared ask Paige for the favor weighing on her mind. "Mind following me home so I can get the car back?"

"Absolutely, Halling. You know I'm good for a favor."

"Yeah, you always are." They finished their meal talking about Paige's ongoing case, and Grace knew she was going to have to have a long conversation with Amya when they both were home and settled in for the night. Neither of them were going to get much sleep.

UNRAVEL

IT WAS near dusk by the time Amya made it home from her shift. It had been a mostly normal day with only a few hiccups, but it had been exhaustingly draining. The individuals who had come to see her that day had heavy issues weighing on their hearts, and she'd broken right alongside them. It had felt as though she hadn't had even five minutes to herself to collect her thoughts.

As she pushed the door open, she smiled when the dogs vied for her attention. She bent down and scratched them between the ears and under the chin. Sighing, Amya dropped her bag by the door, slipped her shoes off, and went straight for the kitchen.

The house was quiet, far too quiet. Normally Grace would have come to greet her at the door along with the dogs if she was awake, but there was nothing to indicate Grace was even home except for the cruiser parked outside. When she got to the counter, she saw the bottle of whiskey sitting on it, still open. Amya picked it up and read the label, one she had read a dozen or two times over the past years.

Shrugging, she grabbed a small glass from the cabinet, poured herself a couple shots and downed them in one gulp. The burn sliding down her throat felt amazing. It had been so long since she had indulged in anything more than a glass of wine at dinner, and that had really only been while she was gone at her conference since Peter was still living at the house.

Her heart sunk. Peter could have very easily brought the alcohol home, but she suspected it was Grace, seeing as it was her favorite label. Pouring herself a couple more shots and adding in cubes of ice this time, Amya took a sip and let out a long relieving breath. She shucked her jacket and threw it over the back of the kitchen chair as she moved toward the bedroom.

The light was off when she entered, so she turned around and narrowed her eyes. The bathroom door was open a crack, and she caught the slight flickering light and the sound of moving water. Sipping her drink, she chuckled as she stepped barefoot down the hall and opened the door.

"Having a bath without me, I see." Her voice was sharp and loud, and it echoed in the tiny room.

Grace, laying in the tub with her eReader zip-locked into a bag and her shot of whiskey on the edge of the bath, jerked with a sudden start and splashed water onto her eReader. Water also sloshed over the edge of the tub and onto the floor below. Amya laughed and smiled as she moved the bathmat with her toe to soak up the water properly.

"You even lit the candles."

"Jesus, Amya."

"Don't say that."

"What the hell do you want me to say? You scared the shit out of me. Again."

Amya pursed her lips. "When was the last time you took this kind of bath?"

"Does it matter?"

"Sure it does. What happened?" Amya sat on the closed lid of the toilet seat and put her feet up on the edge of the tub as she stared down at her girlfriend of three years who very likely moved slower than a sloth when it came to anything relationship-related.

"Nothing happened," Grace muttered and shifted in the tub, her focus going back to the book her device had on it.

"What are you reading?" Amya asked as she took a quick sip from her own whiskey.

Grace sighed. "The same thing I was reading five minutes ago when you barged in here."

"Testy, aren't we?" Amya stared down Grace's form. She'd always admired Grace's body, the way she kept in shape for sure, but more the long lines of her legs and her arms that made her look taller than she actually was, the slight curves moved perfectly to allow her such grace—except Grace was anything but. "What happened today to get you so worked up you had to open the bottle of Johnny and get in the bath?"

"Nothing happened," Grace muttered, her gaze still solely focused on the eReader in front of her.

"Forgive me for not believing you. Where's Peter?"

"God only knows."

Amya narrowed her gaze. "He's not back in jail, is he?"

"He deserves to be," Grace added, her voice barely above a whisper.

"What does that mean?" There was a slight accusing tone to Amya's words, a bite she hadn't intended.

"Nothing."

Amya closed her eyes and downed the rest of her drink before she set it on the edge of the sink. "What happened today?"

Grace's gaze slid, full of contempt, from her eReader to Amya. "I told him not to come home until he was sober."

"What happened, Grace?"

"I was at the diner getting lunch, and Peter was there. With *the boy*." The way she said the last two words were astounding, so much anger and bitterness, so much snide hate.

"I assume he was intoxicated."

Grace nodded. "Yeah, so I told him he wasn't welcome here until he was sober and *the boy* wasn't with him anymore."

Again, that same sneering tone. "What boy?"

Snorting, Grace turned to stare Amya in the eye. "The one from seminary. Apparently he came for a visit, I'm betting spring break, and Peter just failed to share that information with us. So I told him I didn't appreciate him lying—"

"What exactly did you tell him?" Amya's shoulders stiffened. She didn't want Peter to think he wasn't welcome at their house any longer. They were—at least to their knowledge—his only safe place to go, and if he truly wanted to make a change in his life again, they would be there for him.

Grace glared as she set her eReader onto the edge of the tub and grabbed her drink, mimicking Grace downed the rest of it before she set the glass on the floor. Amya leaned over and picked it up, setting it next to her own empty cup.

"I told him not to come home until he was sober."

"Yeah, I got that. But what else did you say to him?"

"I told him lying was an abomination."

Amya choked. "You said what?"

Grace sent her another glare. "I told him lying lips were an abomination and I didn't appreciate him lying to me, that he was only welcome at this house when he was sober and without Dick."

"You quoted scripture at him?" Amya raised an eyebrow, curiosity, humor, and astonishment all warring within her.

Shrugging, Grace scooted into the tub more, her messy blonde hair that was haphazardly pulled into a knot on top of her head daring the loose strands to get wet. "I thought it might help him make sense since that's his go to."

"What scripture did you quote to him?"

"How the fuck do I know?" Grace cut her a look of serious confusion.

"You quoted it."

"Yeah, but I don't know what the fuck it is. My dad used to tell me that shit all the time. You think I actually looked that shit up?"

Laughing, Amya shook her head and closed her eyes. "What did he say?"

Grace let out a puff of air with a hiss. "Same thing you did."

"What?"

"He asked me when I started quoting scripture."

"To be fair," Amya tried to hold in her laughter, "I'm not sure I've ever heard you say something like that."

"I'm not stupid." Grace's defenses went up.

"I'm not saying you are. I would never say that because I don't believe it at all. I've just never heard you quote scripture."

"I know the Bible. My dad was a pastor."

"Yeah, he was." Amya's tone took on a softer quality. Any time Grace brought her father up, it was usually because she was avoiding some other kind of feeling. "And he was a crappy one at that."

Grace huffed. "He made me memorize scripture every night before bed."

"Did he really?" Amya's eyes widened. "You've never shared that before."

Shrugging, Grace moved the water over her belly and chest. The ripples entranced Amya and dragged her gaze down Grace's body when she hadn't intended to look there. "I'm pretty sure he'd be turning in his grave to know I'm gay."

Amya smiled at that. "Not that you'd care anyway."

"Of course I wouldn't care."

Nodding, Amya licked her lips. "So what made you think of your dad?"

Grace pulled her lower lip between her teeth as she stared at her toes, and Amya knew she had her. She was going to push her into talking, and she was patient enough to wait for an answer. She was one of nine children, she could easily wait a century before asking the same question twice. She was also very good at moving the conversation in ways most people weren't expecting in order to get answers.

"Did I tell you I used to steal shit?"

"You've mentioned it here and there. Before Daniel, right?"

"Yeah." Grace still wouldn't look at her.

Amya moved to stand and started on the buttons on her slacks.

"What are you doing?" Grace's dark brown eyes went wide.

"You'll see. Why did your history with stealing come up?"

Grace once again stilled and stared at her toes, clearly not sure if she wanted to answer or not. Amya shucked her pants and kicked them into the corner of the room before pulling at the buttons on her blouse. They remained in silence until Amya pulled at the clasp on her bra, then Grace's gaze was completely locked on Amya's body, causing a flush to rush through Amya's chest and into her cheeks.

"I swiped Peter's keys at the diner."

"You did? Clever."

"Didn't want him to drive. Paige was impressed."

Amya faltered in her movements as she pushed her underwear to her toes. "Paige was with you?"

"Yeah. She...well, it doesn't matter. What are you doing?" Grace's cheeks tinged pink.

"Huh?"

"You're naked."

Amya turned her head up to look at Grace as she grabbed for a hair tie and twisted her own brown locks into a messy bun at the top of her head. "Yeah."

"So what are you doing?"

"Joining you."

The sneer Grace gave her in return to the comment almost threw her into a fit of giggles. Amya popped her hip out to the side and put her fist on it as she stared down at Grace. "I mean, I could just go to the living room, naked, wandering around the house, waiting for you to be done."

"No." Grace's voice was a whisper. "No, don't do that."

Smiling, Amya stepped closer and bent down, her palms on the cold cast iron of the tub. "Then what would you like me to do."

"Get in here," Grace mumbled.

"You sound so thrilled," Amya flirted back as she put her toe into the water, hoping it was still warm. She knew Grace often stayed hours in the tub and sometimes it was cold before she got it. Amya was pleasantly surprised to find a good amount of heat still in it.

Grace rolled her eyes and gripped Amya's ankle, tugging hard as she shifted her weight and forcing Amya to slip and fall directly onto Grace's chest. The splash of water was loud in the tiny room, water overflowing the tub and onto the floor around them.

Before Amya had a chance to catch her breath, Grace's mouth covered hers and Grace's hands gripped her hips to hold her steady. Their tongues tangled, and Amya lost herself in the embrace. The heat from the bath and the room working wonders with the four shots of whiskey she'd had when she hadn't drank in such a long time. Her head spun pleasantly, a buzz in her ears as she moved against Grace to get comfortable in the tiny tub.

When Grace finally let her up, Amya grinned and shifted so her back was against Grace's front. They'd only done this a few times over the years, but Amya loved it. "It's a good thing you put that eReader in the damn bag."

"What?"

Chuckling, Amya grabbed over the edge of the tub where the device had fallen and pulled up a sopping went Ziploc baggie.

"Oh."

"Yeah." Amya laughed again before she set it down and snuggled into Grace's arms. "Why were you out with Paige?"

Grace sighed and ran the edge of her nails up and down Amya's arms, making her shiver. "I had an interview I wanted to do, and Humbard is insisting we work in pairs until the IAB investigation is over."

"How is that going, by the way?"

"Hell if I know. I did my interview. I know I'm not the target of it. Beyond that, I know nothing as it should be."

"I guess," Amya muttered. Her heart still clenched at the idea Grace and Paige had gone to eat together. It shouldn't. She knew Grace wasn't going to do anything to jeopardize their relationship, but she did not trust Paige to keep that same distance. Last winter, her jealousy had come to a head, and she couldn't avoid it any longer. It had gotten slightly better since then, but she'd never been able to make it fully go away.

Grace dropped a kiss to Amya's shoulder, bringing her attention back around. "I used to steal to stay alive."

"I know," Amya whispered, her heart breaking for the umpteenth time that day. She couldn't imagine how Grace had grown up, alone, essentially orphaned, on the streets, with no hope of a better life.

"Okay."

They stayed in the water until it had a definite chill to it. Amya begged Grace to get out, and they spent the next hour cleaning their mess and talking about Peter and *the boy* as Grace had dubbed him. Amya loved to watch and see how attached Grace had become to Peter. Usually she tried to remain as aloof as possible and have no serious attachments to anyone, something Grace continually failed at.

They'd had the entire weekend to themselves. It was such an odd feeling considering they'd had someone in the house with them since before Christmas. The house had felt obnoxiously empty the entire time, and Grace wondered if Peter would ever come back to them.

Sighing, she pushed open the door to her unit and stopped short. Peter sat at her desk, a uniformed officer standing nearby. She nodded at the officer, who glared at her. "Detective Halling?"

"Yeah, that's me." She wanted to ask if Peter was brought in for something stupid he had done, again, but she didn't have the heart to form the words.

"Do you know this man?"

"Yes."

"He wants to talk to you, but I wasn't about to leave him in here by himself."

"Thanks."

The officer left, and as soon as the main door shut, Grace crossed her arms and stared Peter down. No one else was in the offices yet. Grace always got there before anyone else did. She shifted her stance, taking on an aggressive posture. If Peter wasn't going to talk, then she would stare him down. She had no regrets about what happened at the diner, but it was clear by his demeanor he did.

"I'm sober, by the way." His voice was soft, and he refused to look her in the eye.

Grace knocked her chin up as she stared him down, judging him to see if he was telling the truth or not. She could tell he wasn't full-out drunk, but whether or not he was completely sober was a different story. Only a breathalyzer and blood test would tell her that, but she wasn't about to perform that on him and have it on his record if she could avoid it.

"Where's *the boy?*"

"At the airport."

Raising one eyebrow, Grace dared herself not to soften. "What do you have to say for yourself then?"

"I'm sorry. I really am."

She felt like she was talking to a toddler. "Sorry for what?"

"Everything." Peter ran a hand through his perpetually messy hair and shook his head. When he looked up at her, his gaze locking on hers, she knew he was telling the truth. "I'm really sorry. About drinking, about using you, about fucking up everything."

Grace swallowed and stared him down a few more seconds before she gave him a good nod. She relaxed and then stepped over to grab an extra chair from Paige's desk and scooting it so she could sit with him. "Where have you been?"

"Hotel. It sucked. Dick left."

"So you said."

"No, he left. We're over with."

"Because you lied to him?"

Peter nodded, his lips thinning and tears watering in his eyes. "Yeah."

"Happens when you lie."

"Yeah, I get that." Peter let out a breath. "Again, I'm sorry."

"I won't leave you, kid. You know that, right?"

Peter's gaze slid up to meet hers. Grace leaned down, her elbows on her knees as she made sure to stare at him hard but with compassion. She wanted him to understand what she was about to say.

"I won't leave you. You're always welcome in our house so long as you are sober or ready to get sober. We're here to support you in this walk of life. You know that, right?"

"Yeah." He nodded and then shook his head. "I'm sorry."

"Shut it, kid. You've said that already."

"I'll do better next time, I promise."

Grace reached out then, her hand on Peter's knee, she gave him a gentle squeeze. "How many times are you going to mess up before you'll do what you know you're called to do and before you'll let us help you and support you?"

She almost told him life wasn't meant to be walked alone, but she bit her tongue. She'd maintained that for years she didn't need anyone, and it wasn't until Amya that she really started to see the world differently.

"I don't know."

"Are you called to ministry?"

Peter nodded.

"Do you want to do it?"

"Some days."

Grace laughed. "That's good enough for any job. Some days I don't want to be here either. If it's something you want to do most days, then let's get you back to doing it, okay, kid?"

"Yeah."

"But you're going to have to do the heavy lifting."

"I know."

"Good." Grace was just about to ask Peter if he wanted a lift home when her phone rang. Reaching to her hip, she pulled her cell phone off its holder and narrowed her gaze at the name on it. She held out a finger to Peter and answered. "Annabelle?"

"Hey, Detective Grace." Annabelle's voice wavered.

Grace's stomach clenched. "What's wrong?"

"It's...it's Kit."

"What happened?" Grace's shoulders tightened with fear. She knew she shouldn't have let Kit go home. She should have kept her, forced DCFS's hand or something, anything. She closed her eyes and prayed Kit wasn't dead.

"I'm not entirely sure."

"Annabelle, is she okay?"

"I don't know."

Grace let out a sigh. She had to be patient. She could do this. "Where is she?"

"I...that's the thing. I don't know."

"Annabelle." The warning in Grace's tone set Peter to full alert. "What happened?"

"I don't know. She's not home. Her parents kicked her out again. This week...it was bad. I haven't seen her since your house, but she sent me a few texts when she could get to her phone."

"What do you mean get to her phone?"

"Well, her parents found it."

"Found it?" Grace's eyebrows rose. "We gave her that phone—"

"I know, but she had to hide it from them. She doesn't have it now."

"Fucking Christ." Grace shot Peter a glare. "When did they kick her out?"

"Last night."

The biting question on the tip of Grace's tongue died with a bad taste. She wanted to know why Annabelle had waited so long to call her. If she'd known before, she could have driven over and gotten Kit immediately instead of having to try and find her. Again. Grace snapped her fingers at Peter and mouthed "Call Amya" at him.

He was on the phone in seconds while Grace focused on Annabelle. "Did she say where she was going?"

"No." Annabelle sniffled. "Why does this keep happening?"

"Don't worry. This is the last of it." Grace stood and pushed Paige's chair back to her desk and grabbed a piece of paper and wrote two notes, one to Paige and one to Humbard. "You go to school, Annabelle. Let me worry about Kit. I'll find her like I always do."

"I knew you would." The relief in Annabelle's tone was astonishing.

Grace glanced at Peter who gave her a thumbs up sign. Finishing her note, Grace left one on Paige's desk and headed for Humbard's office. "Get to school."

"I will. Let me know when you find her, okay?"

"Yeah."

Grace drew in a sharp breath as they hung up, and she put her the note on Humbard's desk. When she came back, Peter handed her the phone. "I didn't know what to tell her."

"Amya," Grace took the phone.

"What's going on? Kit's missing?"

"Her parents kicked her out again."

"When?"

"Last night. I'm going to go look for her."

"I'm coming."

"Probably better to stay separate and hit multiple places at once." Grace headed for the door of her unit before looking over her shoulder at Peter. "You coming, kid?"

"Uh...yeah." He skipped a step before joining her.

"What's Peter doing there?" Amya asked.

"I'll tell you later."

"Okay." Amya sighed. "Um...I'll take the coffee shop and the school since I'm closer."

"I'm going to swing by her house, the library, and I'll call Peggy to see if she can let me know if she shows up there."

"Sounds good. Call me."

"Yeah." Grace hung up as she slipped into her cruiser. Peter joined her in the passenger seat. Grace started the engine and backed out of her parking space and drove into the street. "You've got more than just me to apologize to, you know."

"What?" Peter's eyes went wide.

"Amya?"

"Oh, yeah, right."

"So you can get on that." She handed his phone back over before taking a left and headed for the library downtown. Kit was adept at hiding in the library. Grace had found her there once before when she'd been kicked out of her parents' house, but Kit loved to sit in the quiet stacks.

When Grace pulled up outside, the library wasn't open yet. Gritting her teeth, she was about to go searching for the emergency number to get whoever was on call to let her in to the building when she stopped short. A lump of a person shoved into the corner of one of the pylons caught her attention.

Grace put her hand out to Peter to stop him in his tracks and her hand over her weapon, though she was pretty sure she wasn't going to have to use it. She stepped closer, quietly, as she tried to figure out who was under the jacket. Grace nudged the boot with her shoe and waited as the person rustled.

Sure enough, Kit's crystalline eyes and dark brown hair shone back at her. Grace grinned. "Kid, we've got to stop finding ourselves in this situation."

"Annabelle?"

"Who else? Let's go."

"Go where?"

"I don't know, but I'm betting you're cold and hungry, so let's start with breakfast."

Kit nodded and pushed to her feet. "I couldn't call you."

"You heard of a pay phone?"

"What?"

"Jesus, kid, you're young. Find a phone, put in some coins, or call collect."

"What's collect?"

"I'm done. You did not just ask that. Get in the damn car."

Peter hesitated as Kit came closer, but she didn't. She walked right up to him and wrapped her arms around his middle in a tight hug before getting into the back of the cruiser. Grace let out a breath and called Amya.

"Find her?"

"Yeah. Library. I'm going to get her breakfast and drop her off at school."

"Want to talk in an hour?"

"You know it. Your office?"

"Yeah."

"See you then. I love you."

"Love you, too, Grace."

It didn't take them long to go through the drive through and order breakfast for the three of them. Grace drove toward Kit's school, and as soon as she pulled up outside with the other dozen million parents dropping kids off and kids parking their own vehicles, Grace let out a breath. She got out of the car and opened the door so Kit could get out with her bag in tow.

Grace put a hand on her shoulder. "I have no answers for you right now. Go to class, listen in class, I'll be by to pick you up when school is done. Meet me here, and I will have some answers for you then, okay?"

Kit nodded. "I'm sorry about the phone."

"It's not your fault, kid." Grace wrapped her arm around Kit's shoulders and pulled her into a brief side hug. "None of this is your fault."

Kit's chin bobbed up and down, but Grace wasn't sure if she believed her or not.

"And I swear, kid, if I have to go find you when I get here after school, I'm not going to be happy. No more running."

"Got it." Kit gave her a smirk.

"See you in a few hours."

Kit stepped away from the cruiser and turned to walk up the front steps to the school. Peggy waved at Grace, who made a hand signal like she was going to call her that day. Getting back into her cruiser, Grace turned to Peter.

"Want to go home?"
"Can I?"
"Always, kid. Always."

FOCUS ON THE FAMILY

HEADING INTO Amya's offices, Grace sat heavily on her couch and let out a huff of air. Amya still sat at her desk, but Khloe had told her she could go right in. Rubbing her fingers over the bridge of her nose, Grace let out another long sigh. Amya shot her a dirty look.

"Give me five minutes."

"You got them." Leaning her head on the back of the couch, Grace closed her eyes. What the hell were they going to do with Kit or even Peter for that matter? Surely they couldn't do what Daniel did for her. Her parents were dead, well, her mom had been dead. Her dad—he was alive technically when she'd been homeless as a teen, but she'd known he wouldn't have been worth her time.

They couldn't just bring Kit to live with them for the next year and a half, could they? Without getting into all kinds of trouble? Peter was a whole different story. She'd allowed him back in the house after he swore up and down he was sober, and she hadn't seen any signs from him that he wasn't. She'd locked the alcohol back up that they'd brought out over the weekend and left him to his own devices for a while.

She and Amya were going to have to set some new ground rules for the house. Rules that would stick and be strict. Both those kids needed the structure in order to flourish. Amya spun in her chair and smiled at Grace, her lips bowing into a curve as her eyes crinkled in the corners.

"Kit okay?"

"I guess," Grace muttered. "Didn't get too much of a chance to talk to her, but I'm not bringing her back to them."

Amya crossed her arms over her chest as she rested against the back of her chair. "I wouldn't think so. No third chances."

"Right." Grace sat up and then leaned down again. "She slept outside last night at the side doors to the library."

"Why didn't she call?"

"They took her phone."

"Wonderful." Amya rolled her eyes.

Grace could tell there was a question on the tip of her tongue, but Amya wasn't asking it. Scratching the back of her head, Grace groaned. "You don't think...I mean...what if...I don't even know what I'm trying to say."

Amya smiled and then stood up to sit next to Grace. "Start with whatever words come to mind."

"What if she does come live with us? Assuming that's what she wants. Can we even do that?"

"I think we could."

"I don't want to call Doreen again. We saw what happened the last time we did that, and I really don't want to make her go back to her parents just to be kicked out again."

"I agree." Amya ran the palm of her hand up and down Grace's thigh.

"Do you think Kit will be angry if there is no punishment for them?"

Amya let out a breath and bit her lip. "She could be. I don't think she will be right now, if that's what you're thinking. She may be at some point in the future, but for now, I think she'll just be happy to be somewhere safe and where she's wanted."

"She'll be eighteen in a year and a half."

"She will be."

They lapsed into a silence. Grace stared at the floor under Amya's desk and rubbed her palms absent-mindedly together. When Amya's hand slid over hers, Grace turned her gaze upon her girlfriend.

"What are you thinking?"

"That I want to do this."

"Then let's do it."

Grace nodded. "Okay. It's settled. I'll pick her up at school."

"Grace, this is going to be different than if we formally fostered her. There's going to be some things she can't do until she's eighteen."

"I know. I've been there, remember?"

"Yeah, but it's a bit different now. We'll just have to make the work around when we can."

"We will." Grace leaned in and pressed her lips to Amya's, smiling when Amya's hand moved to the back of her neck and pulled her in deeper. A year ago, she never would have allowed such intimacy in the offices. When she backed away, she cupped Amya's cheek. "Still got time to go to the hospital with me today?"

"Yes, right now, as a matter of fact."

"Good. I'm driving."

Amya rolled her eyes. "You always drive."

"I have the cruiser. I get front row parking."

"There is such a thing as chaplain's parking, but I'm not going to argue with you." Amya grabbed her purse and slung it over her shoulder. Grace stood up and followed Amya out of her offices. She locked the door to her main work area behind them and told Khloe she'd be back in two hours. Grace sincerely hoped a visit to the hospital wouldn't take them that long.

When they got to ICU, Amya immediately started talking to the nurses. Grace slipped into Joseph's room and sat in the chair against the window and stared at him. She had no idea what to do or what to say. The kid was comatose. He wasn't going to respond no matter what she did, but she wanted to still get a sense of who he was as best as she could.

She let out a breath and focused on the room. Did he have a particular smell other than hospital sanitation? No. Did he have any ticks he did even while in his coma? No. Did he have any items in the room? Yes. There were small trinkets here and there, teddy bears, cards, flowers, but nothing that would tell her who he was.

Grace stopped short when she heard the curtain slide. She figured Amya would be joining her shortly, but instead, she was greeted by a small man in blue scrubs. He looked just as startled to find her sitting there. He looked down at the floor as soon as she sat up.

"Sorry," he muttered. "I'll come back later."

Immediately, he left the room. Grace watched him as he skittered away, curious as to who he was. Clearly he worked at the hospital. He had the uniform and the badge to prove it. He was probably a nurses aid come to change the sheets or something. Amya slid into the room shortly after he left with a smile on her face.

"So Joseph has a whole line of regular visitors."

Grace rolled her eyes. "I know that. I got the list from them the last time I was here."

"Oh." Amya handed the sheet of paper over to Grace.

Grace skimmed the names, curious to see if there were any similar ones or different ones from before. Curiously enough, one of the names did pop up as different and yet familiar. Diego Narvaez. His name was actually listed twice, each time the same day or the day after she had gone to talk to him. Curious, Grace handed the paper back to Amya.

Amya immediately moved to Joseph's side and touched his hand and his forearm, running her hand back and forth over his taped up skin. Grace stared at her in curiosity. This was not a side of Amya she saw.

"Hey, Joseph. I'm Amya, and I'm a chaplain for the sheriff's department. It's so good to meet you."

Grace's lips thinned. She never would have thought to talk to him because he couldn't talk back to her. Watching carefully, Grace stood unmoving, still unsure of what she should be doing.

"My friend here is Detective Grace Halling, she probably didn't introduce herself because she's a bit shy."

Rolling her eyes, Grace turned toward the door out of frustration and embarrassment and caught sight of the man in blue scrubs walking past the door again. This time, she made sure to memorize every feature about him she could. His hair was short cropped against his scalp, near a buzz cut but slightly longer. His eyes were dark brown but had a golden hue to them.

As soon as he saw her looking, his speed increased, and he moved beyond her line of sight. Grace stepped to the door and poked her head out to see where he had gone, but he was already vanished again. "Interesting."

"What's interesting?" Amya said as she came over to stand next to Grace.

"Nothing. What did Joseph tell you?"

"Not much," Amya gave a wry smile. "You should ask him

some questions or say something to him."

"Uh...no thanks."

Amya gripped Grace's hand and dragged her to the bed. Instead of putting her own hand on Joseph's, Amya laid Grace's hand against his arm skin. Immediately, Grace wanted to move. She was not comfortable with the situation, but the only reason she stayed put was the look Amya gave her, the one that dared her to try something new, to test the waters, to stand right where she was in her own discomfort.

"Remember," Amya whispered, "This isn't about you. It's about him. Four years with very limited human contact wears on a person even in a vegetative state."

"All right." Grace drew in a deep breath, held it in her lungs for a moment before letting it out slowly. "All right."

Gripping her hand around Joseph's wrist, she held on.

"Good. Joseph, this is Grace." Amya turned toward Joseph's head. "Like I said, she's a Detective for the Sheriff's Department, and she's actually the lead investigator on your case. Isn't that cool? She's trying to figure out who you are and where you come from."

Amya rambled on for another ten minutes or so, but Grace stopped paying too close attention to what she was saying. The monitors on Joseph's body changed. His heart rate increased, his blood pressure went up slightly before going back down. She was curious about it all, but she didn't dare ask anyone in that moment. That could be a question for later. She made a mental note to find some answers when she had the time.

They were just getting ready to leave after an hour of sitting in the room, when that same man walked by again. Curious, Grace followed him this time, not explaining anything to Amya. She beelined it out of the room and tried to catch up with him, but he was fast and wily. He was gone before she had a chance to figure out who he was or where he was going.

Grunting, Grace went back to Joseph's room and a confused Amya. She shook her head and walked up to the nurses station. "Hey, have you seen that man come by Joseph's room before?"

"What man?"

"The one that has been by three times today since I've been here. That doesn't seem normal to me."

The red-headed nurse glared at Grace. "Every visitor Joseph has must sign in here."

"I don't think he signed in. I think he just showed up. And I've been told that some visitors don't sign the log." Grace's tone was getting sharp, and she knew she was going to have to reign herself in. Luckily, Amya stepped in and pressed her fingers to Grace's arm.

"What did he look like, Grace?"

"He had on blue scrubs. I thought he was CNA at first, but I don't know. They would have just come in and done their job while I was in there. They wouldn't have cared about visitors."

The nurse narrowed her gaze. "Blue scrubs?"

"Yeah."

"Dark blue or light blue?"

"What the hell difference does it make?" Grace snapped.

The nurse popped her hip out with her fist on it and raised an eyebrow.

"I'm sorry. It's been a long day. What difference does the color make?"

"There are certain floors in the hospital that wear certain color scrubs. Maternity wears pink. We wear black."

"So who wears blue?"

"Unfortunately, a lot of departments."

Grace groaned. "Well, that's not very helpful."

"It can be. You know he doesn't work maternity, ICU, or cardiac."

"Great." Grace's lips thinned as she sent a longing look toward Amya. She wanted to get out of the hospital. They were never really her thing anyway, but having been there over an hour, she was certainly hitting her limit of patience.

"I'll keep my eye out for him and see if he comes by again and then give you a call."

"Thanks," Grace muttered. "That's at least a little helpful."

The nurse scoffed and went back to work. Amya took Grace by the arm and led her out of ICU and down the hall. "You have to be nicer if you want answers."

"Don't talk to me about how to interrogate suspects, Amya. I'm a trained detective. I know what I'm doing."

Amya put her hands in the air and stepped away from Grace. "Fine, do it your way. But there are better ways to get answers than trying to push people into it."

"I wish I had been able to get his name."

"He obviously didn't want to talk to you."

Grace pursed her lips. "No shit, Sherlock."

"Maybe stop by again and see if he comes by for a visit."

"I think I'm more interested in finding out why my taxi driver has been paying Joseph visits." Grace held up the visitor log.

"What?"

Grace smirked and handed the paper over to Amya. "Your question did come in useful, thank you. See here?" Grace pointed to Diego's name. "He's been by twice since I first questioned him. The day after and the day of the last time I interviewed him."

"Interesting coincidence."

"I think not." Grace took the paper back.

"I'm inclined to agree." Amya smiled and then gripped Grace's fingers. "This was actually kind of fun."

"What was?" Grace stared down at the paper in her hand as she shoved it into her pocket.

"Going on this interview with you."

"We hardly interviewed anyone today."

"Grace."

Turning to face Amya at the tone in her voice, Grace stopped short. "What?"

"I'm trying to tell you this was fun."

"What was fun?"

"Playing detective."

Narrowing her eyes, Grace cocked her head to the side. "Not thinking of coming back to the dark side of police work, are you?"

"Oh no." Amya giggled. "But it was fun to dabble in it again. Come on."

Amya dragged Grace by the hand out to the cruiser. As soon as they were near enough the doors, she touched Grace's waist with her hand and spun Grace into her, pressing a kiss on her lips. "I think today was a good day."

"What has got you in such a mood?" Grace asked, her lips thinning as she tried to figure it out.

"Nothing. Just ignore me. I'm happy."

"Happy for what?"

"Does it matter?"

Grace paused at that. "Yes. Yes, it matters."

"All right then. Our house is full again, and that, Grace, feels damn good."

"You're right. It'll feel better when I pick Kit up in..." she glanced at the watch on her right hand "...an hour."

"It will. Wait...will we need to get her new clothes? Again?" Amya's tone tensed.

"No. I'm going to make a stop by her house first. I want my phone back."

Amya snorted. "I still have an hour. Want company?"

"Fuck yes."

"Then lead on." Amya moved her hand out in front of her. Grace got into the cruiser and waited until Amya was buckled in before she drove immediately to the Umptree house. This was going to be one of the best conversations and demands she'd had in a long while.

Knowing Diego had been in to visit Joseph twice since Grace had made contact with him set her nerves on fire. There was more to Diego and Joseph than Diego was sharing. She knew it in her gut. The hard part was going to be figuring it out and getting Diego to admit it. She would have to interview him again, no doubt.

Grace sat at her desk for the last hour of her shift before she was set to go pick up Kit at school. She and Amya had discussed it again briefly after leaving the Umptree house with trash bags of Kit's things in tow. It would be what was best for Kit in the long run—hopefully. But anything was better than her living on the street at that point.

Paige sent Grace a look, but Grace ignored her as she booted up her computer and pulled up their reporting system. She ran Diego's name to see what other types of calls his name came up in, and she hoped it was something she could use to leverage him into telling her more about whatever the hell had happened that night.

She found nothing on him. He had never been arrested. He had never been given even a speeding ticket. His driving record was spotless. The only call his name came up on was her case. Cursing under her breath, Grace closed her eyes and racked her brain for what to check next. Diego, but all means, was an upstanding citizen, clearly one with his own demons like they typically all had, but a member who contributed to society in some form and fashion.

Paige sat at the corner of Grace's desk, her toe holding her up as she leaned over to look at Grace's computer screen. "Diego?"

Grace grunted. "He paid a surprise visit—well, two visits—to Joseph in the hospital."

"You're kidding."

"Nope."

"When?"

"Funnily enough, the day after we interviewed him the first

time and the day we interviewed him the last time."

"Damn."

"I know." Grace rubbed her lips together and ran a credit report on Diego. While her computer whirred and searched for the information. She tapped her toe against the floor and stared at the computer and then at Paige.

"Why do you think he'd go there?"

Paige shrugged. "Guilt?"

Grace puckered her lips before turning back to her computer. Diego's credit was shit, absolute shit. He was in debt up to his ears; his business was clearly floundering. She could see where he wouldn't find any hope in surviving or digging himself out of the hole he'd put himself into.

Paige glanced at her screen then did a double take. "Damn."

"Yeah."

"I don't think I've seen financials that bad on a business still running."

"I doubt it's running."

"What do you mean?"

Grace drew in a deep breath. "The vehicles on his property don't run. No one is going to take a ride from a taxi that has broken out windows. There was maybe one working vehicle in the driveway, which I'm betting is mostly his personal vehicle. But he was piss drunk in the middle of the day. He's not driving anyone like that, especially if he's not been arrested for a DWI yet."

"You've got me there. Makes sense."

"Yup. But still doesn't explain why he's going to visit Joseph."

"I'm telling you, guilt." Paige crossed her arms.

"Maybe, but I'm thinking there's more to it than that. And guilt over what?"

"Survivors guilt, maybe?"

Grace shook her head. "I don't think so."

Paige slapped her hands on her thighs. "Well, you'll have to figure it out. I'm going back to missing old people."

Grace ignored Paige's blunt comment. Some days Grace couldn't tell if Paige even liked her job or not. Paige moved to her own desk. Grace printed off the reports she had run and organized them before shoving them into the file she created for Diego. She searched for relatives to see who was supporting him financially, since it was pretty clear to her he didn't have much of an income.

She went through his bank records to see transfers in and out, what he spent his money on. No surprise, a hefty amount of it was at the liquor store six blocks from his house. Clearly it was his favorite place to go. Grace wrote down the name of it to make sure she checked it out and inquired after him. She wanted to know if he shared anything with his bartender, or at least his seller of his drug of choice.

People often confessed random things to cashiers, bartenders, and store clerks. It always surprised her what people would tell random strangers rather than best friends or close family. She would have to go visit them another day because she didn't have the time to do it that afternoon.

Checking her watch again, Grace noted the time and that she'd need to leave in twenty minutes. Finishing up her reports for the day, she filed everything away, wrote up a summary of her day to hand in to Humbard, and prepared for the conversation she was about to have with Kit. Amya was going to tackle the conversation with Peter, or they both would most likely, but Amya was going to take point on that one.

With a plan in place, Grace got ready for the rest of the afternoon and evening. It was going to be a long one, but she knew with her whole heart the decisions they had made were the right ones for everyone involved.

Parental Rights

The drive to the school that day seemed longer than normal, but Grace made it just as the bell rung to dismiss the students from class. Peggy was already outside where Grace parked her cruiser. She stepped out of the vehicle and walked around the back of it to stand next to Peggy with her arms crossed as she waited.

"You didn't call," Peggy started.

Grace grunted. "Got lost in the day, sorry."

"I wish you'd really consider being the School Resource Officer. Getting a new one every year doesn't help the kids, and I think you'd be perfect for it."

Snorting, Grace brushed her hand over her face. "Sorry, that's not funny. I have no desire to do that. I like my job."

Peggy sighed. "I guess."

"You want to be superintendent?"

"Absolutely not."

"See? Now we have an understanding."

Peggy shrugged. "So what happened over Spring Break that you haven't told me about because clearly something happened."

"Hmm." Grace shifted her stance and slid her gaze over Peggy as students filtered out of the front doors. "That's a long story."

"I have time."

"Of course you do." Grace bit her lip, not quite sure how much she wanted to share with Peggy, but they'd also talked to her a lot about their journey with Kit, and she was heavily invested in Kit graduating. "She go to class today?"

"Every single one of them."

"Good. Now to get her grades up."

"You're avoiding."

"I am," Grace admitted. "It's been a strange and stressful winter. I'm glad spring is here, but summer needs to come faster."

"You sound like a teacher."

"Or a student," Grace added.

Peggy smirked and shook her head as she waved at a student who walked by to their parents' vehicle. "Tell me what happened."

"We picked Kit up Friday before Spring Break, brought her home. Everything was fine until Monday morning. Peter has been...not doing well. I'm hoping we're at a turning point, but that remains to be seen."

"Not doing well?"

"He's drinking again."

"Oh, Grace." Peggy turned fully to her, compassion and sorrow written all over her expression.

Tears sprung unbidden into Grace's eyes. She tried to blink them back, but one escaped the corner of her eye. She wiped it away as she stared ahead, trying to maintain her tough woman persona. She didn't want to be weak in any aspect of her life, and crying was for sure a sign of weakness.

"Yeah, anyway, so he was drinking and apparently Kit wanted in on it, so they went out together to get drunk."

"He bought her alcohol?"

"Yeah." Grace scoffed. "We haven't gotten to that part of the conversation yet, but it's happening tonight."

"Why tonight?"

Letting out a long slow breath, Grace lowered her voice and stepped in closer to Peggy. "They were in a car accident. At the hospital, Kit had to go home with her parents, who were...well, they're her parents. I'll just say that."

"I've met them. They were decently pleasant until this last year."

"Yeah. Anyway, Kit went home, and we didn't hear from her again. Annabelle called this morning. They found her phone we gave her, presumably found some texts, and kicked her out again. I found her sleeping outside the library."

"And you brought her to school?"

"Kid needs an education whether she wants one or not. I've been on the other side of that, remember? I dropped out. I wouldn't wish that on anyone. Way easier to just stick through four years and graduate and then do whatever the fuck you want."

"Grace."

She shrugged at the admonition for cussing and barreled straight ahead. "Amya and I went to grab Kit's stuff from the house and had an oh-so-lovely chat with her parents. Kit will be staying with us until she's at least eighteen."

"You think you're up for this?"

Grace turned sharply and stiffly to Peggy. She raised a singular eyebrow in Peggy's direction as she mulled through the question. No one had asked her that. Not the social worker last December, not even Amya. When Kit came out the front doors with her backpack slung over one shoulder and a scowl to scare even the kindest person off, Grace laughed.

"Yeah, I think I'm up for it. Kit's not as walled off as she thinks she is, and she just wants someone there who actually gives a shit. Now she's got three of us."

"Three?"

"Peter."

"Right."

Grace waved at Kit, ready for the full force of attitude that was about to hit her. Surprisingly, Kit didn't say anything as she came to stand in front of Peggy and Grace. Grace stared down at Kit.

"Ready, kid?"

"I guess," Kit muttered.

"Get in the car then."

Kit moved around the two of them. Grace turned to Peggy and raised her eyebrows in excitement. She had never thought she would be this excited about having a kid come and live with them, but something about the adventure of parenting sent a thrill down her spine in a way it never had before. Perhaps it was just Kit and the impact she had already made in her life, but Grace was more than ready to take on the challenge of a sixteen-year-old girl who was kicked out for being a lesbian.

"I'll see you Friday," Grace said to Peggy as a way of dismissal of their conversation.

"See you then. Let me know if I should make an addendum to

the contact on her file."

Grace smiled. "I'll let you know tomorrow after we talk to her."

"Sounds like a plan."

Waving to Peggy, Grace stepped around the front of the cruiser and slipped into the driver's seat. Letting out a breath, she turned to Kit and smiled. "Heard you went to every single class today."

"So what."

"Good for you."

Kit rolled her eyes. "I'm not a dog."

"Nope, but you still have to be trained to be an adult and showing up is step number one."

"Whatever."

Chuckling to herself, Grace put the car in drive and moved out of the pickup line. She had no idea where she was going to park, but she did know the conversation they were going to have should not be happening at their house and should be happening some place a little more neutral. Kit remained stoically silent as Grace drove through the streets and found a nearby park to pull the cruiser up at.

"I wanted to talk."

"I figured," Kit grumbled. "Where are you going to send me?"

Grace drew in a sharp breath and shook her head. "Nowhere, kid. Where do you want to go?"

"Not home."

Snorting, Grace smiled. "I figured as much."

"I'm sorry about your phone."

"It's yours." Grace pulled open the glove compartment in front of Kit and handed over the cheap phone they had purchased for her earlier in the year. "Here."

Kit grasped it tightly in her fingers and stared down at it in awe.

"We won't turn it off until you tell us to."

"You sure?"

"Absolutely, kid. If you need something, I want you to be able to get hold of us."

Kit's jaw clenched, and Grace knew she was holding back as much emotion as she could. In some ways they were way too similar, and Grace knew Kit needed Amya's influence to not fall into the same stupid habits Grace had.

"Here's the other part of the deal," Grace started, staring out the front windshield because she didn't want to see Kit's reaction.

She turned, finally convincing herself she needed to. "I'm not going to call Doreen unless you want me to."

"You're not?" Kit's eyes widened, but there was a touch of hope in them.

Grace shook her head. "That didn't really work in your favor last time. You're sixteen, almost seventeen at this point, and Amya and I agree you should have some say in where you end up and what you want for your life."

Kit nodded, not saying anything in response. Grace waited her out, wanting to make sure Kit had the space to speak. Amya would once again be proud of her for using silence to her advantage in the entire situation. As the car idled, Grace waited.

"What are my options?" Kit finally whispered.

Grace drew in a deep breath. "Well, there's always the option of calling Doreen and you going back into the system."

"Will I get to stay with you again?"

"Maybe." Grace shrugged. "I don't really know for sure. Once you're in the system, I don't have control over anything. That's all up to Doreen and what she thinks is best for you."

"I want to stay with you."

Grace's heart swelled. She had hoped the conversation was going to take that turn, but she wasn't sure Kit even wanted to be with them after everything that had happened. And Grace only wanted what was best for Kit in the long run.

"You're always welcome to stay with us."

Tears raced down Kit's cheek, and she wiped them away harshly before giving up. When she finally turned to stare at Grace, Grace was done for. She unhooked her seatbelt and reached over, wrapping her arms around Kit's shoulders and tugging her in for a hug. Kit gripped Grace's sides, her fingers fisting into the suit jacket Grace abhorred as tears once again reached Grace's eyes.

She had not been expecting this. She'd figured Kit would maintain her tough-kid persona and reluctantly agree to move in with them. The break down was too much. Grace had no idea how long they stayed locked together in a hug, but when Kit eased away, they were both wiping at tears and laughing through them.

"I just want you to be in a safe place, Kit."

Kit nodded. "Thanks."

"You don't have to be thankful. You deserve someplace safe, someplace stable, someplace that isn't cold concrete or a place you're not wanted."

A new wave of tears slipped down Kit's cheeks, but this time Grace didn't lean forward to hug her. Silence slipped into the cruiser, but it was a comfortable silence. Grace knew she was going to have to talk to Doreen anyway, because surely Doreen was going to be doing some kind of follow-up with Kit's parents since their reunification. It hadn't been long enough for them to fall off the radar.

After another five minutes, Grace leaned into her seat and grinned at Kit. "Okay. So one more thing."

"What?" Kit visible stiffened.

"There are going to be some new rules in the house."

Kit rolled her eyes. "You guys are always about the rules."

"Yeah, but these ones are important."

"Because of what happened with Peter?"

"Yes."

Kit's chin bobbed. "I figured as much."

"Good, then this will be easy." Grace's stomach twisted with nerves, but she barreled through them and into the new rules she and Amya had discussed. "You will not go out with Peter without one of us with you under any circumstances. No drinking under any circumstances. No drugs under any circumstances. Peter has his own rules, too, so don't think this is just on you, okay?"

"Okay."

"He's the adult. He should have known better and said no."

"It's not his fault."

"It is in a lot of ways, but don't think you get off easy either, Kit. You made poor decisions too, and there are consequences to those decisions."

"Like what?"

"Grounding."

"You're grounding me?" Kit's eyes were wide.

"Yes, for two weeks."

"I...I don't even know what to say."

Grace inwardly laughed. She had no doubt Kit had not been expecting to move in with them only to be grounded. But it was also a test of how much Kit wanted to stay with them. They weren't going to make grounding awful, but it wouldn't be a free for all at their house either.

"You will go to every single class unless you are sick."

"Figured that."

"You will pass every single class no matter what, and you will graduate on time."

Kit shrugged. "Fine."

"Not fine. I don't care if you don't want to go to college. That isn't what this is about. Education is important. You know how we feel on it. I have a GED, and I barely managed that. Amya has a fucking Master's degree. She's smart. Follow her footsteps, not mine."

Kit shot Grace a look. "You're not stupid."

"Well, I'm not smart."

"You're not stupid," Kit repeated.

"Yeah, okay, we'll go with that. You graduate with your diploma. I better damn well be sitting in that audience when you walk across that stage."

Kit grinned, her eyes lighting up with the humor. "Okay."

"Two weeks, and then we will re-discuss your grounding and what privileges you can have back."

"Okay."

"Shall we go home then? We're on KP duty tonight."

"KP?"

"We're cooking."

Kit's delighted face vanished. "Can't we get Indian?"

Laughing, Grace shook her head and shoved her seatbelt into place. "Nope. Amya doesn't like Indian. We'll have to get it when she's not around some day."

"Fine." Kit crossed her arms.

"By the way, we went to your parents' house today."

Kit froze.

"We got all your shit. It's in the trunk."

"You got my stuff?"

"Well, what they'd let us take."

"They let you take stuff?"

"Yes. You can put it all away when we get home." The phrase felt odd but wonderful coming off her tongue. They were going home for sure. Kit was home, exactly where she belonged.

As soon as Grace walked into the office the next morning there was a buzz in the air. Not only was Alonzo's crew huffing around again, but Paige was there. Narrowing her gaze, Grace set her travel mug of coffee onto her desk and shot Paige a curious look.

"What the hell are you doing here this early?"

Paige grunted. "My turn to be on call. Got a call."

"Figures. What's the case?" Grace slipped into her chair and sipped at her coffee. Before Amya, she rarely ever drank it, but Amya had changed her mind on the effects of caffeine in the morning. Still, she rarely drank more than one cup on a normal day. She much preferred her orange juice.

Paige let out a huff of air, moving her bangs from her eyes only to have them land squarely back where they started. She slapped the folder she had been holding down on the desk and rubbed the bridge of her nose. "It's a custodial kidnapping case."

"Know where the kids are?"

"Yes."

"Gonna untangle that web?"

"Please help," Paige begged.

Grace snorted. "You should do this one on your own."

"Humbard wants us to work together because you know—" Paige indicated the crew shuffling around the office "—we're being watched."

"Uh...yeah." Grace took another sip of her coffee. "You untangle it, and I'll come along for the ride."

Paige grinned. "Sounds like a plan!"

Grace turned to her computer. She had a few more reports she wanted to pull on Diego before she interviewed him again, and she really wanted to know who that CNA was. Gnawing on her lip, Grace bent over her computer and jerked when she felt Paige's hand on her shoulder.

"We've got to go to Johnson County, so we should get going."

"Excuse me?" Grace turned with wide eyes. "Johnson?"

"Yeah."

"Why?"

"That's where the mom is with the kids."

Grace closed her eyes as she wrapped her mind around Paige's case. "Okay, tell me what happened."

"Mom had the kids for the weekend, first weekend since she's been allowed to have the kids unsupervised, and she took a joy ride out of county and missed drop off. Dad called in a panic. I've been up all night. Found her. She's willing to do the exchange, but she's in Johnson County."

"So have them do the exchange."

"Nope."

"Paige, this is ridiculous. This is why we work together as different agencies, not against each other."

Paige propped both her fists on her hips and shook her head. With Paige's slow look around the unit, Grace knew why they were going to Johnson County. It wasn't in search of the kids or to make sure the case was handled correctly. It was to get out of the watchful eye of IAB. She couldn't argue with Paige's logic, and it wasn't like Grace wanted to be there either if there was any chance of Alonzo showing up and questioning her yet again.

"Fine, but I'm calling Blake."

"Who's Blake?"

Grace glared. "Let me finish this up, and I'll be ready."

"Can't you do that on the way?"

"No."

"Fine." Paige went back to her desk.

Grace finished up the files she pulled, printing them and organizing them. She would be ready to interview Diego again shortly. Hopefully Paige would sit in on it as well since she had been there for the previous two interviews. She would be able to give good feedback with the differences in his story. They always expected some differences, especially the further out the event was, but something about Diego's demeanor made Grace think the story differences meant more than just time and forgetfulness.

"Halling!" Paige called from her desk. "I want to get home before dark."

"This isn't going to take that long. It's only an hour drive," Grace muttered.

"Yes, and then all the paperwork at the end of it."

Grace pushed to stand after shoving her papers into her desk in their proper place. Paige's desk was never clean. Grace kept her desk impeccable. "Tell Humbard?"

"Yeah."

"Then onward we go, oh fearless leader." Grace chuckled as Paige gave her a strange look. She liked to tease Paige and make fun of her when she had a chance. Technically Grace had seniority in the unit, but Paige had far more experience and seniority in terms of being a detective.

As soon as they were in the car and driving, Grace worked through her own case in her head. Paige was rambling about the custodial case they were on their way to deal with, but Grace couldn't help but think about Joseph and that CNA who had come by not once, not twice, but three times in the hour she had been there. Surely there was some kind of record of him somewhere. At the very least, she supposed she could stake out Joseph's room for a few hours and see if the CNA came back.

"What are you thinking?" Paige asked.

"What?"

"You're a million miles away. You haven't listened to a word I've said. What are you thinking?"

"That I'm missing something big in my case."

"Talk me through it, then. See if that helps."

"All right." She wasn't quite sure where to begin, but she did have to start somewhere. "When we were at the hospital the other day—"

"We?"

"Amya and I."

"Amya went with you?"

"Yes. When we were at the hospital the other day, there was a CNA—at least, I'm pretty sure he was a CNA—anyway, he walked by Joseph's room three times while we were there. The first time he actually came into the room, the other two were just drive-by."

"What makes him so special?"

Grace shrugged and turned her head to stare at Paige's profile. "Something about him seems very familiar, but I can't place it."

"What is it about him that makes him familiar?"

"I have no idea. That's what's bugging me. But Diego seems familiar, too."

"In the same way?"

Grace mulled the question over in her mind. What was it about the two of them that seemed so familiar to her? It was like it was on the tip of her tongue but she couldn't form the word, and the frustration from it all pressed in on her. "I don't know."

"Think about it then, because I'm betting when you can answer that, you'll have the answer you're looking for." Paige shifted her hands on the steering wheel.

"Yeah, and hopefully it won't be too late." Grace sighed, staring out the window to the passing landscape.

"I doubt it will be. Joseph isn't going anywhere."

"Well, that's true."

"So I went on that date with Crystal."

Grace froze. A chill ran down her spine all the way from the top of her head to her toes. She almost didn't want to dare to turn and look at Paige. Crystal hadn't mentioned a thing, although, they hadn't really talked in the past few days either. "When?"

"Last week."

Grace wondered if it was before or after they talked to Diego last, when Paige had pushed the physical boundaries the last time. She seemed to always do it when she considered herself single. But she didn't ask the question, not wanting to pry or have the answer.

"It went well, thank you for asking."

"Didn't realize you wanted me to ask," Grace mumbled as she stared out the window. Of all conversations she thought they could have, this was not any of them she would have pegged.

"Well, it did. I'm going to see her again."

"Good for you." Grace crossed her arms and wished they were at the exchange already. "Uh...I'm going to call Blake and see if she can meet us."

"Who is this Blake you keep mentioning? Side girlfriend Amya doesn't know about?"

Ignoring the comment, Grace answered, "She's our counterpart in Johnson County. She could have just as easily done this pick up for you, but you insisted on driving the entire way yourself."

"Whatever." Paige rolled her eyes.

Grace grabbed her phone and called Blake's cell. She answered on the second ring. "Grace."

"Blake."

"What's going on?"

"We're in Johnson County."

"We?"

"My partner and I. We've got a case we're working and are doing a pick up."

Blake snorted. "You didn't think to call me or tell me *before* now?"

"I assumed my partner had made contact with your sup."

"Maybe she did."

Grace pursed her lips. She couldn't quite figure out why Blake was being such a hard ass, but it was exhausting already. Between Paige's random conversations on topics Grace did not want to touch with a ten foot pole to Blake's stand-offish comments, she was confused all around.

"Want to assist?" Grace put out there for the world.

"Never thought you'd ask. Where am I going?" There, the gentle and happy tone in Blake's voice was back.

"Paige, where are we going?"

"McDonald's."

"Really?" Grace gave her a blank stare.

"What? It's the universal kid swap place."

"How do you even know that? You know what? Never mind. Which one?"

"What do you mean which one?" Paige gave her a hard look before focusing back on the road.

"Which McDonald's. There's three of them."

"Uh...the one by the college?"

"Are you sure?"

"Yes."

Blake interrupted their conversation. "How much longer until you're there?"

Grace glanced at the clock on the dash. "Fifteen minutes."

"I'll meet you."

It didn't take much longer, and when they pulled up, Blake's cruiser was already parked near the near of the restaurant. Grace got out first and waved at Blake, who stepped out of her car. "Where's she at?"

Paige glanced around, putting her hand over her eyes as she looked. "Don't see her."

"What kind of car is it?"

"Brand new Chevy Suburban. Black."

Grace turned to look around, too. Five minutes later, they saw her pull into the parking lot. She drove right up to them and parked her car. Grace prepared herself for anything. Blake took control of the situation, which Grace was glad for, considering she was the only one with jurisdiction should anything happen.

There were tears for both the kids and the mom. The social worker arrived right on time to take the kids, and the mom stayed back with them as the kids were taken somewhere else and out of sight. As soon as they were gone, Blake and Paige turned on the mom. Grace didn't even feel like she needed to be there except for the connection of Blake and Paige. The two of them worked well together so far.

Blake made the arrest and put the mom in the back of the cruiser. After paperwork was exchanged, they said their goodbyes and Paige and Grace drove back with the mom in tow behind them. This time, Grace made sure to keep the conversation light and steered clear of any sensitive or personal topic, including her case. She wanted nothing to get out beyond her and Paige and her unit.

INTERNAL INSPECTION

AMYA SAT in her office only an hour after arriving. Grace had texted to let her know she was leaving the county for the day to do a pick up, but that she'd in theory be home early enough to still get Kit at school. Amya brushed her fingers through her hair as she researched through some of the newest information on PTSD and Moral Injury she had been gathering in the past couple years.

Ever since Grace had struggled with her own PTSD, Amya had taken to researching as much of it as she could. She was just about to dive deep into an article when there was a knock on her door. Khloe stood with a worried expression on her face.

"What's up?" Amya asked.

Khloe stepped in closer but didn't shut the door. "There's a detective from Internal Affairs who is here to talk to you."

"A detective?" Amya's stomach dropped. There should be no reason they wanted to talk to her. She was rarely involved in anything that would bring them down her way. Perhaps they wanted to talk to her not about her work but about something bothering them.

Khloe nodded, her cheeks still pale.

"Did they say why?"

Shaking her head, Khloe swallowed. Something in her

demeanor put Amya on the edge of her seat. She closed out of the article she was reading and stood up to greet her newest guest. She could only hope whoever was there to talk to her wasn't about to interview her without warning.

"All right, then." Amya smoothed her hands down the front of her suit jacket and straightened her shoulders. She was preparing for whatever may come, which if someone was truly wanting her help, she felt bad about feeling so tense about the entire situation.

Stepping out into the main office, she smiled at the short man who stood by Khloe's desk. She'd never met him before. His hair was dark with salty gray strands poking through, eyes darker, and his skin a caramel color. She forced a smile to her lips as she walked closer to him.

"I'm Chaplain Stone. It's nice to meet you." She held her hand out for him.

Khloe slipped into her own chair and turned toward her computer, but she kept her eye on Amya.

"I'm Alonzo Esparza. I work in Internal Affairs."

Amya nodded. "How can I help you today?"

"Can we talk in private?" He nodded his head toward her office she had just come from.

"Sure." Amya turned around and walked back to the room. She immediately sat in her chair and offered the couch across from her desk to him.

Alonzo shut the door behind him and settled into the couch, crossing one ankle over his knee. He sat relaxed, like he had complete command of the room, which set the hair on Amya's neck straight. She had no idea who he was or what he was there for, but every defense in Amya's repertoire waited on edge for what was about to come next.

"What can I do for you today?" Amya asked, curious as to exactly what the situation was. She had a feeling Alonzo wasn't there to seek help, not with the way he held himself, and his name sounded oddly familiar.

"I wanted to ask you some questions."

"About?"

He smiled at her, and she felt a shiver run down her spine. Amya rubbed the pad of her thumb against her fingers and leaned against the arm of her chair as she waited him out. Two could play at the patience game, and she was willing to bet she had more of it than he did. Then it hit her. Alonzo. Grace had mentioned him. He was the head of IAB. What in the world would the head of IAB be doing in her office?

"You just figured out who I am." He was confident and bold, that was for sure.

Nodding, Amya raised an eyebrow. "I've heard your name mentioned before. It just took me a minute to put two and two together."

"Then you know what I'm here to talk to you about."

"No, actually. I'm a chaplain. I hear a lot of reasons why people come to see me, and the real reason isn't usually the original one they tell me if they even know why they end up in these offices."

Alonzo pursed his lips, and his gaze left hers for the first time since she had walked out of her office. She had him there. He had a secret agenda for being there. What that was remained to be seen, but Amya could play his game if he wanted to. She had been on the police force for ten years before graduating seminary and becoming a chaplain. She'd talked to IAB a couple of times throughout her tenure, and she certainly had learned in the last few years how to get information out of people when they very much wanted to hold that information close to their person.

"Fair enough. You know there is an investigation going on."

"There's usually more than one, which one are you referring to?"

He smirked at her but didn't shift his stance other than to fling an arm out along the back of the couch as he stared her down. "The one in Missing Persons."

"I've heard mention of an investigation, though the reason for it still remains unknown."

"It won't for much longer. We're near finished."

"That's good then." Amya hoped Grace would be able to finally work in peace if their investigation was done, that and she wouldn't be paired with Paige as much.

"But I have a few more interviews I need to do to finish up."

"Oh?" Amya's stomach dropped. She knew she was about to be the subject of one of those interviews. Why, however, was a completely different question. She had nothing to do with Missing Persons investigations other than Grace. Inwardly sighing, she realized immediately why she was there.

"How many Missing Persons investigations have you been a part of since you started your position here?" Alonzo pulled out a notebook and a pen.

Amya closed her eyes as she tried to think. "I honestly don't know. I hasn't been too many, maybe twenty over the course of the four years I've been chaplain here."

He nodded and wrote down the number. "What about in the last year?"

"Maybe five."

"Why so many?"

"That's not a lot. I spend a lot more time with Sex Crimes Unit and with Homicide, but mainly I spent time with officers coming in to speak with me one-on-one here."

"And you counsel them?"

"Sometimes. I'm not a professional counselor by any means, so if they need professional therapy, I send them to Dr. Kissik."

Alonzo nodded as he scribbled something else on his notepad. "The case last year where the Corrections Officer's daughter was kidnapped..."

"Yes, I was involved in that case, though I was originally involved in it from my work at the jail."

"Originally?"

Amya bit her lip. She had said too much and had indicated her relationship with Grace as the tie, not that their relationship was a secret. They'd gone through the proper channels after they'd started dating and informed the right people. They weren't hiding anything.

"Yes. I was called in to the jail for a different reason that day, and while I was there, Officer McDavidson's wife called to inform him their daughter was missing. I stayed to help him through the initial shock and trauma."

Alonzo's tongue dashed out, wetting his lips. Then he stared directly at Amya with a penetrating look. "And Grace?"

"What about Grace?" Amya's heart thumped hard. She had been anticipating this line of questioning, but she had figured he'd take longer to get around to it.

"What was her involvement in that case?"

Amya shook her head. "My understanding is she wasn't that involved in it. It wasn't her case, it was Detective Delwin's case, and while she consulted with Delwin, outside of helping with calls she didn't participate. Beyond that, you would have to ask Detective Halling herself."

"I plan to." He smirked. "There was a call you placed from the jail to Detective Halling's cell phone shortly after Officer

McDavidson's daughter's kidnapping was reported officially. What was that call about?"

Amya drew in a long breath and let it out slowly as she tried to relax every tense muscle in her body, which was near impossible. "Why?"

"Pardon?" Alonzo looked up from his notebook to Amya.

She shook her head. "I'm not obligated to tell you anything. Most of the work I do is confidential and remains outside the bounds of your investigation. Why do you want to know what we talked about?"

Alonzo shook his head. "I can't share that information."

"Then neither will I." Amya gave him a serious look. She was done playing games. "Why is it you are here, exactly? Because you are aware that I'm bound by confidentiality laws that far exceed your capabilities in investigating. You're not here to talk about your investigation into Missing Persons, are you?"

After a brief pause, Alonzo's lips curved into a bow, and he set his notebook down against his thigh. "You're smart, I'll give you that."

"I'm observant. Now, please, answer my question."

"You are correct that I'm not here solely for the purpose of our investigation into Missing Persons."

Silence fell over them. Amya waited it out, curious for what Alonzo would tell her next. She had a sinking suspicion he was really there about Grace, otherwise he wouldn't have brought her up by name, and that was Amya's strongest connection to the unit.

Minutes ticked by, but Amya waited. She wanted an answer more than she was willing to give up information. Finally Alonzo sighed and shifted to plant both his feet onto the floor and leaned forward.

"I've had my eye on Detective Halling since she was still an officer in uniform."

"An eye on her?" Amya repeated what he'd said in hopes of gaining more information.

Alonzo nodded. "She was rarely involved in investigations, but she did call a number of issues to light in her time as an officer and in her time as a detective."

"Are you saying she's the reason you're investigating now?"

Alonzo's lips thinned, but he didn't answer Amya's question. "I want her to join my team."

"She doesn't want to join your team. I think she has made that plenty clear." As much as Amya would like Grace to not be working with Paige, it was ultimately Grace's decision where she landed, and she needed to be happy with the unit she was in.

Alonzo let out a snort. "I'm aware. I had hoped you might offer insight."

"Insight for what? Why she doesn't want to work on your team or how to persuade her?"

With a grin on his lips, Alonzo nodded. "You are smart."

Amya didn't answer. She couldn't quite tell if Alonzo was talking down at her, like he expected her to be stupid, or if he was praising her for calling him out on his roundabout questions. Either way, she was readily understanding why Grace didn't like him.

"The former, although if you want to offer the latter, I would love that information."

"I think this conversation is done. I have actual work to do." Amya stood up and moved to the door, opening it. She gave Alonzo a very pointed stare when he didn't move.

"I'm aware of the relationship the two of you have."

"And your point is what, exactly? Our relationship is no secret."

"No." He shook his head. "I'm aware of the complications it has caused Grace, and I know if she were to transfer to my department, those complications wouldn't persist."

Amya's lips thinned. "I'm not going to convince her to do something she clearly doesn't want to do, and I should think you want people who actually want to work for you in your department, not ones who feel forced into it with no other option."

"Point taken," he muttered as he stood and moved to the door. "Still, should she want to transfer, the offer will remain permanently open."

"What is your obsession with her?" Amya's nose wrinkled.

He grinned. "She's a damn good detective, Amya."

"Chaplain Stone."

"Chaplain Stone," he corrected. "She is a damn good detective, and more importantly, she has something I can't train into someone. She has high standards of morals and ethics. It's rare to find someone who thinks like she does. She would be a wonderful asset to our team."

"Yes, but I think the question you should be asking is if your team would be an asset to her."

His lips parted, but Amya stepped back and brushed her hand

out in front of her, telling him silently he should be leaving and not speaking again. Alonzo took the hint and walked out of the room. Amya shut the door and put her hand against it, leaning and closing her eyes as she drew in a deep breath. That had been one of the strangest and most obscure conversations she'd ever had with someone. If he really thought she could convince Grace to transfer to IAB, he didn't know Grace at all.

Pushing the odd conversation from her mind, Amya sat down and glanced at her schedule. She had another hour before her next meeting started. She could wrap up the research she had been doing before Alonzo Esparza had barged into her office easily enough. With determination set in her mind, Amya pulled up the article she'd been reading and started it over.

Grace had barely gotten back with Paige dragging her feet when Alonzo walked into the unit with a sure step. He went straight over to Grace's desk and bent down. "I need a word."

Her stomach twisted as she stared up at him, and as much as she really wanted to say no, she knew she didn't really have a choice. He was her superior officer even if he wasn't her immediate boss, and he was the head of Internal Affairs.

She pushed out of her chair and stood before him. She hadn't even had a moment to check her email or her phone messages since she'd gotten back. It was as though he'd been watching and waiting for her to arrive so he could grab her before she could check any of that.

Alonzo grumbled as he walked directly out of Missing Persons and down the hall. Grace sent a look over her shoulder at Paige and raised her hands up a shrug. Paige shook her head and mouthed "Good luck!" at her.

With no clue what she was being called in for, Grace followed Alonzo to his office in the other part of the station. She could have done without going in there again and just having the interview in one of their interview rooms, but she knew that wasn't quite procedure.

When he shut the door behind her, she knew whatever it was, it was serious. She sat down in the chair across from his desk, and this time Alonzo sat next to her in the matching chair. Narrowing her gaze as her curiosity grew, Grace bit her tongue to try and wait him out like she knew she should. When he didn't say anything, she gave in.

"Why am I here?"

"Let's begin with where you were today?"

"I was helping Detective Delwin with her case."

"Where did you go?"

Grace sighed and folded her hands into her lap. "We went to Johnson County. There was a custodial dispute and mom took the kids and didn't bring them back. Delwin found her in Johnson County, and she agreed to return the kids, so we went to make the exchange."

"Why didn't you contact Johnson County Sheriff's Department and have them make the exchange?"

Pursing her lips, Grace drew in a deep breath. She wasn't sure she wanted to answer that question because the answer was she had left because of Alonzo and his crew being present in her work space when she didn't really want them to be. "You'd have to ask Detective Delwin that question. I went as a second hand per request of our supervisor."

"Humbard told you to go with Delwin?"

Alonzo's eyes were unnerving. He stared at her like he already knew the answer to every question he asked, which made Grace wonder on earth she was there to begin with. She forced herself not to cross her arms in a defensive manner, wanting to remain as open and as truthful as possible. She had nothing to hide from him, but she was getting annoyed at the constant interruptions.

"Delwin asked Humbard if we could leave, he said yes, so we left." His lips thinned into a line, and Grace had a feeling she was missing something. "Why?"

"What?"

"Why do you ask?" Grace cocked her head up at him, ready to be the one asking questions.

Alonzo shook his head as an answer before moving on. "Since your last conversation with me, how many times have you been out?"

"Can't you look at the logs for that? I don't count up how many times I leave the office during the day." Though if she really wanted to she probably could manage it, especially considering it hadn't been that long since her last interview with Alonzo.

"I could look at the logs. I have them right here." He leaned forward and patted a stack of files on his desk. "However, I was hoping you could give me the simple answer without me having to sit and search for your name."

"Why does it matter?"

"It matters." Alonzo rubbed his hands together.

"Fine. I've gone out at least ten times in the last week."

Alonzo raised a singular eyebrow at her. "Ten?"

"Yes, why?"

"That's more than other Detectives normally go out."

Grace clenched her jaw. "I like to be thorough."

"I can see that. Have you gone with Delwin each time?"

"No."

"Who else have you gone out with?"

"Again, why the hell does this matter?" Her frustration grew.

Alonzo sighed. "Detective Halling, I'm asking you questions as part of an investigation. I need you to answer them for me."

"I don't see the point in asking where the hell I've been for the last two weeks and what fucking difference it makes."

Alonzo's jaw muscles tightened when she cursed. Finally knowing what might set him off, Grace filed that information in the back of her head for later. She tried not to curse in front of her superiors, but if it was a way to get Alonzo riled up enough to change his line of questioning, it might work to her advantage to use it. She was sure he had probably heard worse.

"Did you know you weren't released from restricted duty yet?"

"I...what?" Grace's jaw dropped, and her head slowly shook from side to side. "I was released a week and a half ago."

"No, Detective, you weren't." He leaned forward and gripped a file on his desk and handed it over to her. Humbard had signed her off, Alonzo had signed her off, but Kissik—the resident head shrink—hadn't.

Skimming the file up and down, she flipped sheets, trying to find Kissik's release form, but it wasn't there. She bit her lip and moved her gaze from the file in her hand to Alonzo. "What happens now?"

"Now you tell me why you thought you were released."

"H—Humbard told me I could go back to field work."

Drawing in a deep breath, Alonzo nodded. "I suspected as much. Did anyone else tell you that you could?"

"Paige was the one who asked him originally."

"Paige?"

"Detective Delwin," Grace amended. "She wanted to stop listening to me moping or something like that. When she told me, I went and confirmed with Humbard. He said I could go."

"All right. When was this?"

"Last week sometime." Her voice trailed off quietly as she continued to stare at the paperwork in her hands.

"I need a date, Grace."

She sighed. "Just a few days after the shooting, maybe Friday. It'll be in the logs that I went out."

Alonzo's lips were thinned into a line again. "Detective Halling, I'm going to have to ask you to tell no one of this interview, including Chaplain Stone."

Grace stiffened at that. She stared directly into Alonzo's eyes.

"I spoke with Chaplain Stone earlier today, so I imagine she will speak to you about that. This interview, between you and me, must remain confidential until the end of my investigation. Do you understand?"

"Yes, sir." Grace swallowed, her heart pounding.

"Good. You can go back to your desk now."

Grace stood and walked to the door. When she reached it, she turned around, her eyes wide. "Uh...sir, do you mean back to desk duty?"

He grinned and stood to reach over for another paper on his desk, handing it to her. Skimming the form, Grace recognized it immediately as the one she had been searching for earlier, except the date was that day rather than nearly two weeks before.

"You have been cleared for active duty, Detective, so please, get back to solving your cases."

"Yes, sir." She handed the paper to him and left his office.

The walk to Missing Persons was one of the longest she had taken. She was sworn to secrecy, and she knew why. The answer to everyone's question floated through her mind, and she had to pause in the hallway for a few deep breaths before she walked back into the office and pretended like everything was normal. She couldn't and she wouldn't mess up Alonzo's investigation. As much as she didn't like where it was headed, she had to let it play out. She didn't want to be working for someone who broke regulations.

OLD MONEY

IT WAS the end of the week before Grace managed to get Diego into the station for an interview. He had been very resistant about coming, but with some help from Paige, she'd managed to convince him it was a better idea. Something about showing him a picture of something they had accidentally left in the office, which was a line of utter bullshit, but it had worked.

Grace set Diego up in one of the interview rooms and left the room with a uniformed officer standing by to watch him and make sure he didn't do anything stupid. She had her line of questions all written out and ready to go, but she wanted to let him sit and fester for a bit about why he was there. The room itself would hopefully lend to some different answers than she had been receiving.

Paige sat on the corner of her desk when Grace went back. Her arms were crossed over her chest, and her dark brown hair fell almost to her shoulders around her face as she stared down at a piece of paper.

"Reading something interesting?" Grace asked, surprising Paige, who responded with a start.

"Yeah, your questions."

"Comments from the peanut gallery?" Grace sat in her chair and pulled out the bottom right hand drawer and grabbed a small baggie of dried bananas to snack on.

Paige snickered. "No."

"Well, that's a first," Grace muttered.

"Actually, now that you mention it. You should ask this question toward the beginning."

"What question?"

"This one."

Grace stared down at the paper where Paige pointed.

"Where is the ring?"

"Yeah, ask that one first. Just get it right out there that you want to know that."

Grace spoke around the banana in her mouth. "I'm pretty sure he already knows that."

"So make it clear."

"Why?"

"See what his reaction is to you blatantly asking him. If you want to find that ring, then you have to actually find it and ask about it. And what the hell is this question?"

Grace looked down again at the question on the paper Paige pointed to. She shrugged. "Figured that would be my curveball question."

"We'll see."

They waited another five minutes before they headed in to the interview room. Grace sat on one side of the table while Paige stood near the door with her arms folded over her chest, putting on the bad-guy persona she had kept up with Diego the entire time. Diego stared from one to the other.

"Hey, Diego, thanks for coming in today."

"Didn't have much of a choice. What did you want to show me?"

"We'll get to that. First, I want to know where the ring is."

His eyebrows rose, and again he refused to look at Grace in the eye. "What ring?"

"You know what ring I'm talking about."

He lifted one shoulder in a half shrug. "I don't know where it's at."

"Here's the thing that's confusing me, Diego. You are the only one who has mentioned anything about this ring. No one else has said anything about it at all, so that leads me to think you're the only one who knew about it."

He paled. Grace inwardly smiled. She had him on the right

track.

"So, where is it?"

"I told you, I don't know!" His voice rose, echoing in the tiny room.

Paige shifted behind Grace, and Grace knew she was preparing for anything that might happen. Grace let out a breath and calmed the room considerably. "No reason to get upset, Diego. I just want to know about it."

"There ain't nothing to know."

"Well, if it was the only thing left on Joseph when you found him, then yeah, it's a bit relevant to the case." Grace leaned back into her chair and opened her body so Diego wouldn't feel threatened. She wanted him calm and complacent but nervous at the same time. She wanted to keep him on his toes.

His head shook from side to side. "I don't know where it is."

"Okay, why do you tell me again what happened that night."

"Are you serious, lady?"

"She's deathly serious," Paige interjected just over Grace's right shoulder, her voice lower than it was when she normally spoke to give off the air of command and anger. "Tell her what happened that night."

Diego groaned. "I was driving that night and stopped out back behind the buildings when I saw the kid lying on the ground."

"You stopped because you saw him?"

"Yeah."

Grace sent Paige a look with wide eyes that Diego couldn't see. "How did you see him?"

"My headlights shined on him."

Grace's heart rate sped up. "And that's how you saw him? Not because you had to stop to pee or stop for a smoke break?"

Diego stilled. Grace knew he'd just made the connection about his mistakes in retelling his story, that had she not pointed it out to him, he never would have known he was saying different things.

"Which is it, Diego?"

His lips parted.

"Did you stop for a smoke break and find him? For a piss and find him? Or were you driving by and your headlights shone on him?"

"I...I don't remember."

"Okay, we can come back to that and maybe you'll have some time to remember." Paige grunted behind her, and Grace knew she had done a good job. Shifting her in her chair, Grace prepared for her next line of questioning. "Why don't you tell me about the hospital?"

"About what?"

"Why did you go visit Joseph?"

Diego shrugged and stared down at his hands. He was trying to play off nonchalant, but it wasn't working. Grace knew he was tense, he was scared, and he had no idea where she was going with the conversation.

"I wanted to see how the kid was doing."

"You haven't visited him in four years. Why now?"

"I didn't realize he was still in the hospital. I figured he'd gone home, you know?"

Grace shifted back in her chair to how she had sat before. "Okay, say I believe you, why did you go visit him twice?"

Diego paused for a moment before shaking his head and tossing his hand up in the air. "First time I didn't get to talk to him."

"And you did the second time?"

"No."

"What did you want to tell him?"

Diego slowed down. Grace waited with bated breath for his answer, truly curious as the reason he would give. When he didn't answer, her frustration grew.

"Look, Diego, I don't have all day. Just tell me why you went to visit him. We're almost done with this interview anyway."

"I went to see if the kid was all right."

"Hmm, and what did you determine from that?"

"Kid's in a coma."

"He is. And he likely will be for the rest of his life. Don't you think he deserves a family?"

Diego nodded.

"So where is the ring?"

He glared at her. "I don't know. I don't have it. I don't know where it's at."

Grace paused the conversation. While she wanted him on edge, she didn't want him so close to it that he couldn't and wouldn't answer any of her questions because she still had a doozy of one to ask. Paige shifted behind her. Grace knew they could stay in the tiny room all day if need be. They'd give Diego breaks here and there, but he still wasn't a prime suspect in anything. She was looking for who Joseph was. But something about Diego pulled at her.

Pulling a photo out of the folder she'd set on the table in front of her, Grace slid it across so Diego could stare at it. She said nothing as she watched each and every one of his reactions, no matter how small they were. His eyes widened, his cheeks paled, his jaw clenched and then loosened. Diego's hand on the table fisted then he shifted it into his lap. She heard his shoes rustle against the floor as he moved in his chair. He was uncomfortable—insanely so.

"Who is he?" Grace asked, her voice soft in the suddenly tense air of the room.

Diego shook his head.

"Who is he?" Grace repeated.

Pushing the picture back at Grace, Diego collapsed in on himself. His shoulders tightened, his arms wrapped around his stomach, and his lips were shut tight.

"Diego." Grace tapped the picture in front of her. "Who is this man?"

"I don't know."

She didn't believe him that was for sure. He knew exactly who he was, and frankly, so did she. It hadn't taken her that long to track him down through the hospital system as soon as she had figured out he'd actually worked there.

"His name is Angel. He works at the hospital, and surprisingly, he also has a vested interest in Joseph."

Diego didn't respond, not that she expected him to. Grace slid the photo back into her file and then planted both of her feet onto the floor. Paige was still behind her, supporting her in whatever way she took the conversation.

"What I can't figure out is why you care so much about Joseph to go visit him twice in the last few weeks or why Angel keeps checking in on him. Do you know why, Diego?"

Diego shook his head.

Grace nodded slowly and pursed her lips. "I think you do."

"I don't."

"We'll see about that."

"Am I free to go?"

Grace shrugged. "Do you have anything else to share with me?"

Diego pushed back from the table and stood up. "No."

"Then thank you for coming down today, Diego. I'm sure we'll be seeing each other again."

He rushed from the room. Paige walked him out of the station as Grace went to her desk and sat down, inputting all the information she had learned from the interview. It had been short, but it had been well worth it.

"Are you just going to let him go?"

Grace turned to look up at Paige. "Yeah."

"What the hell, Grace?"

"I need him to tell me what the connection is between him and Angel and Joseph. Without that, I have nothing."

"You have nothing now."

Grace glared. "I'd like to see you do a better job. No one in four years figured this much out. No one even had an inkling about any ring or Angel."

"I think the ring is a bunch of bullshit."

"Whatever. What crawled up your ass today?"

"Nothing," Paige muttered and went to her desk, sitting down with a huff. She scooted her chair in and sent Grace a glare.

"Good, because I need you to go do me a favor."

"No."

"Yes." Grace stood her ground. "I do you favors all the time, you can do this one thing for me."

"What?"

"Go pick up Angel before Diego can call him."

"You should have done that before you interviewed Diego."

Shrugging, Grace turned toward her computer. "Then you better get moving quick."

"Fucking hell, kid."

Grace ignored her and went to work. She didn't have time nor desire for workplace drama. Focusing on her own case, she catalogued the interview and made record of it, and then she prepared for her next one.

It took Paige only thirty minutes to get back with Angel, and she put him in the exact room Diego had been in. Grace finished prepping out her questions as Paige came and leaned on her desk as was her custom when she wanted information but didn't want to ask.

Her arms were crossed, and she gnawed her lower lip as she stared over Grace's shoulder and back toward the interview rooms. Grace sent up a few glances in her direction before focusing on the computer in front of her. She wanted everything to go perfectly this time around.

When she was done, she printed her questions and leaned into her chair, fully staring at Paige. "He give you any issues when you picked him up?"

"No. Quiet as a clam."

"So he said nothing?"

"No."

Grace cocked her head to the side. "Did you ask him if Diego had talked to him?"

"No."

"You know any other words?"

Paige glared, and Grace knew she had her.

"What crawled up your butt, seriously?"

Paige shoved her cellphone in Grace's direction after pulling something up on it. Grace glanced down at the object in Paige's hand before taking it and reading the text message exchanged. She recognized the number instantly even though Paige hadn't put a name into the contact yet.

Raising an eyebrow, Grace handed the phone back. "So you got dumped."

"You made her dump me."

"Really? You think I have that type of control over Crystal? I did no such thing. I haven't even talked to her in like a week. I don't have the time, energy, or desire to mess with your love life."

"She said she didn't want to date her best friend's partner."

Grace closed her eyes and sighed. Crystal had used that excuse before, but it hadn't been with someone she'd slept with or gone on an actual date with. She typically used it whenever some guy asked her out because he clearly didn't get the hint she was gay. Grace gave Paige a soft and empathetic look.

"I'm sorry she said that. I don't care if she dates my partner or not, which I will make clear to her next time I talk to her." Grace wouldn't have that conversation, knowing Crystal most likely used that excuse as a way to get out of something she really wasn't interested in. "You guys only had one date, right?"

"We went on three."

"Seriously?" Grace's eyebrows rose. "And she said it was because of me?"

Paige nodded.

"Got me then. I haven't talked to her in a while. We don't talk every day, you know."

"Fine." Paige shoved her phone back into her pocket. "We going to talk to this kid or not?"

"Yes. Your attitude going to change?"

Paige stood and then stopped as she stared down at Grace. "Maybe."

"Well, at least you're honest."

They went into the interview room and took the exact same stances they had with Diego. Angel looked far more frightened than Diego, and when his eyes lit up on Grace, she knew she had him. He recognized her just as much as she recognized him.

"It took me a bit to figure out your name, Angel," Grace said as she slid into the chair across the table from him. "But you work at the hospital, so it wasn't that hard to figure out who you were."

He nodded. "Why did you bring me here?"

"I saw you walking by Joseph's room three times the other day when I was there. Do you have a vested interest in him?"

Angel's lips remained closed, but his jaw was tight with tension, and his chest rose and fell unevenly. His cheeks paled, and Grace knew he was holding information that would be useful to her. Whether or not she could get that information in one interview was another story.

"How do you know Joseph?"

Again, Angel didn't answer. He remained utterly silent and mostly still. Grace sent Paige a look over her shoulder with a raised eyebrow, trying to silently tell her she wasn't quite sure what to ask next. Paige stepped forward in the tiny room and slid into the chair next to Grace.

"Angel, we're trying to find Joseph's family. Don't you think he deserves a family?" Paige's voice was soft and tender as she spoke, washing away the hard exterior she normally wore and using compassion to her advantage. "He's been on his own for four years."

Angel seemed to completely shut down. He stared at the top of the table, refused to look at either of them. Grace had patience, but after Diego and her conversation with Paige, her patience was wearing thin. She drew in a deep breath. "How do you know Diego?"

"He's my cousin," Angel answered, his voice quiet but it rang through in the small room.

"So you two grew up together?"

Angel shrugged. "When we were kids. I ain't seen him in years."

"Really? Why's that?"

Not answering, Angel continued to stare at the table top. Grace's foot bounced against the cement floor, and Paige moved her hand out to still her knee, giving a gentle squeeze. Grace bit the inside of her cheek and debated whether or not to move Paige's hand but opted not to.

Grace repeated her question. "Why haven't you seen Diego in years?"

Angel gave the slightest of shrugs.

Paige leaned forward, her voice quiet and her hand finally off Grace's thigh as she closed her fingers together and pleaded with Angel. "You're not in trouble for anything, Angel. We're just trying to figure out who Joseph is and where his family is."

Angel turned to look up at Paige, his dark eyes roving over her face before he turned to Grace and stared directly at her. Grace couldn't quite tell which one of them was in charge of the interview anymore since it seemed Paige was going to be taking over some of it and playing the role Grace had originally been meant to play.

"Do you know who Joseph is?" Grace asked.

Angel didn't answer.

"Let's start somewhere else, shall we?" Paige commented and relaxed into the chair, widening her stance to open her body language to listening. Grace watched each calculated move as Paige made it. "How did you first come to hear about Joseph?"

"News." Angel licked his lips but still kept his gaze on the table in front of him.

"That's good. So you saw him on the news and then what? Thought you'd go visit him?"

"A lot of people visited him at first."

Paige nodded and shifted to lean in a little like she was enraptured by his words, which Grace had no doubt she was because she was herself. Curious, Grace kept her mouth shut and her questions behind and Paige took over.

"And did you?"

Angel nodded. "A couple times."

"Then did you stop?"

"No. I kept visiting him."

"Why would you do that?" Paige slid her hand against Grace's under the table again.

Grace ignored her and focused on Angel and every change in his demeanor. He had gone from defensive to resigned. He still refused to look at either of them, but his lips moved with no words escaping, and Grace wondered if he thought he was talking. When the rooms stayed silent, Paige slid her hand from Grace's thigh to her pocket and pulled something out. Dropping it onto the table, she smiled at Angel.

"Where did you get this?"

Grace's eyes widened in shock. The least Paige could have done was tell her. The class ring, red jewel with engravings on the sides sat on the table in front of them, and she had to do her damnedest not to grab it and run to examine it. Paige must have wanted to get back at her for whatever Crystal had said. Gritting her teeth, she focused on Angel's face, knowing this moment and opportunity wasn't going to happen again.

"Is this your ring, Angel?" Paige asked.

He shook his head ever so slowly to the point Grace wasn't even sure he knew he was doing it.

"Where did you get it?"

His gaze flickered from the table to Paige and back down to the ring, where he remained transfixed, not that Grace could blame him.

"Whose ring is this, Angel? Is it Joseph's?"

Angel nodded, his chin rising and falling as he closed his eyes. Grace reached for the ring then and held it in the palm of her hand. It was larger than she had imagined, but it had a date on it, a high school name on it, and it had initials carved into one side.

Taking back control, Grace shot Paige a glare and asked Angel another question. "Angel, you won't get in trouble for this. I promise. Where did you get the ring? Did you take it from him when he got to the hospital?"

Angel nodded. "When he was in the ER that first night."

"Okay. Thank you." Grace shot Paige another glare. "I'm going to keep it, if you don't mind, since it is evidence."

Letting out a sigh, Angel didn't give a verbal answer as his head rose and fell.

"Here's the deal, Angel. I don't want you to talk to Diego."

"I don't talk to him anymore."

"Care to share why?" Grace asked, her voice softer than she had intended, but she was pretty sure it would work to her advantage.

"He's not a good person. He drinks a lot. He's not the same person he was when we were growing up."

"All right, that makes sense to me. Make sense to you?" Grace turned to Paige, who smiled weakly at Grace.

Grace wanted to scream and yell at Paige for the stunt she had pulled, but she knew she wasn't going to get away with that, ever. She finished up her interview with Angel, not finding out much more information from him about anything. She felt confident he wasn't going to talk to Diego any more, but that didn't mean he wouldn't talk to anyone else.

As soon as he was released, she sat at her desk, she ignored Paige who loomed over her shoulder. When Paige pressed a hand to Grace's shoulder and leaned down to point to something on the screen, Grace snapped at her. "I know how to do a search."

Paige stepped back with her hands in the air. "I didn't say you didn't."

"Then let me do it."

"Fine."

Paige moved to her desk, giving Grace the space she wanted. When she looked at the ring in her hand again, Grace shook her head. That had been a stupid stunt, but she had something she had desperately needed, and she had proven Paige wrong. The ring wasn't bullshit after all. She continued to run the search to figure out who made it, and then she called the company to find out who had purchased it. Money always told the truth. Following the money would no doubt get her the answers she needed and wanted.

DO YOU LOVE ME?

WITH THE weekend finally around, Grace was beat. It had been one of the longest weeks she could remember having between Kit, Peter, her case—everything had seemed to be going a million miles an hour with no break in sight.

She settled onto the couch, sipping her coffee while the rest of the house was quiet. Grace was typically always the first one up in the mornings, well before the rest of the world, and definitely before any teenagers. Izzy had opted to stay in Kit's room, so it was just Grace, Roslin, and the cat snuggling on the couch in the wee hours of the morning.

When her phone buzzed, she groaned. She had wanted those quiet hours to herself. Swallowing down one more sip of coffee so she was at least semi-functional for whoever was calling, she grabbed her phone off the back of the couch and smiled as she saw the name flash across the screen.

Answering, Grace moved straight into chiding. "You know, I expect when you use me as an excuse that it's not for someone I personally know well or really even care about, and that you give me a heads up."

"Sorry," Crystal whispered. "Nothing else seemed to be working, but using your name did."

Chuckling, Grace took another sip of coffee. "What happened?"

"I don't think she really wanted to date me either."

Grace knew that much to be true since Paige had told her as much, but she wasn't about to bring that up to Crystal, even though Crystal knew just about damn everything about her life, including last Christmas when Amya had gotten so jealous of Paige's actions, she'd abandoned ship for one night and crashed at Crystal's to deal with her overwhelming jealousy.

"So what happened? Because Paige was in a mood that was never-ending."

"What do you mean?"

Grace sighed and settled the phone into the crook of her shoulder as she ran her fingers through Roslin's fluffy hair. "She was just in a mood."

"No, don't do that. Tell me what happened."

Rolling her eyes, Grace settled into the couch and took another sip of coffee. She had no idea quite how to explain what had happened with Paige other than it hadn't been pleasant for anyone in the nearby vicinity. "She was mad. All day yesterday."

"Mad about what?"

"Well, she said about you breaking up with her and me being the cause."

"Do you think that's what it really was?"

With a deep breath, Grace shook her head and stared down the hall toward their bedroom to double-check Amya wasn't randomly coming out. "No."

"Then what?"

"She told me at one point if she couldn't have me then she would date you."

"Oh."

"Yeah." Grace's heart sank. She'd never wanted to do that to Crystal or end up in some kind of weird love triangle where only one party was interested. "I can't figure her out, you know? One minute we're fine, great work buddies, and then next?"

"The next it's like she's kind of weirdly obsessed with you?"

"Yeah. I guess that's it."

"Well, she's got at least a crush for sure. She's an odd duck, Grace. On the dates we did go on, she is smooth to the point of seduction, but when it comes to actual relationships, she's not at all."

"What do you mean?"

"Has she ever been in a relationship?"

Grace thought back over their conversations in the past year. "Not what I would call a relationship."

"That makes sense."

"To be fair, Crystal, until Amya, I hadn't been in a relationship either."

"Yeah, but she trained you up good and real quick."

"Oh shut up."

"It's true, though! I had no hope for you before her."

Rolling her eyes, Grace took another sip and settled the mug on the coffee table before falling into the couch. Like clockwork almost, the door to their bedroom opened, and a sleepy Amya walked out into the hallway and across to the bathroom. Grace smiled at her sleepy form, no doubt still warm from the blankets.

"Amya just woke up."

"Oh good."

"Why are you awake so early anyway? You're normally one to sleep in on the weekends."

Crystal sighed. "Yeah, I am, but I wanted to catch you while you were alone and you're always up before the crack of dawn."

"You woke up to call me? Aww, how ... weird. You could just tell me you wanted to talk to me alone."

"Not really. You and Amya are a pair now, and I just assume anything I tell you she also knows."

"Well, I haven't told her about Paige and you and your break up yet."

"Oh, that'll be fun conversation today."

Grace grunted. "Surely that isn't what you called for."

Amya slipped from the bathroom and into the living room, falling onto the couch next to Grace and pressing her nose into Grace's neck as she curled into her side. Grace pulled her in tighter and dropped a kiss to her head as Amya shifted so the throw blanket covered most of her.

"Well, yes, I called for that, but I also called to tell you Peter was at my AA meeting last night."

"He was?" Grace's eyes widened and once again she found herself staring down the hall, but this time at Peter's door, which remained firmly shut with the light off.

"Yeah. He was ten minutes late, but he was there."

"That's good, though."

"It is. I was glad to see him."

Amya shifted against Grace's side. "We're going to talk to him today about everything going on, anyway."

"What are you going to tell him?"

"We're going to let him do the talking, mainly, but we'll figure it out."

"I'm sure you will. I want to see him succeed, I really do."

"We all do, Crystal. I hope he realizes that."

"Yup. Anyway, I'll let you go because I'm going back to bed."

"You're a dork."

"Somedays. Also, please don't set me up with anyone ever again."

"I did not set the two of you up."

Crystal groaned. "I'm still going to blame you for this one."

"No. No, I do not get the blame this time. I did not want the two of you to date. I told her as much many times. I am not to blame for this shenanigan you found yourself in."

"You introduced us."

Crystal had her there. Grace pressed her cheek into Amya's head. "Introduction does not preclude dating. Still on you and her."

"Fine."

"Right. I'll see you."

"Love you!"

"Love you, too."

Hanging up, Grace put her phone on the back of the couch and turned into Amya, tilting her chin up so their lips could touch. Amya moaned lightly in the back of her throat, her eyes closed, as Grace deepened the kiss. She skimmed her hand down Amya's shoulder to her arm and back up, tangling it in Amya's sleep messy hair.

Amya said nothing as she moved and dragged Grace with her down onto the couch. Grace's foot hit Roslin, who got off the couch with a huff, the cat already having jumped off as soon as Grace had shifted her position. The dog shook out before laying on the floor next to them, and Grace scooted her hand down to Amya's hip to hold herself up.

Amya grinned up at her. "Early morning calls with your lover?"

Snorting, Grace pressed her lips to Amya's neck. "I like this lover a whole lot better."

"And how is Crystal?" Amya skimmed a hand down Grace's back and then up, pulling the fabric of her shirt with her to expose her skin.

"She's doing okay. Called about Paige." As soon as the name left her lips, Grace regretted it. Amya's entire demeanor changed. Every muscle in her body stiffened, her jaw clenched tight, her eyes narrowed, and her breathing quickened.

Astutely making note of every change, Grace leaned in and kissed Amya's lips tenderly, then her neck, and then she pressed more fully into her body.

"But she also called about Peter."

"Oh?" Amya answered, still not relaxing as Grace made her way down her body.

"He apparently went to a meeting."

"Good."

"Yup."

Grace tried to distract Amya even more by trailing her tongue along Amya's neck, but it was clear their moment was over. Amya pulled Grace's mouth up for a quick kiss. "You going to finish your coffee?"

"Yes, but I will get you some if you want."

"I do."

Huffing, Grace kissed Amya again and stood up to make Amya a cup. When she sat back down, Peter emerged from the bedroom, much to their surprise. They stared at him as he wandered down the hall and came into the living room, plopping down onto the chair across from the couch. Both women had their cups perched to their lips as they stared at him over the rims.

"Don't give me that look," he muttered.

"What look?" Amya asked.

"Like you know what I'm going to say."

Grace snorted. Amya was much more graceful as she moved her cup away. "I have no idea what you're going to say, but you are never awake before eight, and it's six."

"I know." He ran a hand through his hair. "I wanted to talk to you before Kit woke up."

The running theme seemed to continue. Grace finished her cup and debated whether to get another one. "What'd you want to talk about?"

"I'm thinking about going to a program."

Grace's shoulders tensed. "A program?"

"For recovery."

"Like in-person?"

"Out patient."

"Here?"

"Yes."

Grace shot Amya a look. "When?"

"Next week."

Setting her cup onto the table again, Grace melted into the couch and tugged Amya into her side again as she stared Peter down. Silence filtered into the room, and she waited to see if he was going to say anything more on the subject, but when he remained quiet, she gave in. "I think it's a great idea."

"Oh good."

"Under one condition, though."

Peter's dark eyes raised to her and so did Amya's crystalline ones. "What's that?"

"*The boy—*"

"His name is Dick."

"Right. *The boy* can't be in the picture if this is going to work."

"He didn't know."

"Well, that's an entirely different problem, which we can discuss if you want."

Peter's eyes widened. "What do you mean?"

Grace nudged Amya, hoping she'd pick up the conversation, but Amya just turned her chin up and shook her head. "No, you keep going with this, you're doing good."

Sighing, Grace twisted her fingers in the tips of Amya's hair. "You didn't tell him you're a drunk."

"No."

"Why?"

"I didn't want the stigma."

Pursing her lips, Grace raised an eyebrow at him. "Or you didn't trust him enough to tell him. He wasn't safe enough to share that information with. You didn't really want him to know because you wanted to not be the drunk in the crowd anymore."

Peter's jaw dropped.

"Right, so with that in mind, since you clearly don't trust *the boy* enough to tell him these things, he's probably not a good fit for you right now. Not to mention, Peter, you need to focus on your recovery, not dating someone half a country away."

"But—"

"Nope. No buts." Grace tugged on Amya's hair and earned herself a half-amused glare. "No boy."

"His name is Dick," Peter muttered.

"I think what Grace is saying is valid," Amya added in finally. "We want you to succeed, and really, with him in the picture right now, that is unlikely to happen. It's not saying you and he can't date sometime later on when you're far more on your feet and so long as the two of you are completely honest and open with each other, but that's how relationships work. You have to be able to trust each other."

Peter didn't answer, and Grace strongly suspected it was because Peter knew they were right. Switching topics, Grace asked, "When do you start?"

"A week from Monday."

"Good. Then you can clean up your room before it starts."

"I'm not a teenager."

"No, but this is my house, and your room is disgusting."

"You always say that."

"Because it is always true." Grace tugged Amya's hair again as Peter huffed.

"Fine."

"Good."

"What's for breakfast?"

Rolling her eyes, Grace pressed her forehead into the top of Amya's head and closed her eyes. "You wanna cook?"

"I can."

"Thank you."

"Pancakes," Amya announced.

"I'm starving."

"Jesus, not a teenager, but fucking eats like one."

Peter shot Grace a sarcastic look, and Amya jabbed her elbow into Grace's ribs.

"Ouch."

"Have more coffee while you're at it. You're cranky this morning." Peter wrinkled his nose.

"I'm always cranky when interrupted when I'm trying to make a move."

Amya's cheeks flushed as she stood up. Grace watched every move until she was out of sight and behind the kitchen island so she couldn't see her anymore. Peter remained in his chair until Grace raised an eyebrow at him. "You can help."

"Right." He jumped up and dashed into the kitchen.

Settling into the couch once again, Grace flipped on the

television to the news and ignored the chattering behind her. It was not her normal way to start the morning, but it had been worth it.

Monday night, Amya made Grace change out of her worn jeans and into a nicer pair of pants and white blouse. She ran her fingers down the front of it and grinned as she stared into Grace's dark brown eyes as they stood in their bedroom while Kit ran from her room to the bathroom so many times she had lost count.

"This is stupid," Grace muttered.

"It's not. She wants us there."

"How long is it going to be?"

"I'm not answering that." Amya grinned and took Grace by the hand, leading her toward the closed door.

Grace spun Amya just before she reached the door and pressed Amya's back into it. Amya let out a breath, her heart skittering as she glanced up into Grace's eyes. Grace's hands were on Amya's hips, holding her to the door even if she wanted to move, but when Grace got like this, she never wanted to move.

"Why not?"

Amya's chest rose and fell, and she had to focus hard to answer Grace's question. She could barely remember what it was in reference to. "Because I don't want you to complain if I'm wrong."

Grace had that feral look in her eyes that always spurned Amya on. If they weren't careful, they would all be late to the Christmas concert but not because of Kit. Grace went to move away, but Amya tugged her back until she was smooshed pleasantly between the door and her girlfriend's warm and hard body.

Moving her hand from Grace's hip to her ass, Amya smirked. She should have made Grace wear a skirt, which would have no doubt led to them still arguing, but it would have made things faster.

"Are we going yet?" Kit's voice rang through the door, and Amya winced at how loud it was. "I don't want to be late."

"Fuck that," Grace whispered into Amya's ear.

"We can't."

"We could."

"No. We have to go."

Grace groaned and closed her eyes. "You owe me. We'll be right out, Kit."

"We're going to be late!" Kit screeched.

"No, we're not." Amya made her voice clear and she kissed Grace quickly. Speaking softer, she whispered, "Tonight after the concert."

"Don't hold out on me."

"When do I ever?"

"True."

Amya turned in Grace's arms so she faced the door and stepped back to open it. Kit stood on the other side in a dress they had just purchased for her that weekend. Her hair was in curls around her face, and she had borrowed Amya's makeup to put a light coat on. She looked stunning. Grinning, Amya reached behind her for Grace's hand.

"You look amazing, Kit."

"Thanks. We're going to be late."

"We are not. Chill out, kid," Grace ordered. Peter came down the hall in a nice pair of jeans and a polo shirt. Grace grunted. "Why does he get to wear jeans?"

"He has nice jeans. Yours are decades old," Amya answered.

It wasn't much longer until they were all piled into Amya's ancient car and headed for the school. They dropped Kit off at the doors before going to park and heading for the theater. The concert lasted exactly as long as Amya had predicted it would: an hour and a half. Grace had only grumbled twice through it.

When the kids were released from their seats at the end of the concert, Amya, Grace, and Peter all stood up and made their way toward the stage. Kit had said something about meeting them up front as she'd slammed the door on her way inside the school. Grace had her hand at Amya's back, guiding her as they went.

It took nearly ten minutes for Kit to stop talking to some friends and make her way over to them. The friends followed. Kit grinned, and Amya stepped forward. "It was a wonderful concert."

"Thanks! We've been working all year on it."

"I bet." Amya gripped Grace's hand to keep her in place and not lose her.

"Great job, kid," Grace said over the din of the room. "Didn't know you could sing."

Kit flushed, and her lips quivered. Amya was sure Grace most likely missed it, but she could never quite tell. Sometimes Grace was so obtuse to others and other times she was the most observant person she knew.

"Thanks. I've got to put my robe back upstairs, but I'll be right back down."

"Okay, we'll be waiting." Amya forced a smile to her lips, knowing Grace would likely groan about the extended wait.

Kit turned on her heel but stopped when someone called her name. Amya's gaze moved over to the gentleman with balding blond hair and the suit neatly pressed. Kit's choir teacher came closer and put a hand on her upper arm.

"Kit, I wanted to tell you that you did a great job tonight, really. I'm so proud of you this last semester."

"Uh...thanks," Kit answered.

Amya knew Kit wasn't quite sure how to respond, but she wasn't about to step in and save Kit either. The compliment was probably worth a thousand more where Kit's improvement was concerned that semester. She knew how hard Kit had worked to get her grades up and stay focused on school.

"Are these your parents?" he turned to them and extended his hand, his eyes crinkling in the corners.

Amya's lips parted, and she was about to correct him when Kit stepped in.

"Yeah. These are my moms, Amya and Grace, and this is my brother, Peter."

Amya's heart stopped. Grace's hand against the small of her back pressed hard into her and her nails scraped. Amya's jaw clenched.

"It's good to meet you. I'm Mr. Killian."

"Good to meet you, too." Amya held out her hand, surprised her voice had held.

"I'm going to go ditch my robe."

"Right. We'll be here."

Kit nodded and dashed off. Mr. Killian disappeared to the next parents he must have found. Amya turned around and stared at Grace with wide eyes. "Well, that was unexpected."

"Not really," Peter commented.

"What do you mean?"

"She's been calling you guys that for months now."

"Months?" Amya's eyes were wide with surprise.

Peter nodded.

"She hasn't," Grace added in.

"She has. She hasn't been so bold as to tell a teacher that, but she's said it here or there."

"She hasn't even been with us more than a few months," Amya

commented.

Peter lifted one shoulder in a shrug. "She likes you guys, and she feels safe with you."

"Well, that's a first," Grace muttered.

Amya sent Grace a sharp look. "It's good."

"It is. I just...it seems fast."

Rolling her eyes, Amya shook her head. "It happens different for everyone."

"We're not her parents."

"In some ways, Grace, we are more her parents than her parents are."

"In a lot of ways," Peter chimed in.

Grace narrowed her eyes at him, and Amya cocked her head, curious as to what Kit and Peter had talked about that she was not privy to. She imagined it was likely a lot deeper than she had originally thought it might be.

Kit showed back up, and Amya threaded her arm through the crook of Grace's. "We ready?"

"Yeah," Kit answered.

The theater was emptying fast, and they easily made their way out to the vehicle and all piled in. As soon as Amya got behind the wheel, she sighed. They were going to have to buy another car no doubt. Her little sedan was definitely not big enough for the four of them, and since Peter had totaled the SUV she had purchased last Christmas for that very reason, they were stuck with what they had.

As she drove out of the parking lot, Amya reached over and pressed her hand into Grace's, giving her a soft smile. It had been a long day and night, but it had been worth it to find a little more insight into Kit and what she was thinking and feeling.

When they got home and the kids piled into the house, Grace slipped into their bedroom, no doubt to change. Amya followed her, and soon found herself pressed up against the door once again. Grace had a hand on her breast and her mouth on her Amya's neck. Amya's lips parted in surprise.

"Grace..."

"You promised."

"Yes, but I'm pretty sure now is not the time and Kit is going to need to unwind."

Grace popped her head up and narrowed her gaze. "I'm too young to be the mom of a junior in high school."

Laughing, Amya patted Grace's cheek. "And you think I'm old

enough?"

"You are older."

"Not by much."

"Still older."

"Grace, get changed."

Grace moved to her side of the room and pulled her jeans she had tried to wear earlier from the hamper. "Mom?"

Amya sat on the edge of the bed. "It's a compliment."

"Sounds more like an insult."

Chuckling, Amya shook her head. "Compliment for sure. You should take it as such. She trusts us, and she wants to be here. In some ways, that should make the next year a whole lot easier."

"Right. I did call Doreen."

Amya tensed. "Did you?"

Grace nodded. "She's going to check on the Umptree's and do a follow-up visit and see if they're okay with this whole situation."

"Well, they are."

"Yes."

"So what does that mean?" Amya's gaze remained glued to Grace. "Is she going to take her?"

"Not if they say they placed her with us."

"Will they?"

Grace nodded. "I think they will."

Amya let out a breath she didn't know she was holding. She hoped they did say that, and she hoped Doreen wouldn't move Kit to another foster home. If anything, Kit needed the stability and to feel like she finally had a say in where she went. Getting up from the bed, she dragged Grace out to the kitchen to get everyone bowls of ice cream to celebrate.

I'll Forgive You Anyway

IT HAD taken her most of Monday to track them down. By Tuesday morning, she'd found everything she needed and got in her cruiser to drive to Johnson County. She drove in silence the entire way to the Sheriff's Department. As soon as she pulled up outside, she saw Blake's shining face.

"Two times in one month, Halling? Must be some kind of record."

Grace blushed. "Yeah, maybe. Maybe I just like Johnson County better than I like home."

"Bullshit." Blake nudged her arm lightly as they headed inside. Grace checked in with Blake's supervisor before she got into her cruiser with Blake by her side and they headed back out. Blake gave directions as they went so she knew where she was going.

"Give me the run down again." Blake said in between direction changes.

Grace shot her a glance before focusing on the road. "My kid's parents' house."

"And how did you find them?"

Grace let out a breath, ready to dive into the story. "Angel is a CNA at the hospital who I caught sneaking around the ICU room with my kid, and Angel is my kid's brother."

"No shit."

"Yup."

"How'd you manage to figure that one?"

Grace bit her lip. "There was a class ring left on the kid when he was found but it disappeared. When I brought Angel in, he had it on him. It was purchased by the parents. Once I had their names, it was easy to find out the kid's real name, which is Matteo, by the way, and that Angel is his brother. I'm betting Angel kept the job at the hospital when he found out his brother was there. He started his employment only a couple months before Matteo was found and put into ICU."

"But they never claimed him?" Blake's eyes were wide with surprise.

"Nope, and that's what we've got to figure out still. Why didn't they ever claim him?" Grace took a left turn into a new neighborhood. "They have no idea we're coming. Angel isn't supposed to be working today. I already called to check that, but he doesn't live at home, so hopefully we can talk to his parents and maybe go get him before they talk to him."

"You think he was involved?" Blake cocked her head to the side as she waited for an answer.

Shaking her head, Grace shrugged. "I honestly have no idea. I still want look at how Diego is involved, especially if they are cousins. He would have known Joseph as soon as he saw him when he found him."

"Matteo, you mean."

"Yeah, Matteo. Sorry. That one might take me a hot minute."

"A hot minute?" Blake raised an eyebrow. "What the hell kind of phrase is that?"

"Shut up." Grace laughed and pulled up in front of the house.

"What, who's Diego?

"The guy who found Joseph."

"Matteo."

"Yes, Matteo, sorry. The guy who found Matteo. Didn't you read the information I sent you?"

Blake flushed. "Nope."

"Figures. Come on."

It was a small house but big enough for a family of five to live in. It was a long ranch style building with three sets of windows and a pale baby blue siding that obviously hadn't been redone in decades as part of it was coming apart.

When Grace stepped out of the cruiser, she straightened her shoulders and prepared herself for whatever may come. If Angel knew about his brother, she could only hope the parents did. She couldn't imagine living without knowing her son was in the hospital for four years.

She and Blake walked up to the front door, and she knocked on it with a firm rap. It didn't take too long for a small balding man to open the door. Fear etched into his features the moment he saw her. Grace tried to put her own body at ease to relax him. Making them worry or fear would do nothing by way of helping her investigation.

"I'm Detective Halling, and this is Detective Miller. Would we be able to come in and talk to you about a case we have?"

His lips parted and closed. He nodded and opened the door wider. A short woman with wide hips and a flowery blouse came through a doorway and into the hall they entered. She wiped her hands on the apron around her waist and sent the man a worried glance.

"They're detectives," he said by way of explanation.

"I'm Kamila. Is there something we can help you with?"

"We wanted to talk to you about a case we have, see if maybe you knew something about it."

Kamila shot her husband a look. "Joseph and I don't know anything."

Grace gave her a soft smile. "Ma'am, to be fair, you don't even know what case we're here to talk to you about."

Joseph stepped in close to Kamila and led her into the other room. Grace and Blake followed after sharing a look. He sat Kamila in a chair in the living room and motioned for Grace and Blake to take a seat on the couch.

"We will answer your questions."

"Good." Grace sat and Blake joined her. "I've been working on this case for a while now, and your names came up in the course of my investigation."

"Oh really?" Joseph said, curiosity piquing his tone. Kamila gave him a dirty look, one Grace recognized from the many times Amya had given it to her.

Nodding, Grace continued, "Yes, would you mind me asking where your son is?"

"He's at work, I think." Joseph pursed his lips.

"Angel works at the hospital," Kamila supplied.

Licking her lips, Grace glanced at Blake before drawing in a deep breath and letting it out slowly. She knew the next question was going to be hard. "I mean your other son. Matteo. Where is Matteo?"

Kamila shook her head back and forth, shock registering in her eyes. Joseph stared at the floor, his cheeks paling and his breathing quickening.

Joseph spoke first. "Our son is dead."

Kamila didn't answer. Grace couldn't tell if they were lying or not. They might have truly believed it even if they knew to the contrary. "When is the last time you saw him?"

"It's been four years now. He went out one night to a party with his friends and his cousin and never came home. We filed a report, but nothing ever came of it. We never heard from anyone."

Grace felt Blake tighten next to her because it would have been her department who had missed it. She had no doubt Blake was going to go back and look into the case as soon as she got a chance to see what they had all missed in the course of the investigation.

"So what happened then?"

"We waited, and finally had him declared dead. We had his funeral last year."

That didn't fit Grace's timeline at all, which worried her. Maybe she did have the wrong family, although, she was pretty sure she had the right family. It would surprise her if she didn't. "Angel works at the hospital, right?"

Joseph nodded. "Yes, in the next county over. They pay better."

"Enough to warrant the commute?" Grace raised an eyebrow at him.

Shrugging, Joseph nodded. "I guess."

"What does he do there?"

"He's a CNA. Makes decent money for not that bad of a job."

Grace filed the information in her head. "Do you know about a patient there who goes by the name of Joseph?"

Once again, both Joseph and Kamila tensed. Their jaws were tight with tension, and their eyes were wide with fear. Grace knew they had to be aware of something going on. She would be surprised if Angel had known about Matteo and not told them.

"No, we don't." Kamila shook her head as she spoke.

Grace sent Blake a look of disbelief. "There is a patient there who has been in intensive care for four years. They call him Joseph because they have no idea who he is or where he came from. I honestly don't know where they came up with the name Joseph."

"Maybe you should ask," Joseph practically whispered.

"I plan on it. Anyway, this Joseph, in the hospital, I'm trying to find out who he is and his family, and he matches the description of the case you filed for your son Matteo."

Surprise coursed through them both, their eyes widening.

"What doesn't make sense to me, is why your son Angel was seen outside of his room multiple times. Did he ever share that with you?"

Joseph and Kamila shared a look but neither responded. Grace barreled forward with her interview.

"It seems clear to me that Joseph is your son, Matteo, and that Angel knows who he is and where he is. The question for me remains if you knew the entire time and chose to ignore that fact or if Angel kept you in the dark."

Tears streamed down Kamila's cheeks. She shook her head, and Grace knew she was close to her breaking point. Joseph reached out and touched his wife's leg in a moment of comfort. "Angel found out Matteo was there a few weeks after he went missing."

"Which is why you never pursued the missing persons report," Blake commented.

Joseph nodded. "Angel works there to keep an eye on Matteo for us. Neither of us have been there to visit him."

"And why did you leave him there for so long? Why haven't you claimed him? Given him his name back?"

Kamila sobbed. "We can't afford it."

"Afford what?"

"He's in a coma, never expected to wake up. We can't afford those medical bills. We can't bring him home."

Fear and truth rang through her voice. There was nothing they could have down except drown in debt and the overwhelming sense of not knowing what to do.

"We made the decision to abandon our son."

"You did." Grace nodded her agreement. "And Matteo has lived without family for four years."

Kamila shook her head. "No! Angel has been there."

"He's been a ghost."

"He has checked in on him every shift he possibly can. He sits with him sometimes."

Grace's heart broke. "Did Angel tell you how Matteo ended up in the hospital?"

She shook her head.

Waiting for a few more minutes, Grace let out a breath. She was going to have to find Angel and ask him a few more questions, interview him once again down at the station. "Who else knows Matteo is alive?"

Kamila choked back a sob, but Joseph was the one who answered. "No one. Us and Angel is it."

"You said Matteo went to a party with his cousin the night he disappeared. Which cousin was that?"

"Diego. They were close friends, always going to parties."

"Diego is seven years older than Matteo, though, right?" Grace slid her gaze to Blake, preparing to head into the next portion of her interview with the Burgos'.

Joseph nodded and got up, walking over to the bookshelf on the far wall. "He is, but they were always close. Angel and Diego never got along as well. Here."

Grace took the proffered photo and stared at Diego and Matteo, arms across each other. Matteo couldn't have been more than twelve. In the photo, but Diego looked like a grown man. "You let your teenager go to parties with an adult?"

"Matteo never drank. He was a good kid. He would go so he could drive Diego home."

Grace handed the photo back. "What kind of party did they go to that night?"

Joseph shrugged, and Kamila shook her head as she had no answer.

"What did Diego say happened to Matteo?"

"He said he went out back of the house for some air and never came in, and he had no idea where he was."

Grace memorized every word they said. She wanted to grab her notebook to write it down but waited as she was on a roll with getting useful information. "Do you have any idea how Matteo ended up where he was found?"

"No." Joseph's eyes were wide. "We always assumed whoever had hurt him took him there."

Grace shifted in her seat. "Do you have any idea who might have hurt him? Did Matteo have any enemies? Did he make anyone mad? Was he dating someone?"

She knew she had asked too many questions as soon as she saw the look on Kamila's face, but Joseph answered every one succinctly and perfectly.

"No, we don't know. Matteo was a pleasant and happy kid. He never had anyone bothering him, and he made friends with everyone. He was dating a girl for a few weeks before he went missing, but I don't remember her name. Sorry. Angel might remember."

"I'll be sure to ask him." She had a feeling she wasn't going to get much more information out of the two of them. Grace and Blake finished the interview and got back into her cruiser.

Blake got out of the cruiser first as soon as Grace pulled up outside Angel's apartment. They got to the second floor apartment, and Blake put her hand out to stop Grace. "Let me do this one."

"He's not dangerous. Paige picked him up at work last time and he came willingly."

"Let me do it."

"Fine." Grace pouted, but she let Blake take the lead.

Blake knocked on the door as Grace stood off to the side of it. They both heard the curse and the rustling before the lock turned and the door opened. Grace had her hand on her weapon just in case anything happened. Angel popped his head out the door, giving Blake a curious look. When he shifted to see Grace, he groaned and cursed.

"I already talked to you, lady."

"Yeah, and we're talking again," Grace muttered. "Out here."

Angel sighed and stepped onto the balcony area, leaving his door open a crack. Angel crossed his arms over his chest and glared at Grace. Blake stepped in. "Tell us about your brother."

"I don't know anything."

"You know something," Grace demanded. "Why don't you tell us already?"

"Detective," Blake muttered her warning.

Grace took it as it was and went back to playing second fiddle while Blake took over the conversation. "Tell us about Matteo."

Angel immediately stared at Grace. "You know then."

"Of course I know, Angel. I'm not stupid."

He pursed his lips. "If you know, then why are you here?"

Grace wanted to sigh, but she held it in. Blake once again stepped between them. "We're here to ask you some questions."

"What questions?"

"How did Matteo end up in the hospital?"

"Diego."

"We know Diego found him."

"No. Diego put him there."

"What?" Grace demanded.

Angel shook his head at her. "You asked why we don't talk? That's why. Diego and Matteo got into a fight that night, and Diego beat him, tried to kill him."

"For what?" Grace's eyes were wide.

"Taking his girl."

"You're shitting me."

Angel shook his head. "No, it was stupid. He nearly killed Matteo then left him there to die. I was looking for Matteo that night to bring him home, the drunk fuck he was, and when I couldn't find him, I went and found Diego. Diego told me he had no idea where Matteo was, but his hands were bloody. I knew they'd gotten into it. It wasn't the first time."

"It wasn't?" Blake asked. "When did it happen before?"

"All the time. Anytime Diego got jealous."

"Jesus." Grace shifted her stance and shook her head. "How did you find this out?"

"I confronted him after I found out Matteo was at the hospital."

"Where did the fight happen?" Blake asked.

Angel shook his head. "I don't know."

"Was it at the party or was it where they found Matteo?"

"I think at the party. Then Diego took him up there to ditch him."

Blake turned to Grace. "I'm going with you."

"You bet."

They didn't wait much longer before heading to the station. One last check in with Blake's supervisor, and they were off back to Grace's turf.

They raced to find Diego. Grace pulled into his driveway with her lights on. She got out of her cruiser, her gun in her hand as Blake followed close behind her. She'd already called it in to Humbard, but Diego hadn't shown any sign of aggression with her, but since he had a history of it, she wanted to be cautious and called for backup.

"Diego, open up, it's Detective Halling!"

Grace nodded at Blake as she pounded her fist against Diego's front door as soon as the first uniform showed up. Blake held her own ground and gun. Grace pounded on the door again, sure Diego was most likely in a drunken stupor like he had been the last few times she'd seen him.

"Diego. Open the door. Sheriff's Department."

He finally opened the door right as she was about to bang for a third time. Grace tensed.

"Come on out and talk to us, Diego."

Diego stumbled through the doorway, his eyes blood shot, his skin pale, and he reeked of alcohol, stale alcohol and vomit. His shirt was covered in it. Swallowing, Grace was happy she wouldn't be the one driving back to Johnson County for an hour with him in her cruiser. She gripped his arm and held him steady while Blake grabbed his other hand. They wrenched them behind his back, and Blake put a cuff on one wrist. Diego barely budged.

"We should get a bus," Grace said.

"Probably."

"Call a bus!" Grace shouted to the uniform officer still near his cruiser. He nodded and turned to his radio.

"Diego," Grace started. "How drunk are you?"

He didn't say anything, but he slowly turned to look at Grace.

"Diego."

Vomit spilled from between his lips and down over his chin and onto his shirt. Neither Blake nor Grace turned their faces from him, knowing they had to keep their eyes on him at all times.

"Sit down, Diego." She pushed him slightly and lightly toward the front step and helped him sit down. He leaned his head against the post with his eyes closed. More vomit slipped from his mouth. Grace made sure to keep a close eye on him as they waited for the bus. They weren't going to get anything from him, and it looked like Blake would not be taking him back to Johnson County that day.

Blake came over and shook her head. "My only question is why Angel held that secret for so long."

"To not hurt his parents any more than they already were hurting. Simple as that. Every choice he has made has been for his family."

"I guess."

Grace knelt down next to Diego and tapped his cheek. "Stay with me, kid. I'm not going to lose you just after finding Matteo."

Diego's dark eyes slid to Grace's face before rolling back into his head. She grabbed him by the shoulder and slid him to the ground slowly as he was completely passed out. Blake bent down close, but Grace already had her hand against his neck to check his pulse and turned him on his side in case he started vomiting again.

"All over some girl, huh?" Grace muttered to Diego. "There are better ways to solve problems, my man."

Blake snorted. "You talk to all suspects this way?"

"Some." Grace shrugged. "Well, most I guess."

"You're a dork."

Blake grinned. Grace glanced over her shoulder as she heard the sirens. Soon enough, they were swarmed by paramedics who took over Diego's care. Once he was in the ambulance and stable, Blake and Grace followed to the hospital. It was going to be a long day of waiting to see how Diego was doing, but at least she'd get to hang out with Blake for most of it. They hadn't had time like that together in months, and she knew they had quite a bit of catching up to do.

Final Interview

She'd closed her case and had seen Blake off hours after her official shift had ended. Grace didn't care though. Humbard would give her the overtime for breaking a case no one had dared touch for years. As soon as she walked into the station and down to her unit, she stopped. Alonzo stood in the hallway just outside the door and stared at her.

"I've been waiting for you," he said.

Grace snorted. "There is such a thing as phone, Esparza. If you wanted to talk to me that badly, you could have called and told me to come back."

He shrugged. "I knew it could wait. My office."

They made the trek up to his office, which Grace sincerely hoped was for the very last time. As soon as she settled into the chair across from his desk, he smiled at her.

"You helped break my case for me."

"I did?" Surprise edged its way into her chest.

"You did. Unfortunately, I'm not at liberty to say any more than that, but I thought you'd like to know."

"Depends on what the results of your investigation are."

He smirked at her. "You're a good detective. This case you solved today proves that."

Grace cocked her head at him, pretty sure she knew where the conversation was going and that she wasn't going to like it. She curled her toes in her boots as she waited for the dreaded word to slip from his lips. He had asked her so many times already, and she had no idea why he wasn't getting the damn hint about it.

"You're smart, you understand ethics and morals in ways a lot of cops don't."

"Helps when you grew up in a house that was shit with them." Grace bit the inside of her cheek. She hadn't meant to say that, and Alonzo's widened eyes indicating she had overstepped.

"Oh?" he responded.

"Long story. I was taught ethics by Officer Brady."

"Daniel?" Alonzo's dark eyes softened. "He and I went to the academy together."

"Really?" Grace's heart opened slightly more to Alonzo, not enough for her to take a transfer he was still no doubt working up to offering her, but enough that she might consider him an ally at some point in her career. Not then, though. Then he was still the weird IAB officer who asked too many questions and didn't know how to take no for an answer.

"We did. He did mention you once or twice. It's how you first came to my attention."

"Great." If Grace could yell at Daniel in the grave, she would.

"There have been a lot of changes today."

Grace kept her mouth shut. She was far more interested in what Alonzo had to say than in what she was going to say back to him, and if Amya had taught her one thing about interviewing and being a cop, it was that she needed to listen far more often than she needed to talk. Not to mention, silence could be her best ally during an interview, and if Alonzo had called her there to get information from her, she would also get some from him.

He cocked his head at her and grinned. "Why do I always feel like you're studying me?"

Grace shrugged.

"I would like it if you'd transfer to my unit."

Pressing her lips together, Grace debated what to say. Hell no didn't seem like a viable option. Politely declining twice over the last year hadn't seemed to work either. "Why do you want me here so badly? This is the third time you've asked. I'm a new detective. Surely there are other detectives with more seniority, more experience, and better skills than me."

He grinned at her, his insanely white teeth shining in the

fluorescent lights. "I see Chaplain Stone didn't speak with you."

"What?"

Snorting, Alonzo shook his head. "Never mind. You're smart, Grace. You might not have the education or the degree that other officers do, but I don't think that's because you lack the skills or the knowledge to get one. Though, if you do want to be promoted much beyond your current rank, you will need a college degree for that."

Grace narrow her gaze. She hadn't really ever thought about that. She'd never really wanted to be a detective either when she'd joined the force. She'd always thought her heart remained in being a field officer, on the ground running day in and day out. It wasn't until she'd almost lost her life that she'd reconsidered what it meant to be an officer and where her skills were best used.

Drawing in a deep breath, Grace let it out slowly. "I've never considered college."

"Might be something to think about."

"If I even want a promotion."

He smirked. "Why wouldn't you? More money for the same amount of work."

Confused, Grace shook her head. "You certainly do more work."

"Yes, but there are three ranks between you and me, Detective."

She gritted her teeth, very confused as to where the conversation was heading. He must have sensed that because he changed the topic.

"You're smart. You don't need a degree to prove that, but you have some street smarts that other officers lack. You have a very clear understanding of boundaries and ethics. I admire that, and it is a skill very useful to my department."

"No one wants to work for Internal."

Alonzo laughed. He downright laughed at her comment. "That is very true. However, as I recruit most of my team, I find they come to love this unit in ways they never expected."

"I won't do it."

"The offer still stands. If you would like to transfer, the door is always open. Your skills would be most useful here, I'm sure of that."

"No thanks."

He nodded at her and leaned onto his desk and picked up a

piece of paper. "You can go then. Just remember, if you ever change your mind—"

"I won't. Trust me." Grace pushed to stand and left his office without another glance.

Every time he asked her, she felt her defenses and wall breaking down a little more. She headed to her unit, glad to finally be back there. It felt like homecoming as soon as she walked inside, but the feel of the department was different. There was a somber tone to the room, and it wasn't until then that she realized she hadn't been told what the results of Alonzo's IAB investigation was.

She turned toward Humbard's office, ready to give him an update on Diego and her case, which she had officially closed but still had a ton of paperwork to do. Grace got to his door and stopped short. The office was bare. No photos. Hardly any papers. And no Humbard. Instead, Paige sat at his desk, her head bent over the computer as she stared at the screen with narrowed and concerned eyes.

"What the fuck are you doing at Humbard's desk?"

Paige looked up at her immediately.

"What the hell, Paige?"

"Shut the door."

Grace stepped inside and closed the door behind her, but she refused to sit down. Crossing her arms over her chest, she tensed every muscle in her body as she waited with bated breath for an answer.

"I got an unexpected promotion today."

"What do you mean?"

"I'm the temporary commander of the unit."

"You're fucking with me."

"I'm not." Paige stood up and leaned over the desk, both her palms flat on the wood. "Humbard was relieved of duty this afternoon."

"What?" Grace pulled the chair out and sat down heavily in it, all the air in her lungs leaving her chest. "What happened?"

"I have no idea, honestly. Esparza came in here, took him out, and then put me in charge. I'm just trying to figure out what the hell Humbard's been doing so I can keep this place running for now until they find a proper replacement.

Grace looked up at Paige with wide eyes. "You don't want the job?"

Paige shrugged. "I never wanted command. I like going out

into the field, and I can't do that as much when I'm in command."

"True." The conversation Alonzo just had with her flashed through her mind, and she shook her head. "So...I guess I should update you on my case, then."

"I guess you should. Get to it, Halling."

Still in shock, Grace relayed the information from her case she'd closed with Blake that afternoon. If Paige was going to be her new boss, it was going to be a long work day every day. Perhaps she should reconsider Alonzo's offer. Biting her tongue, she shook the thought from her head. That was stupid. She had Paige had worked together for a year, they could certainly manage this shift, especially if it was just temporary.

"Grace?"

"Right. So we arrested Diego."

"Figures."

Grace smirked. Everything would be fine. It had to be.

About the Author

Adrian J. Smith has been publishing since 2013 but has been writing nearly her entire life. With a focus on women loving women fiction, AJ jumps genres from action-packed police procedurals to the seedier life of vampires and witches to sweet romances with a May-December twist. She loves writing and reading about women in the midst of the ordinariness of life. Two of her novels, *For by Grace* and *Memoir in the Making*, received honorable mentions with the Rainbow Awards.

AJ currently lives in Cheyenne, WY, although she moves often and has lived all over the United States. She loves to travel to different countries and places. She currently plays the roles of author, wife, and mother to two rambunctious toddlers, occasional handy-woman. Connect with her on Facebook, Twitter, or her blog.